Daniel Loedel is a book editor based in Brooklyn, New York. His first novel, *Hades, Argentina*, was inspired by his family history and was shortlisted for the Prix Femina and the Prix du Premier Roman and longlisted for the Center for fiction First Novel Prize.

Praise for *Hades, Argentina*

'A voyage to the underworld could easily become outlandish, or, conversely, too familiar – trapped in the worn formulas of myth or magical-realist tropes. In *Hades, Argentina*, though, hell is at once metaphor and setting, literary conceit and emotional reality. Tomas's sojourn there is a fittingly moving tribute to the author's sister and her many fellow victims'
Economist

'An astonishingly powerful novel about the complex nature of guilt'
Colm Tóibín, author of *Brooklyn* and *Nora Webster*

'Elegant, searching ... Amid echoes of the Orpheus myth and swirls of magic ... a descent into an underworld of memory and brutality'
O, the Oprah Magazine

'A remarkable novel, as imaginatively bold as it is morally complex. It will stay with me for a very long time'
Kamila Shamsie, author of *Home Fire*

'Strange, gorgeous, and terrifying – a book for the grievers, and for those of us who wish we could turn back time to remedy past mistakes – and so, for all of us'
R.O. Kwon, author of *The Incendiaries*

HADES, ARGENTINA

DANIEL LOEDEL

B

BLACKFRIARS

BLACKFRIARS

First published in the United States in 2021 by Riverhead Books
First published in Great Britain in 2021 by Blackfriars
This paperback edition published in 2022

1 3 5 7 9 10 8 6 4 2

Book design by Daniel Lagin

The moral right of the author has been asserted.

A CIP catalogue record for this book
is available from the British Library.

ISBN: 978-0-3499-9409-3

Printed and bound in Great Britain by
Clays Ltd, Elcograf S.p.A.

Papers used by Blackfriars are from well-managed forests
and other responsible sources.

MIX
Paper from
responsible sources
FSC
www.fsc.org FSC® C104740

This imprint has no connection with The Order of Preachers (Dominicans)

Blackfriars
An imprint of
Little, Brown Book Group
Carmelite House
50 Victoria Embankment
London EC4Y 0DZ

An Hachette UK Company
www.hachette.co.uk

www.littlebrown.co.uk

For my sister

HADES,
ARGENTINA

PART I
1986

ONE

I'd spent eight years officially disappeared. At least as far as I knew; I hadn't been back to Argentina since '76, and even after the ostensible resumption of democracy in '83, no one from the government ever managed to confirm my existence. Only in the ninth year, when I married an American and had to get certain papers in order for my green card, did Tomás Orilla return to documented being.

But the interval between wasn't merely a bureaucratic absence. I'd shut myself off completely until I met my wife, and even then—by our first anniversary, I was already sleeping on the couch. The affair was hers, but the fault, I acknowledged tacitly, was mine. I'd never been truly present. Kind and available, yes. Committed, too. Even making plans for the long term—a joint savings account, my citizenship application, and, most recently, conversations about children. But it was always an effort, a mask I put on. If I blamed Claire for anything, it was that she saw it for what it was and let me wear it anyway.

That's one reason I went back when I got the call Pichuca was dying: it would mean a break from our problems. But like all things, it was a combination, a messy one. The timing contributed: presumably it would be safer for me in Argentina now, three years into non-military rule. So did the fact that my work was portable. The notorious lure of the past—especially amid all that secretly uncomfortable talk of the future—was certainly part of it as well.

There was also the call itself. Pichuca made it unassisted, rambling half intelligibly through a patchy connection that left her sounding older than her sixty years, and a good deal crazier. Not at first, when she told me it was pancreatic cancer and she had little time left, nor when she gave me the logistical details I needed in order to visit. But at the end, when she told me over an increasingly scratchy line that Isabel could come back as well, despite the fact that Isabel had been disappeared as long as I had.

I chalked up the delusion to Pichuca's illness. But the idea still held symbolic appeal, the kind to do with closure and redemption, putting stubborn ghosts back in their graves.

Only when I hung up did I wonder: My departure from the country had been almost traceless. I left behind no forwarding address or number. I didn't notify anyone, regrettably not even my mother, who died several weeks later. How Pichuca had found me—how anybody could have—was a mystery.

A small one maybe. Getting those citizenship forms in order had led me to fill out others, and more paths to me had opened up than I liked. There were census questionnaires, banks and lawyers contacting me about my mother's unclaimed assets, and requests for an interview from CONADEP, the country's newly founded commission investigating the military government and disappeared persons. Their inquiries had been the most difficult to navigate, as Claire had seen one of the envelopes. She knew more than the broad contours with which most Americans were familiar—Cold War, US-backed authoritarian regime kidnapping and killing tens of thousands at will in the name of fending off communism.

She was aware of my time in detention, had heard me recount certain nightmares, and encouraged me to confront them. Yet my honesty with her remained selective, and the full, fleshed-out story still wasn't one I was eager to examine, much less hand over.

The point is, I could reason out ways of tracking me down if I tried. But mostly they involved big investigative bodies and the kind of resources someone like Pichuca would never have had at her disposal. So the question of how she managed it proved to be its own draw. And though I could have called back—she'd told me what hospital in Buenos Aires she was in, the room number as well—I didn't. Instead I simply told Claire my plans and booked my flight and hotel.

But I must have had at least a hunch that the borders I'd cross on this journey weren't the standard ones. Since, on a semiconscious whim I told myself was purely nostalgic, I wound up packing—stuffed into the bottom of my suitcase as if I were hiding it—the fake passport the Colonel had given me when I fled from Argentina, now almost exactly a decade before.

TWO

I'd never flown into Buenos Aires, and I'd only flown out of it the once, making the experience of returning strange from the start. Everything at the airport gave off a sense of foreignness, uncharted waters. Though I showed my real, recently reissued Argentine passport to the immigration officer, for instance, he stared at it awhile, seemingly uncertain what to do about the fact that I'd never used it to enter Argentina before. There was also the clerk at the currency exchange who looked at me suspiciously because I counted the bills she gave me so many times, convinced the exchange rate couldn't be the nearly one-to-one ratio it evidently was, and the chatty young cabdriver who snuck a similar glance in his rearview mirror when I said I didn't want to talk, citing my fatigue.

That wasn't the real reason, obviously. Neither was my unexpected difficulty with the swirly, up-and-down quality of his accent. It was the sights as we got closer, the city in bright nine a.m. light. That time of day had bad associations for me here, filled me with a Pavlovian kind of dread. The loudness of passing Vespas and motorbikes, so much more frequent here than in New York; the radios broadcasting from car windows; even the sweaters tied fashionably over men's shoulders—mine was crumpled into my backpack with the sleeves sticking out, and it felt like yet another way to mark me as an outsider.

I'd nourished hopes of taking a long walk as I used to, or of sitting under one of those Coca-Cola umbrellas outside a café to have a coffee and reflect, give the journey a full-circle kind of feel. But instead I spent my first couple hours back in Buenos Aires in my stuffy hotel room, working on a translation with the shades drawn and the lamp on, much as I might at home.

And because everything seemed so weird and out of place to me already, I didn't dwell much on the brochure on the nightstand advertising tours of the Recoleta Cemetery, the last place I'd seen the Colonel before escaping Argentina. Nor, when I threw it in the otherwise empty trash, the small, half-drained bottle of Johnnie Walker, his preferred liquor for special occasions. I merely thought, on confirming what looked to be a vacant spot in the minibar, I hope they don't charge me for this.

———

HOSPITAL ALEMÁN WAS JUST a twenty-minute walk from my hotel, but I took a cab nonetheless. I was still uneasy; for all the death I'd witnessed, I'd barely seen any in hospitals, and I lost my way twice looking for Pichuca's room.

It was a private one, probably paid for by Pichuca's sister, Cecilia, and her wealthy husband. They were coldly conservative, the type that had referred to those in the movements fighting the regime as terrorists, and at first I thought that was why they stared at me so intensely when I entered. Then I realized the whole room was staring.

The exception was Pichuca. She was a tiny, hollowed-out husk on the bed, covered in tubes, and her eyes were closed.

"Am I—?" I began, before the answer became obvious: of course I was too late.

"Tomás?" Cecilia said, making a show of squinting at me as she came closer. "Tomás Orilla?"

"Is he the one Abuela was talking about?" a young girl asked behind her. She looked about ten, and though she'd implied Pichuca was her grandmother, I couldn't locate either daughter's features in her—no blue eyes or round cheeks or anything else. She was a brunette with a sharp chin and broad forehead, and she was studying me with even more curiosity than the rest of them.

"I guess he is," Cecilia said, appraising me. "We thought Pichu was hallucinating about you like she was about everybody else. This business about calling you—I thought it was one of her stories. She fell into a coma last night," she added, with a hint of relief.

"I'm sorry," I told her, though I was more than that. All those lingering questions of mine would remain unanswered now. The only mystery solved was how she'd survived the heartache of losing two daughters when my mother couldn't handle the disappearance of a single son: this granddaughter of hers. While I weakly shook hands with everyone in the room, giving terse replies about the last ten years—no, I didn't tell anyone when I left in '76, or afterward; yes, it was strange, and yes, it was strange to be back now, for another death—the little girl never stopped staring at me.

When it was her turn for my poor condolences, she ignored the hand I offered and said, "Abuela said you'd get a do-over."

"What?"

"Like in a game," she said, before Cecilia shushed her aggressively.

"Don't trouble him with that nonsense, Vivi. I'm sorry, Tomás," she went on. "Pichuca raised her—spoiled her, really—so you can imagine it's hard for her. Seeing Pichu like this, hearing all the nonsense she was saying. It's not easy."

"She's Nerea's daughter?" I asked. I knew Nerea had been pregnant when they kidnapped her, but I'd always assumed the baby disappeared along with her.

Cecilia nodded. "Born in a detention center. All these terrible things they say about the military, stealing babies to raise as their own and whatnot, but just think: Some young soldier brought her straight to Pichuca's door. It was such a blessing for her."

It didn't seem to be much of a blessing to Cecilia. Nor possibly for the girl, who'd started pouting, her head low.

"Come on," Cecilia told her, forcing the girl's fingers into her own. "Why don't we go outside and give Tomás and Pichu some time alone together. What do you think?"

She didn't get a chance to say what she thought, and neither did I, since Cecilia was already dragging her away. The others filed after them, and soon I was alone with the woman in a coma. I pulled up a chair and sat at her side, close enough to catch the stink of decay.

—

IT SHOULDN'T HAVE, but it felt so unanticipated. All those exchanges I'd played out in my head on the flight, and here I was, unable to utter a single phrase. I'd seen Pichuca go mute grieving for others, but, stupidly, I'd pictured her own death as a more animated affair. "Are you married, Tomás?" I'd imagined her asking me. "What about children?" After telling her we were trying—it wasn't technically untrue; we'd been trying to have children and now were trying to stay married—I'd envisioned her sighing wistfully, a sparkling, movielike tear in her eye as she said, "It should have been you, Tomás. I wish it was you who ended up with my Isabel."

But Pichuca didn't say a word.

Neither did I; ultimately I concluded it'd be a lie to try, that I should have told her whatever I had to while she was still conscious to hear it. So instead, in homage, I mentally recounted what fond memories I could—dinners in Pinamar and her house in Palermo, the many times in '76 that I called for Isabel and she picked up—until they spiraled to graver recollections, and I found myself alternately watching her slow, aided breathing and the equally slow clock on the wall, hoping the others would come back in.

I left as soon as Cecilia returned, giving her my number at the hotel and saying I'd be back the next day. In the hall I saw the girl lying across a row of chairs, asleep, someone who was a stranger to me petting her hair. I wanted to ask her what else Pichuca had said about me, but I knew it would be wrong to wake her.

⟋

WITHOUT THE EXCUSE of being there for Pichuca, it was as if some protective façade had dropped. I felt exposed, naked before the peering eyes of this city and all those pesky demons of mine I'd presumably come to satisfy. It was like I owed them something, a psychic tax of some kind I'd have to pay now that I'd returned. I stepped through the sliding doors into the twilit air and late-November heat.

At first the sight of her confused me; I assumed it was a look-alike, the product of some mental overreaching. But when she languidly raised her eyes at my approach, there was no question, only a rush of emotions I couldn't disentangle or describe, except to use her name:

Isabel.

She was just standing there smoking a cigarette.

Or had been—when I reached her, she threw it away almost unburned and gave it a stomp, saying, "Tastes like shit."

"I don't believe it," I said.

"Don't you, though? You're here," she pointed out. "Do you want to get a drink? I haven't had one in ages."

She went ahead without waiting for my response. And why wouldn't she? It was the most obvious thing in the world that I'd follow her wherever she went. I always had.

THREE

I sabel was my first love, and in some ways our relationship was as simple and as complicated as that.

We met because of Pichuca. A childhood friend of my mother's, Pichuca had moved from La Plata to Buenos Aires when she married, and stayed when she and her husband separated. My mother had recently suffered her own marital trauma—my father's unforeseen death from an allergic reaction to an antibiotic—and in an attempt to maintain a sense of family that had been illusory to begin with, she organized a summer vacation at Pichuca's house in Pinamar. To entice me, my mother informed me Pichuca had two daughters about my age.

At first, Nerea was the one my fantasies pinned themselves on. She was twelve like me, and her Basque name referred to the Nereids of the sea, making it hard for me not to put it next to mine and imagine a match. Then I met Isabel. She was only a year older, but she seemed lifetimes more worldly and wise.

One of our first days on the beach, I hustled past the begging children in the parking clearance and glanced back to see that Isabel had stopped to chat with them. Afterward, feeling a need to justify myself, I said I'd walked on because I had no change on me. Isabel told me she didn't either. "We can give more than money, don't you think?" she said, and it was clear all of a sudden we could.

Another day, as we sat together in the sandy living room, she asked me point-blank how I felt about my father's death. It was a topic my overly protective mother never touched. "How do I *feel*?" I repeated, dumbfounded, and she laughed: "I'm sure you feel *something*. Everybody does."

I'd never encountered anyone who felt as much as Isabel did. When she was happy, she seemed ten notches more ecstatic than I'd ever been, splashing in the water like an unruly child and laughing so wildly she snorted. When she was upset, she picked bruising fights with her mother and took long, sulking walks along the dunes for which she offered no explanation.

The first few times I asked to come with her, she didn't answer or declined. But once I went anyway. Isabel remained silent, shrugging in response to my questions until I went silent too. Then, without warning, she started jumping away from the water lapping at our ankles, and we turned it into a game, dodging the waves as if they were sent by the evil world just for us, and together we could escape them.

I joined her on all her walks after that. We never repeated that game—one time I tried and instead Isabel turned to the water and walked right in—but the experience opened a door between us. Our heart-to-hearts were probably no more than the usual teenage schmaltz, but to me they seemed cataclysmically special. We bonded over loneliness as if we ourselves had discovered the concept, and dreamed aloud about finding romantic partners with characteristics that to me sounded strikingly like each other's—honest, committed, unafraid.

The main narrative was that we both felt like orphans. Though we still had our mothers, the absence of our fathers weighed heavily on us. Hers had left during the clampdown on universities that followed Onganía's coup in '66, taking a job and a lover in New York, and it made a rebel out of her. While I felt alienated, alone in the universe, she seemed constantly embattled by it.

We hardly left each other's side that summer, making little effort to keep poor Nerea from feeling her third-wheel status. We even started addressing each other as cousins; I called her prima, while she used the diminutive primito for me.

By the end of the season, I was sure I was in love. And on one of our last nights together, stealing off to the beach after everyone else had gone to bed, I tried to kiss her.

Isabel rebuffed me. "We're cousins, Tomás," she said.

"No, we're not."

"Well. We might as well be."

For a time it seemed a self-fulfilling pronouncement. The following year our relationship was confined to letters, and in correspondence we retreated into cordiality and banal jokes. Isabel even confided that she'd developed a crush on someone, an older boy in her school, which was such a betrayal that I had to invent a redhead named Susana to get back at her.

Susana was made up, but others weren't. I soon developed real crushes of my own, and Isabel spent the following summer in the States with her father, so I didn't see her again until I was fourteen and she was fifteen. By then I felt like a different person; I was getting top marks in school, I'd had a growth spurt, I'd fooled around with girls while their parents were downstairs. Enough time had passed that all possibility seemed to have shifted on its axis.

Later, when I moved to Buenos Aires in '76, it was the same thing. I always rediscovered her after such distance that I felt we could start over, that this time we'd get it right, or the world would. With Isabel, I never believed it was too late.

—

WHEN I'D REMINISCED about Isabel during the past ten years, it was primarily about the girl with whom I spent summers on the beaches of Pinamar. How she was in 1976 had gotten tangled up in 1976 itself, and it was safer to keep the doors locked to both if I could. Prettier too: without 1976 in the picture, the rest of it changed. Whole alternative realities opened up, among them ones in which history skipped over us entirely, and we found ourselves married or having an on-and-off affair, thrown together with the same enduring force as in our youth.

As a thirteen-year-old, Isabel had a body inclined toward plumpness, lushness. Puberty shaped her early into a woman, as did the bouts of depression she smothered in jars of dulce de leche. I don't know if everyone would have found Isabel beautiful, at least not in Buenos Aires, which liked its women pencil-thin. But to me that lushness only made her lovelier, as if I alone perceived her as she deserved. As if it testified to the deeper connection between us, an antenna-like link no one else shared.

The plumpness was gone entirely now. From her waist and limbs, but also from the cheeks whose cherubic roundness had remained a defining feature into her twenties. Her clothes were baggy and shapeless on her— bell-bottom jeans under a loosely hanging top with a flower pattern. Her chestnut hair looked thinner too—stiff and brittle, like a wind couldn't toss it if it tried. And her eyes, once a piercing blue, were now a leaden gray.

There were subtler shifts too, differences I struggled to attribute a meaning or broader explanation to. Her stride, quick now, slow then. Her stare, which sometimes seemed vacant and bored, but sometimes darted about our surroundings as if they were new to her, as if she were young to the world and its every mundanity appealed.

For all their darting, those eyes never fell on me. Not as we walked a block to the nearest café nor as we entered it, proceeded to a spot in the back. She gave none of the signs of affection one might expect at such a reunion either. I was reminded of the coolness with which she'd returned to Pinamar at fifteen. She sported a pair of oversized sunglasses at all hours and constantly dangled a cigarette over her wrist as if she were a famous actress. After all, she'd seen New York—snow, Vietnam War protests, Coney Island, freaks on St. Mark's Place, one with a whole spiderweb tattooed on his face—why would she have any interest in us third worlders?

This coldness had to be something worse. I braced for accusations, words of hatred or betrayal. But recriminations were no more forthcoming than endearments. With the exception of our orders—whiskey for her, a glass of red for me (I'd had a rule since '78 to stay away from hard liquor)—we remained silent until they came.

Our gazes flitted from our drinks to the ashtray between them to the bottles behind the bar and the wall decorations opposite—framed jerseys and other tokens of national pride. "I don't know where to begin," I said.

"What? You mean catching up?" Isabel said. "It'd be nicer if we didn't have to, don't you think? Fresh starts and all that."

"I'm not sure I'm so good at those now."

"Really? Don't you have a whole new life in New York?"

I wondered how she knew that. Which is to say, I wondered whether she might have been the one to track me down and give Pichuca my number.

"It's not so new anymore," I said.

She sighed. Drank. Plucked a napkin from the dispenser and crumpled it. "Ten years, no?" she said, as if it were a genuine question. "Hard to believe."

"Why didn't you ever tell me, Isa? Ten years. Do you know what it would have meant to me to know you'd survived?"

She laughed. Waved a hand down the side of her body as if to display it as evidence. "Does it really seem I've survived, Tomás?"

"As much as any of us," I answered hesitantly.

"Well, that's not saying very much, is it?" Her cynicism, that offhand negativity—it was so her, so Isabel, that despite the sinister undercurrent, I felt grateful. "I'm a shell, Tomás. Don't you see I'm a shell?"

"They found you, then?"

"They found us," Isabel said.

"You were in a detention center?"

"The biggest of its kind."

I went silent again. Finished my drink and waved the waiter down for another.

"But let's not talk about that," Isabel said. "Let's talk about you. I hope you're more than a shell, Tomás?"

Recent fights with Claire shuffled through my awareness, along with older ones, nights out with her friends or parents when I was taciturn but insisted nothing was wrong. Arbitrary recollections from further back as well: the United Nations couple who rented me a room in their Parkway Village apartment in Queens and got me my first translating gigs, and whose invitations to barbecues I consistently declined; a girl I picked up at a bar who asked me, in a cutting timbre that suggested she knew how limited the answer would be, what I did for fun.

"Not much more," I said.

"Tell me," Isabel said. "Tell me about your ten years. You did escape, no?"

She gave me an unaccountable desire to echo her: "Does it really seem I've escaped?" I wanted to ask. But I didn't. Instead I told her I'd fled to Rome in December '76, and struggled there enough that I fled again for New York, where I got a job and, later, a wife.

Isabel didn't ask about the wife or, I was no less thankful, how I'd gotten out of Buenos Aires. Only about those struggles in Rome. So I told her how I was unable to find a place among the Argentine exiles there, those former members of the revolutionary movement who still spoke till dawn about Perón and Che Guevara and the country's destiny as if they had any control over it; how I couldn't find work like they did either—the architects who built toys to sell in the streets, the artists who did bijouterie; how I spent all my hours walking those ancient, winding alleys like a ghost unsure what to haunt, confused by the colors of the signs and circling sites like the Colosseum thinking it should have been a soccer stadium.

"You spent all your hours walking in Buenos Aires too," Isabel said.

"Not all my hours," I replied. The irony that I was the one to show resentment did not elude me.

"No," Isabel granted. "But I don't think you were ever much of a ghost haunting anything either, Tomás."

There was no point arguing. Isabel never took my pain as seriously as her own.

"How long are you here for?" she asked.

"I don't know. I got a one-way flight."

Isabel nodded as if that made all the sense in the world. "Are you sure you didn't believe it when you saw me, Tomás?"

"What do you mean?"

"You just always knew more than you pretended."

It felt like a refrain, the secret underpinning of our whole relationship, even though she'd used the phrase with me only once that I could recall. It was shortly after I first moved to Buenos Aires; she asked me if I believed I could ever kill someone, and when I said I didn't know, she told me: You know more than you pretend.

Suddenly I remembered that Isabel had been wearing this same flowered top that day. Drenched after running through the rain, the white and yellow flowers had looked to my clouded mind like bees. It had been raggedy even then, and now, ten years on, was clearly out of fashion too.

Which struck me, since for all of Isabel's talk of bigger things, petty concerns like that had always kept their hooks in her as well.

"You don't live here anymore, I take it?" I asked, attributing the shift to some new lifestyle of hers, a hermetic, off-the-grid existence.

"No," Isabel said. "I don't know how long I'll be here either. Probably not very."

"Why not?" It occurred to me we hadn't discussed her mother yet. "Won't you need to stay to make arrangements?"

"Cecilia and her Nazi husband can handle them, I'm sure."

"But the funeral? All that goes into a death?"

"I didn't come back for death, Tomás. If I came for anything, it's life. I've forgotten the taste of it, you know?"

I thought about reminding her of her endlessly high expectations. Asking how she hadn't learned to lower them yet.

"How about dinner then?" I said. "That's what I've forgotten the taste of—a proper, bloody Argentine steak."

Isabel shook her head. "You don't understand. I want to go back to Pinamar, or tag walls somewhere. You remember when we did that? Food is just food. I want experiences, stories. Did I ever tell you the one about Gustavo at the chicken factory?"

He'd made other unexpected entries into my life, but perhaps none as unexpected as that. The first overt reference between us to the great jealousy of my life.

"We needed cash and he'd take whatever odd job he could get. His first try was in construction. But he lost a tool in the septic tank and—I swear—was forced to fish it out." She laughed; I failed to. "After that, he worked at an understaffed chicken factory in Caseros, preparing the chickens you'd buy at supermarkets. His role was on the assembly line, tying the legs, wrapping the meat in plastic, that kind of thing. But Gusti couldn't keep up, the skinned chickens started piling on top of him. He tried to push them back but—*splat!*—they started falling to the floor. *Splat, splat, splat!* As he bent over to pick them up, some on the conveyor belt got away from him. The result? Let's just say the resistance was fought for a day or two by gifting the Argentine supermarkets of the bourgeoisie a shocking number of unwrapped, unsanitary, and salmonella-inducing chickens."

She laughed again—loudly, like a cackle. *Splat, splat, splat!*

"What happened to Gustavo?" I asked.

"We were in hiding together when they found us. What do you think happened?"

Based on experience, I could guess. The women often lasted marginally longer, thanks to the proclivities of their male captors. The men they tired of more quickly.

"Anyway, you get my point. We could go to the water or some of the old spots from '76. Sneak into the Japanese Garden or visit your old pensión."

"I don't think so," I said.

"What about going to the Bosques? After Pinamar, that was probably where we spent the most time together. We could pick up some wine and drink it out of styrofoam cups."

I waited for a grin or some other indication that she was referring to a specific memory—a night when we drank that way, side by side, on my twin bed before our pain and our clothes came off—but none followed.

"Really? The Bosques at night?"

"Does it frighten you, Tomás?"

I felt as if I were twelve again, staring at her bloody foot after she stepped on a broken beer bottle on the beach and said it didn't scare her. Then I felt twenty-one, staring at her as she said things about her role in the revolutionary movement and what she wanted mine to be. By then, she didn't need to tell me it didn't scare her.

"Don't you want to get a taste of life with me?" she said.

———

IT WAS A HALF-HOUR WALK to the nearest entrance to the Bosques, but on Isabel's urging we took a cab. The whole ride she stared out the window as if she were a tourist and didn't want to miss the sights. She hardly spoke. Hardly moved. Her rigidity was such that I was hyperaware of every movement of my own, from my bouncing after a bump to the sway of my shoulders on a turn. On one, I was forced so close to her, I realized she had scarcely any scent. No perfume, no body odor. Not even the stink of cigarette smoke. I attributed it to the cracked window, the battling fragrances of the city—car exhaust, sweat, the pollen of late-blooming flowers.

I paid the driver and we entered a supermarket off the park. Inside, Isabel seemed to regain her spirits; she went straight to the liquor section and handed me a bottle of Old Smuggler whiskey.

"I thought you wanted wine," I said.

"I can't tell good wine from bad anymore."

So much for my rule about hard liquor. She started back down the aisle, presumably for the cups.

"Do you want to get food?" I asked.

"What? To stay sober?"

"To eat, Isa."

She shrugged. "You get some empanadas if you want."

I did, enough for both of us, despite her declarations. Then we got in line to pay.

"Shit," Isabel said, noticing the fatness of my wallet, which I'd filled at the airport with Argentine pesos. "Are you rich now, boludo?"

Boludo. That most Argentine of all Argentine colloquialisms. Literally it meant you were big-balled, but it was used so indiscriminately, it really just meant you were human. It was wonderful being called human by Isabel again.

"I thought I'd be richer," I said. "Being an American in Argentina."

"I don't know how you can live there," she said.

There was a period I didn't either. When my original reason for coming had evaporated like the whim it was, and I found myself stranded in a purgatorial state and a borough I'd never heard of prior to my arrival. When all those conversations of my youth about the "Yankee imperialists" were still fresh in my memory, and my knowledge of how they'd backed the military and its horrors shadowed every opportunity that arose there, every chance at enjoyment.

But time had dulled that particular shame, or left no room for it. I rarely took a bird's-eye view of my life anymore, burying my head like an ostrich in the day-to-day instead. I hadn't felt worried about my growing Americanness in years.

"Are you a fascist like Cecilia now too?" Isabel asked as we exited the store.

"I'm as bad as Ronald Reagan himself," I said. Isabel looked at me blankly. "US president? Actor from California?" Still no sign of recognition. She crossed the street ahead of me and made her way under the trees.

IT WAS AS IF NIGHT FOLLOWED US IN. Cleared the spaces between the leaves, snuffed them out so that all that was left was the sense of canopy, a tightly woven quilt of shadows. The breeze murmured after us as well—playfully, lightly. Even the clouds kicked up along the dirt path seemed gentle, pretty puffs of red.

I scanned for less hospitable presences—kids with bottles of their own, the glint of a knife in a crack of moonlight, the glow of police flashlights—but spotted none. We passed the botanic gardens and the zoo, where we once secretly met amid the calls of exotic birds, and continued into the Bosques' sprawling heart. Our conversation along the way was fragmented, punctuated by exchanges of the whiskey and more stories: "I can't believe you gave me the fucking code name Penguin," I told her, and she retorted, "Shit, Tomás, I was Mrs. Bitter, you remember?" We recalled asados, late nights singing along to Mercedes Sosa and Piero, giddy flights away from angry, excluded Nerea. The air teemed with nostalgia, the past in all its flawed, flavorful glory.

Here and there we stopped on a bench too, and once Isabel even got me to sit on the grass with her. But it was already cold and dewy, and after a few minutes I could feel it through my pants. Despite Isabel's protests that she didn't feel a thing, I pulled her up by the hand, and we continued walking.

We joked, we laughed. Not in bursts, but with enough verve to feel the woodenness of our earlier interactions being chipped away, peeled off like chunks of bark.

More reminiscences, more refills of the whiskey. Less and less sense of time.

I remembered our last and most important summer together, when she was seventeen and I was sixteen. Again she'd returned with an above-it-all air and an array of tales that made me feel like I had none at all. One was about the week she'd spent in an NYU dorm—her father and his idiot girlfriend had messed up the dates when Isabel and Nerea were visiting and planned a trip to the Caribbean that overlapped with the girls' stay. Rather than cancel his vacation, their father used his connections to secure his daughters a room on campus while he was away. "You don't know the freedom we had," Isabel said, regaling me with stories of the parties she and Nerea had gone to down the hall, and dropping hints that they hadn't slept every night in the room they shared. "And marijuana—you don't have a clue how much fun marijuana is, Tomás."

She was still laughing over an anecdote when she started crying. I got only an inch or two closer on the couch—just enough to stretch my arm across her back. Her head nestled of its own volition onto my shoulder. It was late afternoon, nap time, and not even Nerea was around.

"It's so fucking stupid," Isabel said through her sniffles. "So meaningless. I don't even know what I'm missing."

"You don't have to," I said. I'm not sure I've ever been wiser.

Isabel kissed me then. Briefly, her lips landing lightly on mine without lingering. I could tell it was in thanks, but I was thankful myself all the same.

It shouldn't have been the start of a sexual relationship. But late the next night she appeared in my room, climbed onto me while I was in bed, and woke me with a longer, different kind of kiss. "Shh," she whispered when, despite my ecstatic comprehension of what was transpiring, I couldn't resist asking what she was doing. "You're dreaming, Tomás. Keep dreaming."

If it had been the one occasion it happened, I might have concluded I was, since she left before morning and the whole thing had seemed miraculous. I'd put my hand under her pajama top on my own initiative, but she was the one who slipped my fingers under the waistline of her bottoms and rolled us over to give me a better angle. I'd touched other girls like that by then, but those experiences always had the inverse dynamic, with me leading the charge and them acquiescing. Delicacy had ruled, permission. But here was a smoothness and openness that was new to me, that made it all feel natural and free and aligned the moment perfectly with the dancing spray of those Pinamar waves.

It didn't happen every night—Isabel invoked our mothers and Nerea, exaggerating the risk involved. I figured she liked the excitement, and I was content to drift off knowing she'd soon slip away, tiptoeing back to her and Nerea's room as if the secret could actually be kept.

It's as if that summer existed for me only at night, and only in my room.

Even the moments we returned to our old confessional ways, sharing our anxieties and sorrows, tend to be set across pillows in my memories, the sheets thrown off but our rumpled clothes still on. We were never entirely naked then, and we never had actual intercourse. But to me it has always felt as if we were and we had.

"Are you single?" I asked Isabel now, catching her eye as we crossed from one lantern-lit lawn to another.

"Very," Isabel said. Though I'd told her at the outset I was married, I raised my cup to hers as if I were too. The styrofoam bumped together like cushions. She still somehow seemed sober, but despite having eaten all the empanadas myself, I definitely wasn't.

"Lonely?" I asked.

"Like Dracula," she said, and I felt another punch of youthful, free-flowing intoxication. I had drunk for such different reasons back when I used to get drunk that this felt almost like the first time.

Eventually we came to a large statue on a raised platform. It was a man in nineteenth-century military garb on a horse, with either a lean musket or a sword extending from under one arm—in the darkness it was hard to tell. The horse was as regal as its rider—head raised high, thick tail pluming out behind him. Conquest, more than heroism or sacrifice, seemed to define their stance. Victory.

"Who was he?" Isabel asked.

I tried to recall my Argentine history. It couldn't have been Belgrano or San Martín, since they had whole plazas as their namesakes, and the rest of the figures were forgotten in a grade-school muddle.

"A general, probably," I said. "Who knows?"

We stared at the statue. Then Isabel reached for the grocery bag in my hand. Pulled the styrofoam cups free. They came in packs of twenty or so, and we had used only two.

She took one out and threw it in the statue's direction. The wind caught it and tossed it harmlessly aside like a feather.

She threw another cup.

Another and another, and I didn't say a word. Not one reached the statue. Instead they lay scattered across the ground in front of us like the leftovers of a large picnic or patches of snow that had been melting for days.

"Should have gotten glasses," Isabel said.

I reached into the grocery bag. Drew out the bottle of Old Smuggler and handed it to her. She smiled gratefully. Clasped the bottle by the neck and, despite the thinness of her arms and the off-balance way she wound up, hurled it perfectly. It shattered against the horse, and we could hear the sprinkle of shards as they rained down.

We started laughing again.

What roller coaster were we on? And was it any different from the one Isabel always rode, from flirtatious rebel to insecure lover to whoever she became next?

This aspect was no different either: I felt flat by comparison. I'd become stable as a rock, Claire told me once, before correcting herself: No. A slab of stone. A floor.

Make me swing, Isabel, I thought.

"Isa," I said, taking her hand. It was frigid and jarringly bony. "Will you come back with me to my hotel? Please?"

I watched her ponder. Was it really so wrong to think the universe owed me this? Owed us? After all the years and mistakes. If I can have this, I thought, I'll give back anything. Everything.

I didn't wonder if I could make her swing—if she could even "swing" at all. Her eyes were on the ground, the trail of cups that began at her feet. With the ratty end of her shoe, she gave one a gentle shove into another.

"Only because you said please," she told me.

WE LEFT THE PARK. Waiting at the curb, my hand outstretched for another taxi, I thought momentarily of Claire. I felt little guilt about what I was about to do. More, curiously, about how much I hadn't told her. That in my piecemeal truthfulness with her, I'd discussed only the more obvious injuries, those tied to the horrors of the regime—kidnapping, torture, death. I never told her my more ordinary torments, like my unrealized love or jealousy, or the way they played into those larger horrors. I never traced the intricacies, plotted Isabel's place in all that misery. If I had, she might have understood. Been glad, even, to make some sense of me. But Isabel was just another name to Claire, one more victim on a list so long the names blurred together.

Isabel and I didn't touch in the cab or even in the hotel elevator. Only after I'd fumblingly unlocked the door to my room and held it open for her did I place a hand on the small of her back. I could feel the knobs in her spine.

She stopped near the bed, stood still. Before I even approached, she started taking off her shirt.

There was something mechanical about it. Little sense of allure, of need—it was like she wanted to get it over with quickly. And though I might have hoped for more, if this was all I'd get, I found myself willing to comply, to be mechanical about it too.

I removed my clothes also. Only when we were both naked did we finally kiss. Her lips were dry, cracked. Her tongue careful, slow-moving, without my sloppiness; it felt like it was reading mine and reacting rather than seeking it out. My fingers brushed up her arms, her neck, into her coarse hair. There was still no discernible smell, and among the many out-of-place, drunken thoughts that flew through my brain was the realization that I couldn't recall what Isabel had smelled like in the first place.

Another, vanishingly swift: I knew every scent of Claire's, down to her particular brand of nail polish remover and the distinct sweat of her armpits and her neck. In bringing myself to anger at the news of her cheating—an older, presumably less damaged lawyer at her firm—I'd pictured the man kissing away a bead from her clavicle, as if the salty taste should have been reserved for me alone.

But that didn't matter now—none of these observations or fleeting distractions did. Whatever its condition, this was Isabel's body before me, back in my grasp.

She lay down on the bed, and I lay on top of her.

WHEN IT TURNED OUT TO BE BAD, I blamed myself. Not strictly because of my performance. More because of its apparent irrelevance; Isabel stared at the ceiling through most of it, as if a clock she could count down were mounted there. I wasn't much better, focusing almost as intently on the slice of pillow by her ear to avoid the spins.

The problem wasn't solely physical. Worse was the insecurity, the comparisons with Gustavo and the paths my mind wandered while I thrust. At one point, I wondered what to do with the fact that my poor sex life with Claire had one less justification now that the shadow Isabel had cast over it was gone. At another, what that shadow had been doing there in the first place. My physical explorations with Isabel always had more in common with our emotional ones than I liked to admit. Touching remained about comfort, affirmation. The first time Isabel ever took me in her hand and felt my hardness, she laughed in surprise. And when I came in her grasp moments later, she laughed again, as if sensuality had never been as much the point as reassurance and curiosity, amusement at these bodies we existed in.

This was different. Probably because there was no solace in it now.

I apologized; Isabel told me it wasn't my fault. We reclined next to each other, with enough space between us that it felt like we were the married couple: both on our backs, both of us staring at the ceiling. Sweatless—cold, even. I had to resist the urge to pull up the sheets. The room had stopped spinning and settled, and I wished it hadn't.

"I'm sorry," I said again when the silence got unbearable. "I imagine sex is . . . complicated for you now."

"That's one way of putting it," Isabel said, laughing mirthlessly.

"How would you put it?"

"Fireless. Bloodless."

"That's somewhat ironic, no?"

"No," Isabel said sharply, and I wanted to slap myself for being such an idiot.

She got up, went naked to the window. Pulled the curtain a few inches aside to peer out, making herself a reddish silhouette in the soft city light. It should have been beautiful. But the skinniness of her limbs was thrown into relief as well. She seemed so small, suddenly.

"Hotels," she said.

"What about them?"

"It's like the whole world is nothing but a fucking hotel."

Her back was still turned, so she couldn't see my eyebrows rise. "You've gotten philosophical in your old age," I said. It seemed better than saying she'd gotten cliché.

"My old age," Isabel repeated. That same resigned, hollow laugh followed.

"You sound skeptical."

"Let's just say I don't see such a thing in my future."

I felt no shock, or even alarm, necessarily. It was all too predictable, too Isabel. I remembered one of our pillow talks from that pivotal summer when she teared up talking about her father and the pain he caused her—its smallness and the smallness it made her feel in turn. "I want to care about bigger things," she'd said. "Not this meaningless shit."

"Don't we all?" I had asked.

"No. We don't," she'd stated confidently. "It chases you down, doesn't it? Meaningless shit. There's no way to escape, is there? Except death."

I couldn't recall the argument I'd given in response, or if I'd given any at all. Only that I curled her closer and she breathed appreciatively into my arm, and I believed we'd always keep each other safe.

"Do you think about that, Isa?" I asked her now.

"What?"

"Suicide."

That mirthless laugh again. "No. Not the way you mean it."

How many ways could one mean suicide? I wondered.

"I don't anymore either," I said.

It wasn't a lie, practically speaking. But it felt like one at that moment, such a bumbling, obvious attempt at finding common ground, shareable sorrow. I waited for her to ask the story, prepping the details in my mind— another hotel room, my moist temple, voices of I don't know how many phantasms arguing with one another over whether I should—but she never did. She didn't even turn around.

"Do you want to sleep?" I asked.

"You go ahead. I can't sleep."

"What can you do?"

"Not a lot," Isabel said. "What a disappointment I must be to you."

"You were never exactly the most chipper person I knew." I must have been hoping for the kind of response I sporadically earned in the Bosques, amid all that whiskey and nostalgia. Or else I'd simply grown tired and stopped thinking my words through. "It's nice to know in some ways you haven't changed."

"In some ways I have," Isabel said. She didn't explain, and the meaning of the whole exchange started to become muddled, sleep-fogged. What ways were we even talking about? What had she said about hotels, and why did it feel like we'd been speaking in a code I'd never learned to translate?

"What?" I asked, and she turned around. Smiled like I was a sweet, sleepy boy and she was my mother. I didn't want Isabel to look at me that way.

"Go to sleep, Tomás," she said. "Have some dreams. I'd love it if you would."

"It's not like I don't have my own nightmares, Isa," I said. But it was as if I'd caught the drift of some old conversation we were no longer having, and the statement seemed out of place, clunky and unwelcome.

"Well," she said, "don't have any tonight for me, please?"

I had another impulse to echo her, to say something like, "Only because you said please." But I didn't. Soon enough waves of fatigue were rolling me back under, and I fell asleep before she came back to bed.

⸺

WHEN I WOKE IN THE MORNING, she was gone. She'd left no number or note or any other trace, not even next to me in the sheets. It was as if she'd never lain down with me.

I can't say it was a surprise—this was our routine from Pinamar, after all. But I can say it hurt. More than one might think, given that for a decade I'd believed her gone. I even, for the first time in almost that long, found myself starting to cry.

FOUR

There was a dreaminess to it the next day, a whiff of the surreal. I remembered the night's events vividly but felt as if I'd blacked out, opened gaps in my recollection. Again, like a dream, a nightmare you have only the sensation of in the morning, the apprehension.

Claire was part of it. As justified as I'd felt hailing that cab, I wasn't prepared for the sense of rupture I woke to, the panicky feeling of writing on the wall and wheels set irreversibly in motion.

My hangover didn't help; it'd been years since I suffered one so severe. When the phone in my hotel room rang—I was still in bed, my face buried between pillows to block out the glare—it sounded shrill as a baby screeching in my ear. I picked up in a clumsy rush and heard my voice: hoarse and so sluggish I seemed drugged.

It was Cecilia's husband, calling to tell me Pichuca had passed away around dawn. I ineptly offered my condolences, and he promised to pass them on.

"Is Isa there?" I asked. She seemed a balm to me still, indeed maybe a drug. Something to keep reality at bay.

"Isa?" the man said. His confusion was audible. More than confusion—blankness.

"Yes, Isabel," I said. Maybe she never came around when they were there, I thought. Maybe they didn't know she was alive, the way they hadn't known I was. "Isabel, Pichuca's daughter."

"Hold on a second, Tomás, I'm sorry." It sounded somehow like he was sorry for *me*. That he didn't realize I was in—whatever state he thought me in. Broken by grief? Simply broken?

"Tomás?" Cecilia said, coming on the line. "Are you okay?"

I was embarrassed. That was what I told myself: I'd misunderstood something, and I was embarrassed. That was all.

"Pichuca mentioned Isabel on the phone to me, and I . . . I wondered if she—"

"She mentioned a lot of things at the end, Tomás," Cecilia said. "I wouldn't make too much of it."

"I'm not. I just"—I stammered, correcting course—"I just want to know what else she said about me."

"What she said didn't make any sense, Tomás."

"A lot of things don't make sense, Ceci," I replied.

She sighed irritatedly. "Pichu said you needed to see that colonel friend of yours, okay? Felipe Gorlero?"

He was someone else I'd underemphasized to Claire. Just another name on that list, not "the Colonel," as he'd long since been to me.

"Why doesn't that make sense?"

"Because I thought he was dead. I read he had a heart attack last year or maybe the year before, I don't know. When all those accusations started coming out about death flights and whatnot. He wasn't as high up in the army then, but it didn't matter, they pinned what they wanted on him. It sounded like he was in bad shape."

I remembered the bottle of Johnnie Walker in my hotel room trash. The brochure on the nightstand for tours of the Recoleta Cemetery.

"Was it the Colonel who gave Pichu my number?"

"I don't know, Tomás. Honestly, I don't care."

Before I could press—my mind was careening too rapidly, struggling to pick a point of entry—I heard the click indicating she'd hung up on me.

———

I DIDN'T CALL BACK. I told myself it was because I'd be embarrassed again—and rude and selfish as well. Instead I went downstairs to a confitería for coffee and medialunas, hoping my head would clear when my hangover did. But it wasn't nearly as palliative as the greasy American breakfasts I'd gotten used to. Bacon and eggs and butter-slathered toast—I first had such a meal at a diner in Kew Gardens a few days after arriving in New York. The Colonel had pontificated to me about their benefits for hangovers, and I'd been desperate to confirm another of his teachings.

I didn't set out with the intention of finding him. As I staggered into the sunshine toward his neighborhood, there was only the instinct, the reliability of a first step along a well-trodden path. Simply a long, dazed walk like the ones I used to take here, amid the cruel, sprawling beauty of Buenos Aires.

The swaying greenery and Parisian architecture, those charming specialty shops like umbrella stores—the city remained completely unmarred by what happened within it. Buenos Aires never showed its scars, never let its surface be ruffled; it was a city made for forgetting as much as for nostalgia.

It was only in taking specific turns as I got closer—off Avenida Libertador onto Scalabrini Ortiz, left on Cerviño—that I acknowledged what I was doing. Seeking him out as usual, for help or guidance. The last time I'd done so was in '76, as hungover and distressed as I was now. "All I'm saying is you can always come to me," he'd told me some months earlier. "Whatever it is. You need never be afraid with me."

I never was. Not even when I first met him as a ten-year-old boy at Atenas, a men's club in La Plata. Most of the guests went there for smoky pleasures like whiskeys and cigars and prostitutes—I lost my virginity there years later—but I went because Atenas was also the only real chess club in the city. I was good for my age, and my father finagled a membership for me to get some proper competition. The best players in the city and some from farther away came for matches, among them a colonel named Felipe Gorlero, who happened to watch me beat an elderly math professor from the local university. Intrigued, he challenged me next, and I impressed him enough that he offered to give me lessons whenever he returned to town.

Those lessons quickly expanded beyond chess. Books, science, history—knowledge bubbled off him as much as his personality. Though he was slim as a twig, he seemed so much grander than my parents—than anyone. "You seem different from people in the army," I said to him once, in a state of youthful awe.

"Do you know many people in the army, Tomasito?" he asked. After an interval, I confessed I didn't. The Colonel laughed proudly. "Don't worry: I *am* different from people in the army. Most of them—they're pawns. Most people are, Tomás. And if I have a creed, it is not to be a pawn in anything."

He was a patron as much as a tutor. Hosting me on trips to Buenos Aires, getting permission from my mother to drive me to Mar del Plata to see Najdorf play in a tournament. As I got older, he started mentoring me academically as well, steering me toward both medicine—his father had been a chemist and wanted him to be one, and my mother wanted me to be anything with a stable paycheck—and English. Through the army, he'd become exposed to many high-level Americans (including at the School of the Americas in Panama; he never told me what he trained in there but his light references to stuffy CIA types and counterinsurgency tactics from Vietnam gave me ideas), and he'd developed an infatuation that rubbed off on me. "Such a pretty, hunky language," he'd insist, and, convinced, I studied it from middle school through college. "Cloaked in those words, you can be who you want. The American Dream. What's the Argentine Dream, meanwhile?"

I didn't even know my own dreams. Maybe if I'd had firmer ones, my relationship with the Colonel wouldn't have morphed again the way it did when I moved to his city. But by then, what dreams I had involved Isabel, and her dreams involved fighting the military, and there was no getting closer to anyone, only more entangled.

———

I STOOD IN FRONT OF the Colonel's building for several minutes before entering. There was a doorman in the lobby whom I didn't know, despite his advanced age and air of having worked there forever. Haltingly, I asked for the Gorleros, sixth floor—6A, I clarified, to prove I wasn't a stranger.

"They moved out years ago. Separately," the doorman said, eyebrows raised, I assumed because divorce remained illegal here. My own disappointment was of a more basic sort: when I was growing up, no couple had seemed as perfect or happy to me as the Colonel and Mercedes.

"Where'd they go?"

Those eyebrows rose again—bushy and white, with long, sprouting hairs that highlighted his skepticism. "Afraid I can't tell you that," he said. I toyed with making up a story to get myself upstairs—journalist or executor or something—but out of awkwardness or some more latent reason, I opted not to.

I went afterward to Plaza San Martín. It was one of the Colonel's favorite places—the sole one he claimed he could keep quiet in. For over an hour I watched the middle-aged men reading in the shade of the ombú trees, and when there was no sign of him, I continued southwest several kilometers toward Balvanera, the less ritzy neighborhood where I'd lived in '76. Skirting my old building, I wound up on the corner of Jujuy and Yrigoyen, staring into what used to be the café Parada Norte—a dank, old-fashioned spot to which the Colonel had introduced me. Now it was named the Roxy and sported a bright, modern ambience and an American-influenced menu—french fries with everything. At least it was the kind of food my stomach needed, I told myself as I went inside.

There was a newspaper on the table. All the headlines seemed to be about the aftermath of the dictatorship—the languishing trials of military officers; the likely passage of the Full Stop law, which mandated the end of all prosecutions of people accused of political violence under the junta; the general atmosphere of anger and unfulfilled justice. On one of the interior pages, I caught sight of an article about an assault at a ski resort in Bariloche on an army lieutenant named Rodrigo Astral—or, as he'd apparently become known, the Blond Angel of Death. A small photo beside it showed his aquiline features and slicked Prince Charming hair, which I recognized instantly: Rubio, one of the soldiers who worked at Automotores while I was there. The place was also identified in the article, with the strangely formal-looking abbreviation CCD—Clandestine Center of Detention.

I folded the paper neatly and set it back down, then left the restaurant without a word to the waiter. It pressed heavily on me—the vendetta-like feel of events, the sense that Argentina had summoned me back for a reason. There could have been other occasions for my return—those letters about my mother's assets had stipulated that I claim them in person, and the interview requests from CONADEP had alluded to airfare reimbursements—but those requests had been faceless, impersonal, confined to administrative communiqués I could ignore. This by contrast was one face after another, and it seemed clear whose would inevitably be next in the procession: I could already picture the Colonel's grin beneath his mustache as he raised a whiskey to his lips.

I thought once more of the bottle of Johnnie Walker in my hotel room and the brochure for the Recoleta Cemetery. Suddenly they seemed to constitute a message for me. Of course it was there, in the last place I'd encountered the Colonel ten years ago, that I was to meet him again. The past was swinging violently back around, and for me personally.

———

I REMAINED ON FOOT, and the cemetery was closed when I arrived. But instead of going back to my hotel, I went to a nearby café and stayed until dark. Then, semi-drunk on the two liters of beer I'd consumed, I took a seat in the plaza outside the main gate.

I had no fondness for the place. Even at the start of my stay in Buenos Aires, I considered it a tourist trap, a gaudy homage to some of Argentina's most abusive institutions: the aristocracy and the Catholic Church. Only the military was missing. Which was why its having been one of the Colonel's stomping grounds was characteristically peculiar: they weren't his people entombed there, nor were they his people traipsing about taking photographs. I'd never been able to square it. But then the Colonel was not exactly right-angled to begin with.

Night had settled in, and there were no streetlights in the cemetery proper, making the sky above it marginally blacker than it was over the rest of the city. The only lamps hung from wrought-iron fixtures on the outer wall, and cast barely enough light to illuminate the gate's white Greco-Roman columns. The austere Latin sign above—REQUIESCANT IN PACE—was shadowed to the point of illegibility, and the bell tower of the colonial church beside it was hazy enough to seem merely another mausoleum spire.

Still, the scene was sufficiently lovely that a man dressed like a carica-
ture of Gardel, with a fedora and a red rose pinned to his vest, was playing bittersweet notes on his bandoneón and asking for money. Scrawny
stray cats padded past him as if drawn by the music, but more likely by
the hope that anyone generous enough to give him a peso would be generous enough to give them a snack. One was a scruffy gold, another spotted black-and-white, the third a sleek Siamese with eyes that shimmered
like chips of ice. Purring every now and again, they made their circu-
itous way back to the cemetery wall and slipped past the bars of a smaller
gate farther south.

That gate, I noticed, was slightly ajar. I rose and, without looking around
to see if anyone was watching, slipped past myself.

I'd never been inside at night. With all the regal details of the architecture and sculpting obscured, its splendor was diminished, along with any
sense of upkeep; it seemed more like a ruin, a genuine city of the dead.
Overturned flower vases caught my attention, the reediness of dried stems.
Broken angel statues and Gothic crosses cast wild, ghoulish shadows, and
my steps resounded eerily behind me, loose tiles snapping back into place
with quick, frightful clicks under my weight.

One of the cats sat licking itself in the middle of the lane. Silhouetted,
it looked black at first, adding to the Halloween decor; then it glanced up
at me cross-eyed and I realized it was the Siamese. It took off to its left,
and when I reached the corner, I turned after it.

That was when I saw him—a man proportionally as skinny as the animal he was petting, stooped in a narrow alley beyond a crumbling ancient
crypt belonging to some forgotten aristocrat named Dasso and the cracked,
noseless Virgin Mary that peered down from atop it.

He was dressed in civilian clothes—a gray suit the color of the stone
around him and his thinned-out hair. Only his bushy whiskers retained
the rich brown they'd had a decade before. Even his eyes—little beady

things that, because of the rest of his highly cultivated personality, seemed to demand a pince-nez—had dampened and become cloudy.

"Colonel," I called, and the Siamese darted off, leaving his hand to stroke the air.

"Señor Shore." Straightening, he took me in from head to toe with a familiar smile of amusement. "You have a beard."

He said it like I was still a teenager, wearing it in an effort to seem grown-up. The impression bothered me—maybe because it was right.

The name he used bothered me more—haunted me, really. He'd always enjoyed showing off his English with me, and one trademark way was translating my name. I don't remember if he started calling me Thomas Shore before or after he told me about the nineteenth-century British writer of the same name, but I do remember what he said when he did. It was the summer I moved to Buenos Aires, not long before the '76 coup:

"Wrote a book called *The Churchman and the Free Thinker*. Interesting, no? If it was anything like Argentina, the two probably didn't get along. In fact, if it was anything like Argentina, it probably would have been called simply *The Churchman*. I'm the closest thing to a freethinker this country can tolerate, Tomás. Er, excuse me—*Thomas*. Señor *Thomas* Shore, that's what I should call you. Since you, in your own way, are a freethinker like me."

It was the name he had put in my fake passport eventually. And it became, through a special twist of casuistry and hindsight, a kind of curse for me, the spiritual reason I became a translator when I moved to New York. Granted, it was medical texts I translated for a living, certainly nothing too free-thinky, but still. It was as if with his christening my whole identity got tangled up in translation, lost in the proverbial way between two worlds.

"Are you some kind of ghost?" I asked him.

"More like an angel, really. I'm your angel, Tomás, don't you know? Always have been. All that's changed is your . . ." He took me in again, before gesturing vaguely from cheek to cheek, like a parent instructing a child to wipe his face. "Your . . . *chin*." He grinned at finding the word, then came close to pouting when he saw I didn't share his satisfaction. "Come, Tomás, you know it's true. I've saved you from this place in more ways than one, haven't I?"

He spoke as he had in life: Inflected with a certain strain of power, the kind that enabled his idiosyncrasies. His conversation seemed to have a freewheeling nature, but he was always headed somewhere, even when you couldn't divine the destination.

It was also the way he played chess. Or perhaps more accurately, chess was the way he played everything: with bold, random-looking sacrifices, moves so inexplicable they seemed taunts. It used to rattle me. Apparently, it still did.

"And what are you here to do now?" I asked.

"Not save you from this place. Rather the opposite, in fact."

The hint of foreboding I felt—I found myself drawn by it. It was the same dark gravitational pull the Colonel—Isabel too—had long exerted on me.

"What do you mean?"

"My morality has always been . . . complicated. You know I never went in fully for the hero-villain stuff. Yet . . . it finds its way into you, doesn't it? For some of us?"

"You mean guilt?"

"Sure. Penance, guilt," he said, as if nuance among such notions was needless. "You want to go back and change things. But in life you can't go back and change things, can you? Not in life. All you can do in life is try to make up for it in other ways. I know you know about that, Tomás."

It should have been a good thing, arguably, trying to compensate for past wrongdoings. But he lobbed the observation like it was the reverse—a moral failure, a testament to the irredeemable size of those wrongdoings.

"Do *you* know about that?" I asked.

"Of course. Why do you think I sought you out?"

"You're going to make it up to me?"

"To *you?* Ja! You're so selfish, Tomás, really." He tsk-tsked. "To her, Tomasito. We're going to make it up to *her*."

Moments from the day before with Isabel started to replay in my head and on my senses: I could feel her cracked lips, her dry hair on my finger-tips, the unfamiliar boniness in her thighs. Sniff the scentless air and hear that elusive laughter of hers.

It's nice to know in some ways you haven't changed.

In some ways I have.

And it was only as these moments unspooled that it became concrete for me. Only then did those ghostly wisps of logic and feeling thread to-gether into hard fact and certainty, the strange, grainy reality of ghostli-ness itself. The Colonel belonged to it. And Isabel—despite my denials, I'd known it all along, from that first, unmiraculous instant—she belonged to it too.

Ten years. Do you know what it would have meant to me to know you'd survived?

Does it really seem I've survived, Tomás?

"How?" I asked.

"You know how," the Colonel said smugly. Maybe that was all it was, that quality in his speech I'd attributed to some mix of freedom and cal-culation, some eccentric kind of foresight—maybe it was simply smug-ness. "We took her life away, Tomás. Wouldn't you like to give it back to her? To give her back to life, I mean?"

"Give her back? You mean get her from . . . ?"

"Get her, bring her, take her—what difference does that word make? The important word is *back*. Back here. From there."

"But *there* is . . . ?"

"You think it impossible? Even now, after seeing her? After seeing *me*," he emphasized proudly. "Just look at me—fresh as a daisy. Or something a little more wilty, I admit, but lively enough for the purpose of this proposal. The border, it's very real. But it's thin, porous in a way. There are more ways to cross than you might think."

"If it's so easy, why can't she just come back on her own again?" I asked, catching more echoes from the previous night, watching the whole interaction turn further upside down in my recollection.

You were in a detention center?

The biggest of its kind.

"Easy? No, no, you mustn't leap to conclusions, Tomasito. There's the way she came back, the way I did. But what I said was that there are *more* ways. *Other* ways. We came here, your darling little rebel and I, essentially by slipping through cracks. Taking advantage of some fleeting, flimsy loopholes, like the rest of those miserable phantoms you read about in stories. But you have to understand: that place, the underworld—it changes you. Kills you all over again, really, every moment. It's not just your life that's lost after enough time, it's *you*. So, to come back, this way—it's no good, you see. You're missing something, missing everything. It's a technicality, not real. Not life."

"But you've found another way," I said, allowing an edge into my voice, something sharper than sarcasm or skepticism. It still seemed too easy to me, too much like a pawn thrown my way as bait. He did it so often, I occasionally lost games because I was afraid to take it, to discover the net he'd made me weave around myself.

"Don't believe me, Señor Shore? Fair enough, I admit. We are scientific men, the both of us, rational to a fault. But whatever my record with morality, you know it's much less spotty when it comes to honesty. You know I have never lied to you."

I did. Though the distinction between technicality and reality felt appropriate here too: you don't lie when you offer up a piece in service to a greater design; but you do deceive.

"Besides," the Colonel continued, "scientific type that you are, don't you want to know for sure? To know there's nothing more you could do for your penance, your guilt, whatever you'd like to call it? What do you have to lose?"

I thought of Claire, crying in the shower the night before I left. I'd listened from our bedroom for several minutes before undressing and joining her. By the time I did, I couldn't tell the difference between the water on her cheeks and the tears. We soaped each other without saying anything about her affair or my departure, and when we got out, she dried my back for me, since I never did a good job. "You know, if this ends, you'll literally go to bed cold every night," she said, and laughed. I'd laughed mildly too.

"How do you cross the border?" I asked.

"How do *you* cross the border, you mean? But you already know that too, Señor Shore. The path—you almost took it once, after all."

Another pinch of suspicion. More than that, a kind of grabbing of the neck or seizing of the intestines—a deep, twisted clawing. I glanced up at the noseless Virgin Mary and the other statues looming over us and felt the same kind of penetration in their gazes, as if they saw the images competing before my eyes, the memories: the last time I was here at the Recoleta Cemetery, so dizzy from the darkness of the hood over my head I couldn't even see the car I got out of; or that night in Rome several months later, when I got a hotel room and, with a shaking hand, pressed a revolver to my temple.

I felt dizzy again now.

"It was more than once," I told him, covering my eyes and closing them, hoping I'd get my bearings back in the darkness. I should have known better.

"What, Rome? Rome was nothing. You only came close once in truth, and it wasn't in Rome. Only in Buenos Aires did you really look into the darkness of that other world. And only here. The car dropped you off, you made your decision . . . But you could have made other decisions, couldn't you? Gotten back into that car and wound up in a different kind of cemetery . . . ?"

I reopened my eyes. Saw the Colonel smiling.

"And this time I will?" I asked.

"Just go to where that path began, and then go down it. Nudge the door to death open a little bit and it'll swing wide, you'll see. By the time you get back into that car, well—it won't just be a car you're in anymore."

"But the path," I said, focused as usual on the practicalities, the minutiae. Never the bigger picture. "If you mean Automotores, won't it be closed? Locked?"

"Tomás, Tomás," the Colonel sighed. "Don't you know I take care of these things in advance? It's like chess, it always has been for me. True, in this case you were a little slower taking the bait than I expected, but oh well. You're here now, aren't you?"

"I came as soon as I got the message," I answered.

"Please, Tomasito, I've been sending the message for years. Request for an in-person interview with CONADEP in '84? My finagling. That follow-up on your mother's assets? Mine too. I've been trying ever since I arrived in that wonderful world of secondary education. My little ploy with Pichuca was just the first one that worked."

Perhaps the conclusion should have been that there was nothing particularly special about this moment, if he'd been trying so long to get me here without success. Mere timing, coincidence. But the only coincidence I could discern in my relationship with the Colonel was meeting him randomly at a men's club when I was ten. Something stickier had kept us bound together in life and—apparently—beyond it.

"I'm here now," I repeated, to a satisfied nod.

"All you'll need on arrival is your passport," he said. "Your real one, the one I gave you."

"That one's fake."

"Ja—I don't think you think that, Tomasito. You brought it, didn't you? Brought it to Argentina without my saying a word about it to you?"

It took me a moment to return his nod, as if by doing so I would admit more than he'd implied.

"See? Don't pretend to be so naive, Señor Shore. You knew where you were going as soon as you set off for this country. You knew what it was to you, what you came looking for. In some ways, Tomasito, you've started the journey already."

What could I say in response but that it was true? That I was, without realizing it, ready to continue.

He told me to meet him again tomorrow, the way he'd explained, and from there we'd go down together. "Romantic, almost, no?" he said, laughing, and I tried to think of Isabel and tell myself it was. Yet something, his laughter or my desire to turn and leave and get to the end of this journey as quickly as possible, told me it wasn't. It wasn't romantic in the least.

FIVE

It wasn't so different from the morning before: hazy, spotty, fogged. Hungover, too. Only that aura of unreality had been shed, the drapery of dreams and wishful illusion.

I called Claire. We'd agreed not to talk for a few days, to give ourselves some space, some time. But that feeling of irrevocability had returned to me, the fear that, even if I came back from this journey, some part of me might be left behind, the bridge burned in my wake. It had been so long since Claire and I had really spoken, besides. In that sense, the notion of my absence, my being only half there, wasn't such a new one.

Her voice was tired, lazy, as if she'd just woken up. The two-hour time difference, I reminded myself, when the hypocritical suspicion that she'd been indulging her affair this morning crossed my mind. She asked me how I was, and I told her fine. She asked about Pichuca, and I told her I was glad to have seen her. She asked me what it was like to be back, and I told her it was the same. Then different. Then that I had no idea, really.

"Have you decided when you're coming home?" she asked. I'd booked my room for two weeks, figuring I could stay longer if needed.

"No," I said. "Not yet."

We were silent for a time.

"Have you decided about Roger?"

"No. Not yet," she said.

Again, we were silent.

"What are we doing?" Claire asked.

"What do you mean?"

"We're not talking. This isn't talking."

"Well," I said slowly, with the kind of deliberateness she'd have reprimanded me for when our problems were smaller, "didn't we say we weren't going to talk until we figured out what we wanted to do?"

"And did you figure it out?"

I held the phone close to my cheek. "No," I said. "I didn't."

"Well," she said, without finishing the thought.

Until recently, I might have described Claire's defining characteristic as lightness, her ability to foster it. All that weight I carried around on my shoulders—sometimes she massaged it in the usual manner partners did, with tenderness, consolation; but more often she tried to flick it away with a joke. "Tom," she'd call me, having taken a liking to my name in English, much as the Colonel had. "Feeling grumpy today? Need some ice cream? A blow job?" Nothing was sacred or off-limits to her, which might have been why we could convince ourselves of our openness, our total acceptance of each other. "I know you were having nightmares last night, Tom. But you were also pooting up a storm." She barreled through my bashfulness at every stage of our relationship, starting with the first: when I knocked on her apartment door and had to tell her, awkwardly, that I had the wrong one, darting my glance self-consciously away from her long, bare legs in running shorts. Claire—still sweaty, wiping her brow with her shirt so I got a glimpse of her toned torso—invited me inside. "Tom you said your name was?" she asked, and I was too embarrassed to correct her or, on that initial invitation, to accept. That took two years and another accidental encounter uptown. She grinned at me then as if she'd been waiting for me on 103rd Street and Amsterdam all along.

It had seemed a miracle, her resolute interest in me. I couldn't understand it, and once even asked her outright what made her want me. She jested about having a duty to bestow her gifts on the saddest sacks she could find, but I told her I was serious. "I know. So serious. What can I say, I like to make you chortle." "I don't chortle," I replied, though I was already starting to laugh. "You're the chortliest," she said. "How do you say that in Spanish, Tom? Chortliest?"

She didn't call me Tom much anymore.

"I just," I began. "I just wanted to say you've made me very happy, Claire. That's really why I called."

"'Very' seems like a strong word," she answered.

"Fine. You've made me as happy as anyone could, how about that?"

"That's fine," she said. "We'll talk in a few days, okay?"

"Okay." I don't know if either of us said good-bye before hanging up.

———

THE COLONEL HADN'T SAID when to meet him, but I knew: First thing in the morning, time to go to work. Since work was, to use his language, where that path began.

The route wasn't so different from the one I used to take: bus to Estación Once, train to Floresta. Back then, I walked to the station, skirting the Plaza Miserere, with its sparse, seemingly never-blooming jacarandas.

On the platform, men sold medialunas and other pastries, repeating the names of their goods with the practiced cadences of chanting monks. The wait was short, as was the commute—three stops, a mere half hour. Too short.

"Your dreams," Claire had said a few months into our relationship, having seen me wrestle with them in my fidgety, anxious sleep, "your nightmares. Do you want to tell me about them, Tom?" I'd outlined their general sources by then, couching them in impersonal language, as if for an introductory lecture or generic documentary for Americans. For twenty years, I'd told her, there'd been a cycle in Argentina of democracy, dictatorship, protests, democracy, dictatorship, protests. This time the dictatorship wasn't going to fall to protests or democracy. They established these detention centers—they were illegal but run by the armed forces and government with the goal of terrorizing the population and repressing threatening ideologies. In some five hundred of them across the country, probably thirty thousand detainees had disappeared.

"They're nothing," I said of my nightmares when she asked. "Usually it's just the train. On the way there."

"They took prisoners there by train?"

"Yes," I lied, telling myself it was for simplicity's sake.

Mine had been a reverse commute, away from the city's center, and it wasn't unusual for me to have a car to myself, as I did today. I looked out the scratched-up window. There was graffiti on the walls on either side of the rails, which was new, as well as on the rusted, abandoned train cars farther out. But the rest of the scenery had barely changed: the uncared-for backsides of decrepit buildings followed by taller, more modern ones with awnings and balconies, the residences of rich and poor alternating with little apparent logic. Lush, green parks emerged behind the platforms at Caballito and Flores, making the ride seem charming and picturesque. Indeed, maybe it was; maybe that was the problem. The world remained stubbornly, indifferently beautiful despite my destination in it.

I got off on Avenida General Venancio Flores and made the familiar five-minute walk. On one side were the tracks, on the other mostly residential buildings; depending on how early I arrived in the mornings—or on night shifts, how late in the day—I'd see parents taking children to school or to the soccer field a couple blocks away. One evening I'd played on it myself, not two hours after I'd had to resuscitate someone with a defibrillator. I wasn't much of a player to begin with, and I spent most of the game watching the ball move among others' feet as if they had some dazzling magnetism I lacked. But I never so lost myself in the dance as I did that day.

Automotores was known in the public record as Automotores Orletti, I'd discovered in that article about Rubio. The name on the sign out front had originally read AUTOMOTORES CORTELL, but the C had fallen off, and apparently when the escape happened, and the reporting fugitive looked back for a terrified instant, the words he saw were AUTOMOTORES ORLETTI.

To me it was always simply Automotores. But to the other men who worked there, it was also El Jardín—the Garden. Someone in command probably thought that was funny.

It'd been an auto repair shop in its last incarnation, a train-car repair shop in its first, and from the outside retained the look of a garage. To the left of the large roll-up metal gate was the regular entrance, which in those days was unlocked only after radioing the absurdly unoriginal password *sesame* to the guard booth. Now it hung open, and a man I recognized stood at its side with keys in his hand. It was the Gringo Carlitos. His big, child-like face beamed when he spotted me.

"Verde!" he called. "La puta madre, Verde, is that you?!"

Verde was what they called me at Automotores, because of my inexperience. Carlitos we called the Gringo, since he'd been stationed briefly at a base in North Carolina and bragged ceaselessly about having had his own US counterinsurgency training. He'd always been meaty, but now he was more so; his shirt was too small and had one too many buttons undone, revealing his hairy chest and a gold cross and allowing a whiff of talcum powder to drift from his neck. For all his unbounded liveliness, there was still something bumbling and pitiable about him—or at least there might have been, if I didn't know he'd been a torturer not long ago.

"Never would've guessed you were the one I was supposed to let in," he said.

"Me neither," I told him.

"Couldn't stay away, huh? You never could, really. I remember at the end—"

He broke off. It was possibly the first time I could remember him stopping himself before saying something he shouldn't.

"Seems like you couldn't either," I said.

"Huh? Oh this," he said, as if he'd forgotten he was holding open the door to a detention center and we'd run into each other randomly, at the train station or some intersection. "I haven't been in years, not sure anyone has. The downstairs became another auto-repair shop, and a little clothing manufacturer took over the second floor after we left—as a matter of fact, I heard she kept some aspects of our setup, had people locked in the closets at sewing machines twelve hours a day and that kind of thing—but both closed down again back in, oh, '83, '84. I just came to do the Colonel this favor. He did plenty for us, you remember."

I preferred not to. "The two of you stay in touch?"

"Shit, Verde, you want to go in there and interrogate me for real? Ja!" He laughed grandly, from deep in his belly. "I'm kidding you, don't worry. I just got the one letter asking me to be here this morning. For the Colonel, I figure why the hell not? A couple hours standing guard, what's the harm? Truth is, I don't stay in touch with anyone from the old days. Sad, no? What happened to us all? Just take the Colonel—that whole news frenzy a while back, I guess he won't show his face anymore. And Triste—puta madre."

I didn't ask about the Colonel's letter, assuming it was like those he'd arranged for me over the years, and we wound up making small talk. The Gringo asked me how long I was in town, and I told him briefly. He asked me where I lived, and I told him that too. I tried not to ask him anything.

"We missed you in '78," he said, referring to the first World Cup Argentina won, right as the dictatorship reached the peak of its power. I was in New York by then, but couldn't help tuning in to the radio and, for whatever disturbing, inexplicable reason, quietly cheering on my homeland. "We all watched together at Olimpo—that's where most of the crew was stationed then, just ten minutes away over on Coronel Lorenzo Falcón. Everyone yelled the goals when we scored. You should have been there, Verde."

He still had that weird-seeming innocence, like a child who didn't know better. I remembered when he'd asked me, in an almost frightened voice, if it was true what they said, that the Jews were taking over Patagonia. He was too oblivious to realize I was Jewish myself.

"Everyone watched?"

"Of course."

"Even the prisoners?"

"Of course. That would have been real torture, not letting them watch that. You should have heard them screaming 'goal' with us. *Goooooal! Goooooooooal!* It was like we were all on the same side, I swear."

"The prisoners screamed *goal* with you?" I asked, though I needed no clarification. I'm not sure what I needed.

"We told them not to be shy—it was a special occasion. And you wouldn't believe it, Verde, once we gave them permission? They could have blown the roof off that place with their screaming, I swear. Now that would have been an escape, huh? Not like the shit you pulled." He didn't say it like an accusation, but we were quiet for a moment all the same, as awkward as exes who had bumped into each other.

Knowing the Gringo, I guessed he would break under the weight of too much silence soon enough, and I was right. He would have done terribly in a detention center.

"You watch this year? Pah, that Maradona! The Hand of God! Incredible. The war against subversives is the best thing that ever happened to Argentine soccer, I swear. And you know why? Patriotism. We wanted it more for the country after that. We'll see if it lasts, now that the patriots are being hung out to dry by the bosses. You know, they won't give some of us promotions, blame what happened during the war on our type? The Colonel—they basically made a fall guy out of him for Campo de Mayo. Rubio, he was attacked, can't even leave the country because the Spanish will extradite him for those nuns. And Triste, fuck, you hear about him?"

I didn't want to hear about Triste. About any of them.

"I should get going, Carlitos," I said, before realizing I couldn't claim to be pressed for time, that Automotores had waited for me for ten years, and would go on waiting another ten minutes.

But to my surprise, the Gringo stepped aside with an understanding nod. "Got to pay your respects, right? I get it. Truth is, I did come back once, when the women's operation here was shut down. Having the place to yourself—goddamn, what a thing. But anyway," he went on, "we should get coffee while you're in town. Talk old times, watch a game."

"Sure, Carlitos."

"I'm serious. That American girl—pah. I understand. I could've done the same."

"Sure, Carlitos," I said again.

"What? You don't think I have nightmares? You don't think I cared?"

I couldn't help but recognize, with no small amount of disgust, the resonances of my conversation with Isabel. *It's not like I don't have my own nightmares, Isa,* I'd said.

"I do, Carlitos," I said, giving in to his whims as if it really were old times. "I'll give you a call later, after I'm done here," I assured him, though I didn't have his number and wasn't asking for it. "We'll get that coffee."

He smiled sadly before walking off. I'd be lying if I said I didn't feel bad about it. Even when I considered how hard it must be for Argentines who hadn't left, having to go about their daily lives with the possibility of bumping into their torturers at train stations and random intersections or having to wonder, because they'd been blindfolded back then, if the man giving them a funny look on the bus had raped them—even then, I felt bad, like I was running away again.

But now the passage into Automotores was unbarred, and I remembered I wasn't running. Not any longer.

———

JUST GO TO WHERE THAT PATH BEGAN, the Colonel had instructed, *and then go down it*. Instead of taking the staircase up to what had been the officers' quarters—the bottom half was wooden, the top marble, as if you were ascending toward royalty—I went through the guard booth into the garage itself. It had barely changed: car parts remained strewn about the front, and the smell of engine oil was thick and strong, as sticky in your nostrils as the concrete floor was under your feet. Only the curtain that hid the back end was missing, and the space looked wider and emptier than I'd ever seen it in my six months here. Darker too—the bulbs dangling from the ceiling were off, and no sunlight snuck in through the garage door.

I waited for something to happen, a flash of memory or fear, or the prickling of the hair on my arms at least, but there was nothing. It was like most of my nightmares: oddly practical, the trauma conspicuously offstage.

There was a staircase here as well—this one entirely wooden, and no doubt as creaky as ever; it had a flimsy appearance, like it would cave in at the first step, but I knew from experience it wouldn't. It was the staircase prisoners were taken up, and the one I went up the last time I was here, and for that reason I went up it now.

The white paint over the brickwork upstairs had always been cracked, but now it was peeling off; gray showed through in dirty patches. There were still loose threads and lint from the sweatshop on the floors, and the roof was corrugated metal, browned over the years. The windows remained tightly covered and sealed, but there was more light upstairs even so, seeping in from the terrace. It stretched far enough for me to see the doors to what had been the three isolation cells, and the one to collective holding. Farther down, the corridor became more shadowy, like the end of a black, unlit tunnel. But I knew what was at the end.

The torture room. The door, mercifully, looked closed.

I turned instead toward the nearest isolation cell. Its door was shut too, but unlocked. I pushed it open tentatively, as if someone might be inside.

No one was. But in the light from the balcony I saw that there was something on the floor besides lint and thread: two red bandannas and a larger piece of thick black fabric that, despite its shapelessness, I still recognized.

"Anything else?" Claire had asked me in that conversation about my nightmares. I'd stared at the bedroom wall. Cliché, I remember thinking in the delicate silence as Claire looked at my cheek, gently kneaded my shoulder with her fingers. This is what a wounded person is like. This is what a refugee is like.

"The radio. Trucks parking in the garage. Capuchita."

"What does that mean?"

"It means 'little hood.'"

Her look was puzzled but kind, as if I must have been confused. "Never the machine, that electric cattle prod they used?" she asked. "What was it called?"

"The picana," I said. Shrugged, then shook my head.

"I thought they— Didn't they use it on your balls and things, your sensitive areas?"

"Your sensitive areas. Yes."

"But they didn't touch you while you were in that . . . that hood?"

"They didn't touch you much, no."

"Well, what did they do?"

"They didn't have to do much of anything."

What I couldn't explain was that you did it to yourself. That to escape that darkness you clawed out of your self. Out of your mind.

Nudge the door to death open a little bit, the Colonel's directions had continued, *and it'll swing wide, you'll see.*

I closed the door behind me and sat cross-legged on the ground. I used one bandanna to tie a blindfold over my eyes, put the hood over my head, and, by feel, as if my hands had never forgotten how, used the other bandanna to tighten it around my neck. Not too tight—just enough to block the light from climbing in through the bottom and up my throat. Some air still got through. But nothing more.

I lay down, with no need to close my eyes.

———

THERE ARE NO SHADOWS in that darkness. No silhouettes or outlines. Even when you do eventually press your eyes shut in the hope of catching a swimming speck of light or two behind your lids, it seems they've all fled too.

The sounds, though—they're amplified. Most are your own: ugly, grossly biological. You hear yourself sniff or swallow or accidentally lick the gag in your mouth and it's like you can hear every bit of liquid moving, every slimy gear in the action turning. It feels like such a flimsy, haphazard device, your body. You think it'll fall apart. And for most people experiencing capuchita, it already has.

That's not the worst part, though, or it wasn't to me. It was the other sounds, the other things falling apart. Time was one. The hours stretched, snapped, and scrambled, and I didn't know when I was: '86 or '76 or fallen out of the cycle completely.

Ask me something . . . please ask me . . .

Another was—how do I put it? Knowledge? Assumptions? Locked doors started opening in my thoughts: *So what if it's wrong? What does love matter? What does death?*

They hadn't asked me a question when they gave me the picana, not a single question. I cried into the gag, desperately wondering why. Why hadn't they asked me anything?

El tiempo no lo cura. Locura.

Random phrases, recollections seeped through me. It was less like a dam that had burst than a leak, a steadily spreading puddle. A mess of unconnected thoughts and memories, at least at first: A game of chess—when? against whom?—in which I experimented and failed with the French defense. A chicken soup so thick with onions you couldn't find the chicken in it—who cooked that? A couple fighting and one of them replying, *El tiempo no lo cura. Locura.* Was it my parents? A movie? The expression meant, Time doesn't cure you, but makes you crazy. Or, in my rendition: Time doesn't heal you. It steals you.

Lo-cu-ra.

Even words crumbled into their component syllables, rearranged themselves like wicked children playing a trick on you.

Cura.

The Priest. I thought of him then. The way he not only called the

torture room an operating room but seemed to actually believe it sometimes, as if the extraction of information by violent means was something
surgical, medical. He dreamed of having gowns and latex gloves, tiled
walls instead of the styrofoam coating used for sound insulation. He had
us clean it compulsively, spray it with deodorizer and even, occasionally,
bring in aromatic herbs and flowers. What is a hospital without flowers? he
would ask.

Che, Verdecito. You're a medical student, no? My patient may need your help . . .

I could hear their muffled voices in the hallway. They had a name for
that too—the Avenue of Happiness. Everything had to be inverted; down
was up, up down. Prisoners weren't killed, they were "transferred," or "got
their ticket." Or, if they were out of earshot—perhaps—"sent upstairs to
heaven."

*Merlo. Now to López. But Tarantini with a clean tackle. Morete gets there but is
offside. Keeper kicks it deep. Passarella . . .*

The voices—they didn't belong to the other guards. Was that the
radio? A soccer game? It was close and loud, as if just outside the door. My
skin crawled at the sound of it.

*Passarella, back to López. Passes it wide, looking again for Merlo. Marked by
Pernía. Waiting, waiting . . .*

Only our aliases weren't inverted. The Priest was an actual priest. The
Gringo had spent time in America, Rubio was blond, and I was green.
Triste's name was Félix, but he was unhappy and dour and made it sufficiently clear that the job got him down to earn his title too. All of them
except the Priest and me were army men, supposedly there to help bring
discipline and organization to the place.

A few others rotated in and out, including two hairy look-alikes called
Goat and Nose. There were also the foreign operatives—Automotores
was a base of the international Operation Condor, a program sponsored
by the United States to repress South American communist tendencies,

and we often had nearly as many Chileans, Brazilians, and Uruguayans as we did Argentines.

We also had some higher-ups from the Secretaría de Inteligencia del Estado (SIDE), since they ran the place in conjunction with the Federal Police. Aníbal Gordon, designated Black, was in charge. The others from the intelligence agency similarly went by a color: Red, Gray, Brown. No one except me was Verde.

The rest were from the Federal Police, or handpicked monsters of Aníbal's. And with the exception of me and Rubio, all were at least in their thirties. The two of us were the kids of the place, occasionally summoned as nene when our superiors got too lazy for distinctions. It grated on Rubio, since he was older than me, and he didn't like when we were grouped together; I was too soft for his company.

. . . Counterattack now. Boca pushes forward, River's on the defensive. Veglio on the left wing, knocked out of bounds. Tarantini with the throw-in. Down the wing again, looking to cross . . .

You could mostly tell who was at work based on the use of the radio. Whether he left it outside the room or brought it in, and by the station he put on. The Priest chose classical and, if he could find any playing, opera. I even got the impression he occasionally picked his shifts in order to catch a recording from the Teatro Colón. Often he'd belt out arias himself—Puccini, in particular—his hearty tenor a contrast with the nurselike, feminine voice he used when asking prisoners to confess their sins.

Triste liked tango, which fit his name but little else; he had the quietest personality of the group, the most nondescript features too: lean, relatively short, a typical set of shaggy Argentine sideburns, overlarge shoes, and tortoiseshell glasses. For the Gringo, it was American tunes, of course. His big body would swing to everything from Elvis to the Ramones, and the picana with it, making his sessions slightly more tolerable to his victims since the bronze double-pronged tip of the machine would skitter briefly off their skin now and again.

Rubio didn't care; for him, the music that mattered was what went on inside the room. He'd leave the radio on a chair outside, give the knob a quick, careless turn, and go straight in. So sometimes you heard the screams over the news, sometimes over static. Sometimes . . .

. . . and the ball goes back to Veglio, careful, careful, ball to Russo, careful now, he makes it between two outside the box, nice gambetta, Felman goes in, he finds him in danger, takes his shot—GOAL! GOAL! GOOOOOOOOAL!

The common denominator was soccer. When a game was on, it was a mystery who was inside.

GOOOOOOOOOOOOOOOOOOOOOOOAL!

Until Automotores, I'd been as indifferent a fan as I'd been a player. Nominally my team had been Estudiantes. But there I learned to root for the clubs from Buenos Aires, River especially, since the session was worse if they lost.

GOOOOOOOOOOOOOOOOOOOOOAL! GOOOOOO—

The radio shuddered off suddenly.

Footsteps thudded in the hallway.

Ask me something! Please! Ask me anything!

No one did. When the men came, they just grabbed me silently by the arms and dragged my limp body across the floor and down the stairs. I didn't resist, not even when I heard the sounds of a car door opening. The men shoved me into the backseat, pushed my hooded head down so it couldn't be seen through the windows, and sat to either side of me. The muzzle of a gun pressed against my ear, and the car drove off.

I wept. Then—muted, filtered in by the thickness and blackness of the hood—light. It seemed to thread through the fabric and into my eyes, as

if it was seeking them out. There was nothing salvation-like about it—
I still believed I was at the end—but it was warm and sweet and all okay. It
was *all okay*. Wasn't it? Was I no longer crying?

The car stopped. The men tugged off my hood and blindfold, removed
the gag. I struggled to make out the face of the one who said, "Go on." His
silhouetted chin nodded in the opposite direction, as the other guard
opened his door and let me out. "There's no point trying to run."

Standing on my own two feet with the sun bathing me—it was incomprehensible at first, as disorienting as lying down in a tight space in the
darkness. Then the shapes in my vision straightened, found detail. Paths,
grass, a giant gum tree, people having picnics and making out on benches,
curiously without noticing me or my stench. The wall of the cemetery and
the tall gate at its front and, right underneath, his smile inexplicably per-
ceptible despite all the surrounding fuzziness, the Colonel, waiting for me.

I steadied myself and went toward him.

———

SOMETHING SHIFTED AGAIN. Time or consciousness or some more mystical
dimension I had no grasp of yet. I recalled where I was headed, what I was
supposed to be doing. The Colonel was the same as I'd seen him the night
before, and, placing a hand against my cheek, I felt my beard.

"This again?" I asked when I reached him.

"Again and again, Tomasito. Isn't this place one of your hells?"

I looked around. Sun shining, throwing pretty little sparkles on the
pavement; big palm leaves hovering overhead and casting shadows over
the spires. Tourists snapping pictures, cats purring at my heels. It might
not have seemed hellish to someone else. But the sky had an unnatural
spectral flutter, the slippery iridescence of fish scales. And those cats—
among them was a cross-eyed Siamese and another with scruffy gold fur;

I could have sworn they were the same ones I'd seen the night before. That is to say, for lack of a better term, in reality.

"I thought we were going to Isabel's," I said.

"Death is not quite so neat as that, I'm afraid—it's both a very lonely place and a very crowded place, if you get my meaning. Besides, you can't just descend to another person's darkness willy-nilly, Tomás. That'd be very inappropriate, like going to the bathroom with them or something. For this journey you have to—what's the expression in English?—*go your own way?*"

He started humming the Fleetwood Mac song. If it wasn't so creepy and out of character, it might have been funny.

"You've come a long way from tango, Colonel."

"I won't say I did it out of choice, Tomás. It's not hard to teach an old dog new tricks down here." He sang some more. There was revulsion in his face, in the twitching of his lips in particular, as if he were trying to stop their movement but couldn't. "Blagh, guachula!" he spat, as if coughing up the tune and hurling it to the cemetery sidewalk. "Tastes like a smelly brothel, that sound. Let's go."

I followed him. With the sunlight, I could make out the different sizes of the caskets in the crypts—some small enough for ashes, others obviously for babies—and their varying conditions too, from glossy and pristine to ramshackle and caved in. More than a few had crashed to the floor and splintered, but there were no skeletons or loose bones in the spillage. Had they disintegrated? Run off? There was a peaceful breeze, and pinkish mourning doves were chirping on the mausoleum ledges.

"So it's hell then?" I asked. "This place?"

"A version of it. Hades, Argentina, if you will. I can't say for sure, but I believe it is one of the oddities of the netherworld that national borders still exist. At least for us, we Argentines are so particular, as you know. I've only seen some Uruguayans and Brazilians down there too, but that's it. No one else would put up with us."

We arrived at a run-down crypt that looked like it hadn't been cared for in ages; no ornaments, its engravings worn away, leaving a flattish wall discolored by rain. The name on it was almost illegible, and I soon wished it had been entirely so.

In lean, plain script it read: THOMAS SHORE.

"I meant . . . is this where the dead reside?"

"A version of them." The Colonel smiled. "You know there are no dead in Argentina, Tomás. Only disappeared."

He opened the crypt door. The cats padded softly around our legs and started to descend. It was dark enough inside that I quickly lost sight of them.

"Ready?" he asked. I nodded, then covered my ears when he screamed: *"Wrong answer!"* More softly, he continued, "No one here is ready. No one ever will be. Some of us, we thought we might be. Oh, it seemed pleasant enough, that dreamless, dreamy little land beyond the borders of the known and whatnot. But I don't think even the suicides were quite prepared."

"They regret it?"

"Regret? No, I wouldn't say that exactly. Much too simple a notion, your regret. Do something, don't do something—as if actions could be reduced to such measly forks in the road."

"What do they feel then?"

His hand went to his brow, skipping over his mustache; they were the two places his fingers went when pondering a chess move.

"I would say they mourn," the Colonel said. "What was, what could have been. That is what death is: we are confined to what was and what never had a chance to be. And we mourn for them. Ready?" he asked again. Chastened, this time I told him I wasn't, but proceeded down into the crypt—my crypt—all the same.

PART II
HADES

SIX

Fields swept past, broken up by unpaved parking lots and billboards for Lucky Strike and the Citroën Ami 8. Mostly flat earth beyond them, a plain, ordinary blue horizon. Nothing was particularly striking about the sights. But on some intimate, bone-deep level I recognized them, even before I saw the empty bleachers of the rugby club or the signs for Tolosa and Gonnet on the highway running parallel to the tracks: it was the train from La Plata to Buenos Aires. And also—I gathered from the Citroën advertisement, which was for a model that debuted in the seventies—no longer 1986.

There'd been no transition, no physical reallotment of my body that I could pinpoint. It was more like a dream, the break in continuity somehow perfectly natural: there I was on the train, the Colonel's ghost beside me in his gray suit and hair, the other commuters reading papers and tapping their knees against briefcases. "Are they . . . ?" I began, my voice small and squeaky. I cleared my throat, and the Colonel finished for me: "Other *arrivals*? No, Señor Shore. This train is solely for you."

I looked back out the window at the uneventful montage, remembering long-ago trips when I had been so excited at the prospect of what lay at the end of this journey.

"Your passport," the Colonel said, holding out his hand. "You did bring it, didn't you?"

I removed it uncertainly from my pocket. "What are you going to do with it?"

"Well, I can't exactly stamp it and give it back to you, can I? It's like leaving your ID when you rent a boat, that's all. You get it back when you pay."

"When I pay?" I repeated. Logic felt as jumbled to me as space and time. "What do I pay with?"

Numbly it occurred to me he might answer, "Life." But the Colonel shrugged, plucking the document from me and tucking it away in his suit pocket. "That depends. Most ferrymen here like cash bribes. Being as this is still Argentina, after all . . ." His inflection was wicked and pleased, and, perplexed, I reached for my wallet. "I'm kidding, Tomás! Joder," he muttered exasperatedly. The swear was more common among Spaniards, but the Colonel had adopted it in his eccentric cosmopolitanism. "In this world, Tomás, you pay the right price for everything . . ."

———

THE TRAIN PULLED INTO the station at Constitución, and we got off with the rest of the crowd, pushed along by its current as on any other weekday. I walked stiff-armed, whether out of misplaced concern about pickpockets or a more general feeling of protectiveness I couldn't say. The buzz of activity grew as we approached the main hall, then became a throb, the tall, arched ceiling amplifying the sound. The round panels dotting it were more ornate than I had remembered—shaped like the sun in the Argentine flag and containing small murals I couldn't fully make out from below: military figures and men carrying crosses, haloed women outside fortresses with what looked like gargoyles standing guard on their ramparts.

"I don't recognize those," I said to the Colonel, still gaping upward as bustling apparitions brushed by me.

"I'm sure there will be much you don't recognize here at first," the Colonel said. "But don't worry. This place, it recognizes *you*."

He led me to the exit, expertly navigating the crowd on quick, clicking heels. "What do you mean?" I asked.

"Denial," he said. "You were always quite gifted in this arena, Tomasito. Me, on the other hand—I was always more honest."

"Only with yourself," I pointed out.

"Yes, that's fair. One of my great sadnesses, or should have been, perhaps: no one ever really knew me."

"It should have been," I agreed.

"Don't worry, it is one now. As I said, this place—it's quite intimate. Specific. Nothing assembly-line about our pains here, I promise you."

"I can see that," I said as we reached the street, its frantic, moblike swarm filling me with uneasiness.

"As they say in your language, Tomás, *you ain't seen nothing yet.*"

"My language?"

"You aren't going to tell me you're Argentine still? Remember what we talked about with regard to denial. You are more gringo than the Gringo Carlitos."

Outside it was hot and just as crowded. Constitución was known for its seediness, and I recalled the panicky way I'd rushed toward the buses the first time I arrived on my own, my huge suitcase dragging behind me ridiculously. What I felt now was something closer to the resignation of my final return to this station, the solemn, ponderous step-after-step of someone going through the motions.

We went down Lima, where blaring horns and engines prevented conversation, then turned down a squalid-looking side street I didn't know. It was narrow, parking technically illegal, but halfway down the block, I saw a car sitting brazenly next to a hydrant. A green Ford Falcon, no license plate. It was the staple vehicle of the regime, the one the kidnapping task forces used most frequently. I'd seen many at Automotores, their trunks or back doors opening to reveal a hooded head. I had ridden in the backseat of one myself, too.

"What?" the Colonel asked, jangling his keys cheerfully as he approached. "Don't like the color?"

I ignored that. Pulled the passenger door open and got in.

"Where are we headed?" I asked.

"Memory lane," he said in English, and guffawed, a loud, typical "Ja!"

———

DESPITE ITS SEVEN LANES, there was traffic on Avenida 9 de Julio, the thick, somnolent kind, and soon I felt my eyes closing.

It must have been a dream. But it didn't feel like a dream. Nor even like a memory, exactly; though there was a musty flavor to it, like living out a black-and-white film, the sensations seemed new. Precise, photographically crisp. The press of bodies in a crowded doorway, the smell of perspiration and perfume. The music, the low lights, the taste of Fernet and Coke. An acquaintance's grimace after taking a shot, the inelegant shuffle from the kitchen bar to the makeshift dance floor in the dining room.

Easter break, 1975, my visit to Buenos Aires the year before I moved there. I'd been seeing my next-door neighbor in La Plata for over a year, and we were getting serious: not just spending time together when her parents were out, but all of us at dinner, like we were a family and going to be one in the long term. We'd even gotten to talking loosely about an engagement, and I had started to feel a need for certainty about it I lacked. Which is why I went to the capital with some friends and wound up one night, not entirely coincidentally, going to a party where Isabel would be.

Our romantic summer had turned out to be our last together, and our parting that February had been similar to our first. No outright rejection or talk of cousins, but the peck on the cheek in front of our mothers when we separated, the promise that we'd write each other throughout the year. Again, our correspondence had flattened and dwindled, and again Isabel had returned to the States in December. She never gave me any explanation as to why she chose not to go back to Pinamar; my mother told me about the decision, and despite her argument that it'd still be fun with Nerea there, I never went back either. For three years Isabel faded beyond my horizon. I didn't hear about her outside the gossip of my mother and mutual friends, and I didn't see her until that night.

At twenty-one, Isabel still had those round cheeks, but there was something mature about her eyes, an air of experience our peers lacked. She appeared to be looking past us all, with our frenetic inattention, to those "bigger things" of hers.

She had a boyfriend, I saw. But for the first and last time in my history with Isabel, I didn't feel threatened by my rival. He was short, a petty demerit I clung to; another was the American-style button-down he wore, with its angular, starched collar. Most significant was Isabel's mutedness around him, and that wandering gaze that, after I cast my own on her long enough, landed on me.

The jolt of electricity it sent through me was sufficient; though my decision wouldn't fully coalesce until the drive back to La Plata, on some level I knew my current relationship, which had never sent such a quiver through me, was bound to come to a close.

It took a good amount of hovering and chatting with others to come in direct contact with Isabel, since I was determined to wait until she was by herself. Clumsily, I asked how she was. Fine, she told me, but she didn't seem convinced. There was no allusion to the boyfriend who'd caressed her hip minutes before.

"As always, something's missing," she said, going on before I had a chance to pry. "And you, Tomás? How are you?"

"I'm happy," I told her, but didn't mention my girlfriend either.

"Really? And here I thought you were a pessimist like me."

"I am. What allows me to be happy. Low expectations."

She indulged me with a smile. "How long have you been working on that line?"

"Haven't been. I lifted it from a book."

"Did you? The whole exchange?"

"Want to know how it ends?"

"Probably not. My expectations remain high, sadly. I'll be disappointed."

I was the one disappointed then, of course. "You just like the sense of mystery," I told her. Pressed, really.

She shook her head. "I think *you* do, Tomás."

At some point, probably before the boyfriend circled back and we parted, she said I should come spend some time with her in Buenos Aires and get to know her again. Or did she? That part of the recollection didn't rise up with the rest. When I'd gone down the rabbit hole of self-reflection in the past, I sometimes wondered if I'd been the one to make the suggestion, if I'd said I'd like to get to know *her* again. Lying next to Claire, unable to sleep, I'd wonder if in fact Isabel had told me I shouldn't come. Since I did remember this: She said—joking presumably, but still—I might not like what I found. "Low expectations," she reminded me. "Best if you keep them."

———

A HORN HONKING. Gardel's gravelly tenor fittingly belting "Volver" over the radio. We were in Recoleta, driving past the upscale jewelry shops on Avenida Callao, and I gathered we must be headed to the Colonel's building.

> *Volver con la frente marchita*
> *Las nieves del tiempo platearon mi sien*
> *Sentir que es un soplo la vida*
> *Que veinte años no es nada—*

"How do you translate that bit into English?" he asked. *"Un soplo la vida?"*

I thought for a minute. It was useful for clearing my head. "Life is a puff of air?"

"Puff," he repeated. He shook his head distastefully. "What a silly little word. Silly little word for a silly little thing."

We parked in his garage, and I followed him upstairs. Then into his apartment, after he unlocked the door. All the furniture was covered in clean white sheets. I put my hand on the nearest, over the entry table, and discovered it was hot, as if recently removed from the laundry.

"Now that's odd," the Colonel said, pinching the fabric after I did. "Even for this place."

"You don't remember what you said to me? It was my first visit after I moved. You gave me a gun." I went to the cupboard from which he'd taken it and pushed the sheet aside. When I pulled the drawer open, I found the exact same revolver again. The metallic, goosefleshy feel of the handle—I'd never forget it, after the hours-long grip with which I'd held the gun to my temple in Rome. "I asked you if it was to protect me," I said.

The Colonel smiled. "Ah, yes. I said maybe not, but it would ease my conscience."

It felt like we were rehearsing a scene in a play. "When I accepted it, you sighed as if I'd removed a five-hundred-pound gorilla from your back."

"Ah, the sleep I'll get tonight, I said, didn't I? It's like fresh sheets or a fine whiskey before bed, a clean conscience."

"Fresh sheets," I repeated skeptically. Then and now.

"Surely you know the joy of fresh sheets," the Colonel said, and I could no longer tell if it was his ghost speaking or my recollection. "Ah, Tomás, Tomás. You have so much to learn, Tomás."

A recollection. Unambiguous now: It was the younger version of the Colonel in front of me—hair darker and richer, mustache still skinny but a little straighter, sturdier. Seeing him, it was like a switch inside me clicked, and I was the younger version of myself too. Then I was there again—fully, bodily—at the end of February 1976.

SEVEN

I had been to Buenos Aires numerous times before that month, but I had never lived there, and I had certainly never lived there alone. I was an only child and fairly coddled, even before my father died. As a boy, I'd always needed much soothing: dogs howling after ambulances at night scared me, as did the roars of lions during the day—our house was on the corner of Calles 54 and 1, right near the zoo—and my mother often had to remind me that, even if the beasts could escape their enclosures, they didn't have the key to our front door. I also had asthma: growing up, I was constantly out of breath, and even when I outgrew it, I still had enough of my mother's warnings in my head to decline cigarette offers.

She tried to develop an iron fist as I got older, but at signs of resistance she tended to melt like butter. Which was how I won the debate over moving to Buenos Aires.

My arguments were full of holes. The university of La Plata was arguably better than that of Buenos Aires, and I'd put in two years there already. I had relationships at the local hospital where I'd been volunteering over the summer, and a circle of friends that dated back to elementary school. I'd also been lucky enough to get out of obligatory military service in the lottery and had fairly little financial pressure. In short, I had all the trappings of a good life, and in Buenos Aires I didn't even have a home, since I couldn't ask the Colonel to host me for such a long period.

But in La Plata I felt smothered. By my mother, by our home, by the mildewy odor of the wallpaper and its dreary tan shade. By the city, with its uneven cobblestones and junk carts pulled by clip-clopping horses, the claustrophobic everyone-knows-everyone mentality. I wanted independence, and I wanted Isabel Aroztegui, and it seemed to me that only in Buenos Aires could I pursue both.

The main excuse I gave my mother was particularly deceptive that way: After my recent breakup—from my poor next-door neighbor, with whom I'd talked marriage one moment and my desire for freedom the next—I needed distance, someplace new, a fresh start. I told my mother my heart hurt, which was relatively honest at least.

She protested and pleaded, but ultimately gave in after a reassuring call with the Colonel. She only refused to let me take the car. She wasn't using it, I pointed out, but she countered that she would already be using my father's life insurance to pay for my room in a pensión. Not a thing more, she proclaimed, crying, and I was too self-absorbed to realize how much larger the cost was for her already.

"I just wish I understood it better," she said the day I left. She'd helped me pack the previous evening, refolding several shirts and rolling my socks into such perfect round balls that my massive suitcase, at her forceful push, closed seamlessly. "You're my only son. I don't want to get things wrong."

"You haven't, Mami. I promise," I said, lugging my suitcase toward the door and trying not to show how strained my arms were. "Your son's probably the one getting things wrong."

"You're a child to me still. I know," she added hastily. "You'll say I'm cliché. But they have truth to them, Tomás, clichés do."

"Well," I said, frowning at her misty eyes and—awkwardly, my body lurching in the opposite direction—giving her a quick kiss on the cheek, "you speak very truthfully, Mami."

———

DESPITE THE AIRS I'd put on with my mother, I was a nervous wreck on the train ride. From comparatively small-town La Plata, heading for a life of my own among the porteños of Buenos Aires who infamously, because they fancied themselves so European, turned up their noses at anyone from the rest of the continent. I tried to keep my attention on the window, but an armed police officer in a bulletproof vest hovered conspicuously at the end of the car, and every two minutes someone came through the aisle selling something in a loud, practiced voice: gum, alfajores discounted from the kiosk, aluminum wallets. The last seemed like an ominous sign, as bad as the zippered pants pockets I'd noticed on some of the regular commuters— what could one need an aluminum wallet for if not protection from thieves?—until I realized that any pocket-size wallet, even one made of adamantine or metal from the moon, would still be susceptible to theft.

Clumsily pushing my way through the station at Constitución, I got a cab and gave the address of my pensión. It was in Balvanera, a half-hour walk from the UBA School of Medicine and all of my classes, and it lay just south of Avenida Rivadavia, so I could contend to Isabel and her ilk that I lived in the real Buenos Aires, not the upper-crust areas north of that line. The neighborhood also had a Jewish history, something my mother was happy about; Orilla was my father's name, but tagging sneakily along behind it, under varying amounts of obfuscation, was hers: Zimmerman. She'd fled with her parents from Germany in '35 after the Nuremberg Laws stripped them of their citizenship, and the many Nazis who followed after the war on the church's secret ratlines kept her wary of anti-Semitism (and highly alert to the perils of raising a son generally).

My arrival at the pensión didn't alleviate my anxiety. The Gran Atlántico was a converted hotel, but there was nothing grand about it: three stories, two windows wide, no balconies or architectural ornaments, the walls an ugly pinkish brick. It had a shoddy feel inside too—tiny rooms, communal phones and bathrooms, a locker-room-like funk. Taking me upstairs, the landlady rattled off a short list of rules primarily focused on kitchen usage and washing the glassware. "Just don't make any trouble, and all will be forgiven," she said, and I assured her she needn't worry about me.

After unpacking—no housemates knocked to introduce themselves—I went out walking. First, I practiced my route to the university, so I wouldn't get lost once classes started. Then I wandered east, familiarizing myself with the big avenues and memorizing as many street names as I could. I even stopped by a few tourist destinations, relishing the big crowds and anonymity, telling myself I wasn't lonely but free.

In the evening, I called the Colonel from a pay phone and arranged to stop by his apartment. He let me use his shower and prepared a spread of cured meats, nuts, and olives. "Mercedes is out and last week we had to let go of our housekeeper, otherwise we'd give you a more proper welcome, of course."

"Of course," I said, wolfing down a handful of peanuts. I hadn't eaten all day.

"I promised your mother I'd fatten you up. Quite the fearful heart she has, doesn't she? Reads too much news—all this stuff about Montoneros and other guerrilla bands."

I nodded. It had been one of her arguments against my move, the armed revolutionaries supposedly operating in Buenos Aires. There had been a raid on a General Motors factory recently, she'd noted in alarm, and before that the kidnapping and ransoming of an Exxon executive. To which I'd reminded her that I, as a lowly medical student, was probably not at too much risk of abduction.

"That does remind me, though," the Colonel said, rising suddenly and going to the cupboard. "I promised your mother I'd take care of you too, and—well. You won't need it, but I'll rest easier knowing you have it."

He came back to the table with a compact, dark object in his hand. It took me a second to comprehend that it was a revolver. He set it down gingerly next to my plate of olive pits.

"This is going to protect me?" I asked. In addition to the news of guerrilla raids, there'd been growing talk of counterintelligence operations and government death squads, and the little gun seemed somewhat ridiculous against that backdrop.

"Maybe not," the Colonel said, "but like I told you, it'll ease my conscience."

I nodded, and he gave a huge sigh, followed by the speech about fresh sheets.

The revolver remained on the table the rest of our meal; I finally picked it up only when it was time to leave. I wasn't wearing a backpack and worried about letting it stick out of my pocket, so I bought something at a grocery store around the corner and carried it home in a paper bag.

———

THE NEXT DAY I had nothing to do. My housemates—most of them students, many foreigners—continued to take little interest in me. The only one I spoke to for more than five minutes was a Colombian named Beatriz with glassy red eyes and glittery constellations of expensive-looking jewelry. She informed me we shared a wall. "Sorry in advance," she said, her bracelets jingling. "It's not very thick."

It was Saturday, and I'd slept in. Going out for lunch that afternoon, I saw kids my age gathering in parks and plazas with bottles of wine, and when I returned, the pensión was already coming alive with music and laughter. Unable to resist any longer despite my having told myself not to be pushy, I called Isabel.

Her mother answered. "Tomás! I can't believe you haven't been by yet."

"I only got in yesterday."

"Well, why would that stop you? Are you busy? Everyone's already here."

"Everyone?" I asked.

"You know how the girls are—always holding court," Pichuca said. "They've been so looking forward to your coming. Isa especially," she added, and I could almost hear her wink as she proceeded to give me directions.

———

IT WAS THE FIRST TIME I took the subway. I was afraid I'd show up sweaty if I walked, but the train was little better, and I waited under the trees outside their building for five minutes to cool down before ringing the buzzer.

Pichuca took me inside in a flurry of kisses and exclamations. She was a bundle of energy, with unruly curls and darting eyes the same color as her daughters'—fondly I recalled her driving in Pinamar and gesticulating so wildly that we'd gasp in the backseat because her hands had flown from the steering wheel. Handing me a tray of sandwiches de miga, she steered me to the basement and practically shooed me down the stairs.

The room was dim and smoky, with discombobulated furniture that suggested it had been taken over by the girls for socializing some time ago. I spotted Nerea first, on the sofa with two young men and a collection of ashtrays and empty bottles on the coffee table in front of them. A trio of girls sat opposite in cheap metal chairs. Isabel was in the far corner; she'd just pulled another wine bottle from the rack when she turned and saw me.

"Tomás!" she cried, with more of a squeal than was customary for her. "Primito!" She hugged me when I reached her, so closely the sandwiches nearly spilled. "Oh, just put those here," she said, resting them on a nearby filing cabinet herself. "I'm so happy to see you!"

"You seem good," I told her.

"I am, Tomás. I am. And you? I can't believe you're really here!"

"I can't either," I admitted.

"Don't worry, I'll take care of you. We all need taking care of in these times, no?"

Seeing that grin on her face, I asked, "Why doesn't it seem like you do?"

"You'd be surprised." She laughed, lighting herself a cigarette and offering me one. I waved it away regretfully. "Ah, I forgot. Who am I kidding? Take care of you—look at me already corrupting you!"

"Corrupt away," I told her.

"No, no," she said, blowing smoke straight into my eyes. "Your mother would kill me."

I smiled, picturing that brawl. "And your boyfriend?"

Isabel shook her head. "No longer, I'm afraid. Nerea is the one on the happy track to marriage and convention. Marriage, anyway—I've finally broken through her conventional streak. Come say hello," she continued, pulling me along with a delectably moist hand to the couch where Nerea sat. "Here she is—my rebel little sister."

Nerea rolled her eyes. "Don't listen to her, Tomás."

"You do," Isabel said.

"I never had any choice. Family." Nerea shrugged. "Not like you, Tomás, you do this to yourself. Oh," she said, standing to greet me properly only then. Nerea had always been staid and timid, and she looked that way too, with her glasses and fastidiously straightened, pulled-back hair.

But she seemed more at ease and confident now, less the left-behind little sister I remembered running from with Isabel.

Nerea introduced her fiancé, Tito, a heavy, disheveled boy with a sweet face who clearly adored her in a goofy, puppy-dog way. Like her, he was studying journalism, and like her, he seemed to lack the personality for it, the fierceness necessary to ferret out the truth in a country uninterested in a free and independent press. The rest of their friends appeared to be cut from the same cloth—intellectual and eager but soft, cushioned by their upper-middle-class upbringing. Only Isabel didn't seem made of that same mush.

A drink was passed to me, and Isabel proposed a toast. "To the future," she said.

"To a passionate future!" Tito elaborated endearingly. Chin-chins followed, and I caught Isabel's eye as we clinked glasses.

"Is that what he offered you when he proposed?" someone asked Nerea, laughing. Rodolfo, the only other man there, a mustached philosophy scholar who wore a blazer despite the heat and claimed to be named after the journalist Rodolfo Walsh.

"Most men can only offer passionate pasts," snickered another girl in the circle, who had a bob and wore denim overalls. I hadn't caught her name, only a lecture she'd given earlier on the virtues of free love.

"And here I was thinking innocently of our activism," Isabel said.

"You? Thinking innocently?" Nerea scoffed.

"She was thinking of a passionate future fucking the country's fascists in the ass," Rodolfo remarked, rather aggressively. "Tomás, have you read *Seven Pillars of Wisdom*? T. E. Lawrence's account of the Arab Revolt . . . ?" I pretended that I had, and the conversation went on predictably from there, getting caught up in politics and news and affording few opportunities to branch off into more intimate one-on-ones. Not until the end anyway, when Nerea and Tito had passed out on the sofa and the others started trickling out. But by then it was late enough that I felt I had to tell Isabel I'd better be going too.

She walked me to the door. "Any plans the next few days?"

None, I told her, except that at some point I'd likely visit the Colonel again. The name seemed slow to register, like she'd missed a line in a book and was striving to re-create it from the surrounding text, so I went on. My old mentor? Chess player? She remembered my mentioning him, didn't she?

Gradually her mystified expression gave way to a definitive nod. She remembered him perfectly.

———

I WAS STILL VERY MUCH ASLEEP the next day when someone knocked—grumpily, apparently for the second time—telling me I had a phone call. "Who is it?" I asked, still in my pajamas. My unhappy alarm clock—Beatriz, whom I'd heard in the throes of a late-night dalliance when I came home—gave a shrug before returning to her room, and I shambled downstairs lackadaisically, believing it was my mother.

"I've been trying to reach you all morning, boludo," Isabel said.

"Sorry," I told her, in what felt like a massive understatement. "There's only one phone line at the pensión, and—"

"What are you doing today? Want to come with me on an adventure?"

Bleary-eyed and uncaffeinated, I looked at the time: Who went for adventures before ten a.m.?

"Okay."

"Great. I'll meet you at Estación Once, and we'll take the thirty-nine bus, okay? Oh, and can you bring some food?"

"Food?"

"Empanadas, pastries, whatever you like. Maybe enough for ten people? And a couple bottles of Coca-Cola? Sorry," she said, though I could tell she wasn't in the slightest. "An adventure, boludo. Trust me, will you?"

I couldn't say I did especially. But neither did I care. At least not until I picked up the groceries and realized I should have brought my suitcase to carry them all. The Cokes in particular were a pain in the ass. I was parched and I'd drunk one myself by the time Isabel showed up.

"Sorry, let me help you," she said, though she had several large, blocky-looking bags of her own.

"Enough for ten people?" I finally had the wherewithal to ask, after we'd heaved the stuff onto the bus and—luckily—into the seats we were able to procure.

"Well, really it's for a lot more. But I tried to go easy on you."

"Thanks," I said.

"You're welcome. These people—they make do. You'll be a hero for bringing anything at all. Did you a favor, really."

"Thanks," I said again. But the gratitude was more genuine than I let on: there was something couplish about our exchange—the preempted complaints, the jokiness. Besides, it seemed like a privilege to me to be chosen as her workhorse.

We got off on the outskirts of the city—jumping, almost, since the bus barely stopped; one of my Coke bottles flew to the grass with a loud plop. Then we walked for a stretch on back roads and underpasses. Isabel had kept where we were going a surprise, and though I typically would have felt unease in such surroundings, I found I did trust her a little, after all.

The destination turned out to be a shantytown. Or, as we called them in Argentina, a villa miseria. The reason for the designation had always been evident to me, but our approach—on foot, down the unpaved lane—underscored it. Shacks made of tin and wood and scrap metal and roofed here and there by tarps; trash and the lack of trees; the overpowering stench; the skinny children in tattered hand-me-downs rushing to greet us, cheering Isabel's name.

She doled out some of the food and treats we'd brought, saving the rest for "class," and directed me—I just stood there gaping, as if in admiration of some magical creature—to a makeshift porch outside one of the hovels, to let the grandparents know we'd arrived. (When I had the chance to ask her where the parents were, Isabel said, "Dead or looking for jobs usually.")

From their gap-toothed smiles, the elders seemed as pleased at our arrival as the children. An overturned cart was readied for use as a table, and Isabel started spreading the food and Cokes around it, as well as the other items she'd brought: pencils, notepads, elementary textbooks. Then Isabel began her lesson, for young and old alike.

The old were especially enthused. One woman with pudgy, wrinkled hands, which Isabel steered in her own with methodical sweeps across the paper, looked at the result with indescribable awe.

"Beautiful, no?" Isabel asked me of the childlike scribble. "The first time Flor ever signed her name."

I could only nod my assent, since I was awestruck too—not so much at the signature or the woman's proud smile as at Isabel's astounding glee. It made me pick up a pencil and ask the girl on my right her name. "Evita," she said, "like Perón." I took that to be a lie, but I wrote it out for her half-heartedly all the same.

After an hour in the shade of that porch—the tarp providing it tinted everything turquoise, like the bottom of a pool—and a chorus of waves and hugs, Isabel and I got on another bus. As soon as we did, it was like she deflated: allowed herself to appear tired, distracted, her gaze firmly locked on the window.

"You do this a lot?" I asked. It was a dumb, needless question, but I'd have said anything to get her talking again, and my story about the girl calling herself Evita hadn't gone over the way I'd intended. ("What's wrong with her wanting to be Evita? Peronism is for everyone, Tomás, illiterate eight-year-olds especially. That's why we subscribe to it," she'd said, not unfairly including me in that sweeping "we.")

"Not as often as I should," she answered. "It still can feel so small, you know? Flor has her signature, great. What the fuck paper will she ever put it on?"

I was surprised at how sudden yet entrenched this glumness seemed. Had it been there all along, underneath the displays of joy and teacherly encouragement?

"It's still something, Isa. Hope, self-esteem, whatever. You're giving them a lot."

"I know. Sometimes I do, anyway." She laughed at herself, shaking her head. "It never seems to be enough, though. You find that bigger thing to care about and then—boom. Something bigger's still out there."

"Boom?" I repeated teasingly. "Is it a bomb going off, this realization of yours?"

Isabel smiled. Not like before, but widely enough. Then she nestled close and put her head on my shoulder. "Maybe it is," she said, her voice a sweet, sleepy hush. She closed her eyes, and so did I.

⸺

WE DIDN'T RETURN TO THE VILLA over the following days—I fretted again about my fraught show of enjoyment and whether the mocking tone of my Evita story had cost me a second invitation—and Isabel didn't summon me to any other gatherings. I saw only Rodolfo, who'd taken a perplexing fraternal interest in me and invited me to a boliche. I went, hoping to run into Isabel, but neither she nor the rest of their gang was there, and the dance music wasn't loud enough to drown Rodolfo out; for the better part of an hour I had to listen to him wax on about Cuba and Che Guevara. ("The Che was Argentine, don't forget! That's why they called him Che, they didn't know it was just the way we greet each other.") But eventually I found him a law student to preach to instead, and I made my way home alone.

It was Saturday again when Isabel called, inviting me over for a family lunch that included Tito and Cecilia. Afterward, the two of us went for a walk in the neighborhood. It felt almost like an urban version of that first summer in Pinamar: hot concrete instead of sand and scurrying waves under our feet, rambling conversations that touched on everything except our feelings for each other. Passing Plaza Güemes and the children playing on the church steps shadowed by palm trees, I said, "It's lovely here."

"It's wealthy, you mean," Isabel replied.

"Not everything has to be political, does it, Isa?"

"No? What else can it be?"

"There's the personal side of things too, isn't there?"

She shrugged. "They're the same to me—the personal and political. They always have been, Tomás."

Truthfully, I couldn't disagree. Even as a teenager, she'd called her mother hypocrite more liberally than most. "You complain, you want change," she'd rail, "but you don't do anything for it," and it was hard to know if she was referring to the country's state or her mother's, after her father had left them.

Had Isabel become a Peronist because she was a rebel, or a rebel because she was a Peronist? The chicken-and-egg of it was hard to determine, but I tended toward the former explanation. Peronism was the ideal vehicle for those like her who wanted change but didn't necessarily possess a full-fledged ideology or agenda. After the man himself was booted from the country in '55 and his party proscribed, their right-wing aspects were widely forgotten and the label evolved into a catchall for populism of every stripe, a handy banner for anyone who wanted to step on the battlefield. (Indeed, the Montonero guerrillas originally took up arms to bring Perón back from exile, before growing into a broader insurrection against state oppression.) The word almost had spiritual connotations now; for some, it was a moral lifestyle as much as a fight against injustice. As Isabel had said on that same walk, "Peronism is like poetry—it can't be explained, only recognized."

For me, it was about a different kind of poetry. The headlines, Isabel's activism and volunteer work—in a sense, that was all background, the stage on which everything else was meant to happen. I believed in the leftist cause, the fight for liberty and justice, et cetera. But I tacked on that "et cetera" willingly, indifferent to the details. I was more interested in the forest than the trees, and more interested still in getting lost in it, catching the contagious energy that would lead Isabel to bounce off me in exactly the right way.

"Well, I'm glad to know you take your personal life seriously, then," I said.

"Deadly seriously," Isabel said, linking her arm in mine.

That night, her friends came back to Pichuca's basement. We drank and smoked and talked until midnight, and then someone put on a Sly and the Family Stone album.

"You don't still just listen to the Beatles, do you, Tomás?" Isabel said, rising from the couch, her hips swaying. I shook my head and followed her. Jiggling and jumping with the others, tittering at the more preposterous moves, we danced for hours, as if it was pure fun the revolution depended on.

"I didn't think you'd like it," Isabel said to me during a break, drinking water for a change because we'd been at it long enough to start sweating.

"Dancing? I don't."

"You smile a lot while dancing for someone who doesn't like it."

"I'm not smiling because of the dancing."

She smiled too. Then she refilled her glass with booze and led me by the hand back into the fray.

Nothing happened between us that night, or the two other nights like it when we danced in her basement. But the horizon continued to shimmer with possibility, political and otherwise. In Isabel's presence, existence had a quicker-seeming pulse, and the signs piled up in such profusion that I couldn't help but seek a pattern in them, a confirmation. Soon, I told myself, soon we'd get caught up in that slice of the future as well.

EIGHT

As March rolled around, the tremors of fear became harder to ignore. You'd see more television screens with showily waving Argentine flags and catch more speeches from admirals and generals about the war for liberty and democracy, the exact terms their opponents used. You'd see more soldiers in the street, more police barriers. (The ID checks came later, along with unexplained street closings and the need to have your documents on you in public at all hours.) You'd notice the first trickles of inflation, the stress of shoppers in grocery stores deploring the rise in prices. You'd read headlines about shoot-outs in which only the "terrorists" were killed, and none of the soldiers or officers were so much as wounded. You'd hear the voice of a famous activist priest like Mugica on the radio advocating for volunteer work in the villas and arguing on behalf of Peronism or socialism or some other ism that ran counter to the government's increasingly reactionary stance, and a few days later you'd hear another famous voice on the radio say he'd been killed. In these cases, it was the terrorists who were said to have done the killing, and in these cases alone, they somehow always escaped.

You heard rumors. Someone hadn't been heard from in a couple days, hadn't shown up at home either. Someone else, a professor, had suddenly taken a post abroad—in Mexico, the tale usually went, but occasionally there were more outlandish destinations, like Switzerland or Norway. You remembered the stories parents told kids about how an aged dog had been taken to some arcadia in the country where it could run free, and you wondered if these tales were like that.

The one thing you never heard were the shots. For all the talk, death and violence and war remained off-screen. But the forces behind them seemed no less powerful for that. To the contrary, they had more the aura of magic as a result, a sorcerer's unstoppable reach. Again, if I startled when the Colonel gave me his revolver, it was probably less because of the gun itself than because, against such invisible might, it seemed a puny, pointless sort of shield.

———

NOT THAT I FELT terribly in danger myself. On subsequent visits, the Colonel had been nothing but reassuring, telling me it was just a lot of noise, soon enough Argentina would return to its normal level of insanity. "Don't worry, Tomasito," he'd say, gesturing at the plush armchairs and glossy green plants around his living room while talking heads fearmongered on the TV about the Montoneros. "The truth is, life here is more under control than we pretend." Mercedes plied me with wine and food and questions whenever I came over, the Colonel with his whiskeys and soliloquies. They'd insist I stay the night in the spare bedroom if it got late, and took it on themselves to be the unbroken, loving parent set I hadn't had for nine years.

There was also the resumption of classes to distract me, the immersion in a new routine. Biology labs with fetal pigs suddenly consumed my time, organic chemistry assignments and reading for an English literature seminar at the Cambridge Institute the Colonel had suggested I sign up for. I had a physics class too, and I was surprised to find my housemate Beatriz there in the front row of the lecture hall, taking diligent notes as if nothing could be more important.

Of course, it was Isabel who most kept the sense of peril at bay. History came and went, especially in this country. But love? Once in a lifetime, boludo, if you were lucky. And I believed I was.

Her buoyancy in spite of everything was infectious. Once she asked me over to help her and Nerea cook a casserole for people in the villa after one of them had been arrested, and, laughing, she blamed the tears in her eyes on the onions she'd been chopping. Another time, she took me on a long walk past Colegiales and the cemetery in Chacarita to a run-down neighborhood I didn't know the name of, and when I joked that a lot of our strolls lately had been down streets where I worried we'd be killed, Isabel told me, "You're not worried, Tomás." Then she opened the backpack she'd been carrying and pulled out two cans of spray paint. "Are you?"

Taking one, I watched her go to the door of the boarded-up house we'd stopped at and spray a long blue line that curved at the bottom. A *J*.

"What do I write?" I asked, joining at her side.

"I was going to do 'Justice for All.' How about you do something a bit more serious, like . . . 'Fatherland or Death.'"

"'Fatherland or Death,' really?"

She shrugged and laughed, focusing on the loop of her *U*. Hesitating a moment, I gave the can a shake and sprayed. But I held it level too long and then overcorrected, making a thick white dot with a jagged tail that looked like an elongated comma. "Shit."

"Boludo," Isabel said. She took my wrist with her free hand and, moving it in a swift but measured arc, completed the *P* for *Patria*. "You got it?"

My heart was beating fast and pleasurably, and Isabel was looking at me with that sly smile that made my limbs tingle, and I shook my head. "I think you're going to have to help me the whole way," I said.

She laughed and grasped my arm again, and I wasn't worried about a thing.

———

THE FOLLOWING SUNDAY AFTERNOON, Isabel called and proposed the two of us go for another walk—"The Bosques this time, don't panic." I pointed out the sky was ominously gray, and she replied, "Who cares?" She didn't want to be "cooped up," rain clouds and the demise of the nation be damned.

Neither of us wore jackets or boots or even brought umbrellas. "Thank God you're as ridiculous as me," Isabel said. "Caring about bigger things and all that."

"Rain is tiny," I agreed. "Speaking of which . . . what ever happened to your ex?" I segued gracefully, earning a chuckle.

"Nothing happened with him. Literally," she said, to my immense gratification. "It was like dating a fish."

"Not one of those Japanese fighting ones, I take it?" Cecilia's husband wanted one for his tank, a trend among upper-class porteños lately.

"I wish," Isabel said. "More like a trout. But let me guess—your girl-friend, what was she? A goldfish?"

"That's cruel even for you, Isa," I said.

A thunderclap serendipitously thumped its approval. We smiled at each other just as the first fat drops landed on our upturned palms, then took off running back to Pichuca's. Too late by a long shot—we arrived soaked, Isabel's shrieks and snorts of laughter disappearing prettily into the rocky symphony of the storm.

Neither Pichuca nor Nerea was home, so we felt no need to go to the basement. Or to turn on the lights, though it was nearly dark enough out-side to be night. Isabel didn't bother changing on getting home, and her nipples, erect with cold, were visible through her wet top. It was black, with little white and yellow flowers that looked like happy honeybees. At least to my fogged mind, they looked happy. Isabel had rolled a joint—Rodolfo apparently had connections in Punta del Este with rich international types—and, deciding marijuana posed no risk to my asthma, I'd taken several deep hits. Isabel had also prepared a *mate*, and the smoky smells mixed, giving the usually stuffy living room a cabinlike ambience. It reminded me of Pinamar: our sitting across from each other on the shag rug like when we were teenagers, Isabel moving her wet hair from one side of her neck to the other the way she used to after a swim.

"Why'd you stop going? Pinamar, I mean," I clarified.

"I knew what you meant," Isabel said. "It didn't feel very grown-up, I guess. Not real, you know?"

"I don't," I confessed.

"It was like something out of a movie. God, your mother's bathing suits—she looked like she'd walked out of a catalog from the twenties. The whole thing was a bubble, and I had this urge to pop it. You remember that piece of glass I stepped on?"

It had been a pivotal moment for me that first summer. Isabel had returned from a solitary stroll on the beach with a bad cut in her foot from a broken beer bottle, and during the hectic rush to get her medical help, she kept insisting not to make a fuss, she was fine, better than fine. After she got her stitches, I asked her how she could have been okay with a gash the size of something out of an American slasher flick, and she laughed and said it was hilarious.

"Hilarious?"

"Please, did you see the look on their faces? It was like they'd never seen pain. You, though—you were no more scared than I was, were you, Tomás? No," she continued with such authority I believed her. "You and I—we're not scared of pain."

I'd never understood why that experience was so seared onto my memory. Something about being hoisted up to her level at the very moment when I was certain I couldn't be further from it, possibly—nothing had felt more like real love to me.

"What's the piece of glass got to do with anything?" I asked, after a minute listening to the rain patter against the window.

"Don't you know why I stepped on it?"

"I assume you didn't see it."

"I saw it. It was sticking straight out of the sand."

"You're saying you cut your foot on purpose, Isa?"

"Crazy, no? I was such a mess. And here we are talking about it like it was the greatest time of our lives. Don't get me wrong, there was happiness. Fun and joy and the rest. But even that, even us"—it was the closest she'd come to overtly acknowledging our history—"it came out of a kind of flatness, you know? A kind of emptiness. I wanted to feel—what, I didn't much care."

"So, sleeping with me was like stepping on a broken bottle?" I said, hoping for a laugh.

But Isabel shook her head. "I don't know what I'm saying," she said softly. She was fidgeting with the straw of the *mate*, digging it up and down in the yerba grounds. "Anyway, we never actually slept together."

"Happy to correct that oversight," I said, surprising myself. Thankfully, I could make out the faint, shadowed smile on her face.

"We're very different, Tomás. Why we're such good friends, isn't it? I just worry sometimes you wouldn't understand. The instinct that made me step on that bottle, that's made me do much worse. There are ugly, violent parts in me that I don't know that I want you to see. You, for instance—what's the worst thing you could ever do to someone?"

"The worst . . . ?" The question caught me completely off guard.

"Do you think you could ever kill someone?"

"Kill someone? Shit, I don't know, Isa. Do you?"

"You know a lot, Tomás. More than you pretend."

I tried to reconcile this with what she'd said moments ago. She didn't want me to see who she really was, but I did—was that the issue?

"You don't need to hide from me, Isa," I promised her. "Never. Don't you know? I'll always—"

"*Shh*, Tomás," Isabel said. It was the same whisper with which she used to enter my room in Pinamar, and I was powerless before her again, a toy in her grasp. She rose and offered me her hands. I took them, and she pulled me to my feet and started leading me toward her bedroom.

"Another dangerous walk, after all," I said, and now she did laugh. Then she shushed me again and closed the door behind us.

I'd never more than glanced inside her room, and the youthfulness of certain furnishings struck me: the small red rocking chair in the corner and the stuffed monkey sitting in it, the hummingbird-decorated coverlet on the bed. So not the Isabel I knew.

"Who's the monkey?"

"You're the monkey," she said, and I turned to find her smirking. I stepped closer. She put her hand on my neck and brought me closer still. When we kissed, I could taste the earthy, bitter traces of the *mate* on her tongue.

She gave me a shove toward the bed, and I allowed myself to fall back. She straddled me, and I clutched her waist. I was about to remove her top when she slid to my side, and her fingers wandered over my jeans. She unzipped them and took hold of me with such a firm grip I gasped. As had happened more than once in Pinamar, I barely lasted a few seconds.

She continued holding me some time afterward, until my breathing eased and my muscles stopped their tiny spasms. Then she let go and rolled over, her palm tilted toward the ceiling so as not to make a mess.

"I'm sorry," I said at length, finding her smile across the pillow.

"Don't be. I'm glad," she said, and I tried to be glad too. To revel in the release, the lush, sinking feeling of my body next to hers.

"You sure it's okay?" I asked her, suddenly aware of the dampness of the sheets under us.

"Of course, Tomás. I just need to wash my hands."

She got up and went to the bathroom. It felt like an eternity that I listened to the faucet running. I zipped my pants back up and sat forward to wait for her.

When she returned, she stopped at the threshold. "The other Aroztegui ladies will probably be home soon. See you later this week?"

"Whenever you want," I said. She lent me an umbrella and gave me another long kiss before seeing me out, her teeth ever so gently biting my lip.

———

MY CLOTHES HADN'T FULLY DRIED YET, and on the bus ride home I felt chilled and out of sorts. The experience had been so contradictory: too fast but also incredibly drawn out, abrupt yet clearly the result of a long simmering in us both. When I got back to my pensión, I found out I'd gotten a phone call, and my heart fluttered for an instant. But it was only my mother, calling for her Sunday-night check-in.

I went upstairs. The smell of incense drifted from under Beatriz's door. On a whim, I knocked. She answered in a fluffy bathrobe with a towel wrapped around her head like a turban, her eyes as red as usual.

"What's up? Need some physics help?"

"I was wondering if you had marijuana."

She blinked at me. "I'm seeing someone," she said.

"I am too," I said. "I really just want to buy if you have any to sell."

Beatriz pulled her robe more tightly closed and nodded slowly. Then she went to her dresser. Putting a dent in my allowance, I asked for enough to last me the week.

I CAME DOWN WITH A COLD and had to fight off the temptation to skip class and stay in bed. Not that it did me much good; I was so distracted that the notes I took turned out to be useless. In the evening I went for a walk, telling myself it would help clear my sinuses. But the truth was, I felt I had to put off calling Isabel until at least that night, and I worried whether I could restrain myself if I stayed home.

When I finally rang, Pichuca answered. Isabel wasn't home, she told me, and, sick as I sounded, I shouldn't be trying to see her then anyway. "Stay home, have some tea," she said. "Be kind to yourself, Tomás."

Isabel didn't call me back the next day or the day after. I tried to blame it on her classes, and once even loitered on the steps of the School of Engineering, pretending to wait for a friend under its daunting white columns, but there was no sign of her. I started replaying our afternoon together, analyzing it for mistakes I'd made, gestures of hers that in hindsight felt off or disappointed. *You're the monkey . . . I just need to wash my hands . . .*

I went through another day of classes. When I ran into Rodolfo at the Cambridge Institute after my English class, I proposed going straight to a bar for drinks. We barely ate, and after a few Fernet and Cokes, during which he lectured me about Mao, I was insisting we go to a boliche.

"I want to pick somebody up."

"And what, sneeze all over them, boludo? It's barely dinnertime and you're sick."

"I'm not sick."

"What about you and Isabel, eh? I've seen how you look at each other."

"It's—you don't—" I stammered incoherently. "You don't know her like I do."

"I know women, though!" he exclaimed, a typical machista porteño. "Isa's like any of them. Likes playing games. A bit crazier than most too, you ask me."

"I'm going," I said, sliding from my stool and stumbling out. Rodolfo must have followed me, since some blacked-out interval later, I was sitting on a curb bent over a pool of vomit with his hand rubbing my back.

"It's okay, boludo," he said soothingly, with a lilting intonation that made me think he'd been saying so for a while. "It's okay. I'm sure she loves you plenty, boludo."

He put me in a cab. I'm not sure how I got into the pensión or upstairs, only that I brushed my teeth for ten minutes before going to sleep.

———

ON FRIDAY, I went to a confitería to eat and recover, then spent an hour trying in vain to make sense of a spinning set of organic chemistry diagrams. When I returned home, Beatriz told me I'd gotten a call from my girlfriend.

"My what?" I said, before I remembered my lie. I went back downstairs and found the phone free.

"I was hoping you'd call," I said, too breathlessly, when Isabel came on the line.

"So I heard," she replied with a mocking, flirty edge.

"Rodolfo told you?"

"Rodolfo? Nerea told me. You don't remember calling last night?" Suddenly I felt nauseous again. To my relief, Isabel laughed. "Don't worry, boludo, you didn't say anything bad. I should have called you sooner anyway. I've been meaning to, I just—I had to figure it out."

"Figure what out?"

"I'll tell you when you get here," she said.

———

PICHUCA WAS THERE—I forced a nod when she asked reprovingly if I was taking care of myself—and directed me to the basement. When I went downstairs, I found Isabel on the couch, picking uncharacteristically at one of her nails. Her hug was quick and loose, with what felt like deliberate space between us.

I sat down beside her, lacing my fingers in my lap.

"I've been feeling guilty, Tomás," she said.

"About the other day?"

"We're friends. It's high stakes. Not to say I didn't know what I was doing. It's just—that's not always a good thing, me knowing what I'm doing."

"Is this where you enigmatically tell me about your dark side again?" I teased, but Isabel didn't laugh.

"I'll try not to be enigmatic this time," she said, giving me such a steely, unwavering look that I felt a flutter of nervousness in my stomach. "I'm not just a member of the Peronist Youth anymore, Tomás. I'm with the Montoneros."

The guerrilla group. All those news bulletins about raids and shoot-outs with officers came back to me, the photos of dead "terrorists" usually left in their wake. My mother's anxieties about them too, how preposterous they'd seemed to me. Yet here was a Montonera sitting next to me, her beguiling eyes intently awaiting my reaction.

"I don't know what to say."

"My role is low-level," she assured me. "Gatherer and distributor of information only. Reports about government activities, that kind of thing."

"What's so bad about that?" I asked sincerely.

"It can put people in uncomfortable positions. You, for instance," she continued regretfully, as if she were not the one about to put me in such a position. "You're close to Colonel Felipe Gorlero. I'm sorry, Tomás, but I have to ask: Would you be willing to collect information from him for me?"

"Collect information," I repeated slowly. "You mean spy on him?"

"It's okay, Tomás, I understand if you don't feel comfortable. Forget I asked, forget everything I just said. We'll go back to being innocent cousins. No compromising secrets or sneaking around. It'll be safer, I think. In more ways than one."

"I don't want safe," I said. With Isabel, I never had.

She smiled. Then leaned closer, inquisitively almost, her face halting inches from mine, as if she wanted to see what I would do. I did nothing, and after another instant, she closed the distance between our mouths entirely.

Almost instantly our legs were entwined, our hips thrust out toward each other. Our fingers clasped and grabbed, and sofa cushions slid to the floor. Isabel guided my hand underneath her dress, and I slid it past her underwear, listening to her ragged breathing until the rhythm of my own movements mirrored it, and both sped and swelled, and I felt nearly the same dizzy rush she did. She covered her mouth when she came.

"Thank you," Isabel said quietly as we disentangled our bodies. "Thank you so much, Tomás."

———

WE SAT SIDE BY SIDE on the couch again afterward, Isabel stretched out jelly-like with her legs resting on the table while I stroked her hair.

"Do you want to tell me what you need?" I asked.

"I think you just gave me what I needed," she said languidly, taking a deep, relaxed drag of her cigarette.

I smiled. Her hair was so soft under my palm, so soothing. "Tell me," I said.

A minute passed. She moved the ashtray to the armrest and slid one of the fallen cushions under her feet. "We're just looking for little things, really. At what stations he puts in time, what their relationship is with other bases. Does he mention speaking with police, federal or municipal? Gossip can be useful, unsavory characters with political ties, tensions between the branches of the armed forces."

"And I'm supposed to just ask him these things?"

"More or less. Be subtle, work your way toward them. Pay close attention to your conversations and report what you hear, that's all. Leave it to us to do the interpreting."

"Anything else?"

"You stay over at his house sometimes, don't you? If you feel comfortable, and the chance arises organically, maybe you could see what kind of papers he has lying around. I'm not saying pick any locks or anything— just check whatever's on his desk or in his drawers, you know. Reports on counterintelligence tactics and campaigns, classified memos, personal notes from other officers—you know," she said again, though it should have been clear I didn't know a thing.

"And us?" I asked.

"Us," she repeated, with a sigh and a laugh, as if the notion were hopelessly romantic. She pushed herself up with a hand on my thigh, then put out her cigarette and kissed me. "Don't worry about us, Tomás."

NINE

I already had dinner plans with the Colonel and Mercedes the following week. When I called the day of to confirm them, Mercedes told me to come over at nine thirty, adding the caveat that the Colonel might be held up a bit later at work.

I was nervous. Out of both fear of reprisal and the more ordinary concerns that come from prying into another's affairs. I knew the Colonel would be a slippery target, what with all his tangents and topical cartwheels, and I could easily imagine getting tripped up.

Despite Mercedes's warning, he was the one who met me at the door, and my greeting came out sounding shaky and unnatural to my ears. "But I thought—didn't you have work to do?"

"Mercedes thought I'd be coming from a base an hour's drive from the city. Usually I do. But today I was just downtown."

"There's an army base downtown?"

"It's a police station, technically. Coordinación Federal. The tangles of bureaucracy, all very complicated."

He handed me a glass of wine, and, steeling myself with a sip, I asked, "What's your normal base again?"

"Campo de Mayo." The Colonel laughed. "Though I don't know that I'd call it normal necessarily."

Mercedes emerged from the dining room and hugged me, sidetracking our conversation. We sat down to shrimp and hearts of palm with salsa golf. Soon the first bottle had been emptied and the second opened, and in the convivial, safe mood of the evening, I almost forgot what I'd come to do.

Their new housekeeper cleared our plates, and Mercedes followed her into the kitchen. Alone with the Colonel again, I imagined having to explain to Isabel how I'd let this opportunity slip. "In talking to you about the bases," I began tentatively, swishing my wine, "I realized I don't know much about what your work entails."

"And do you think that an accident, Tomasito?" the Colonel said. "You know I'm in counterintelligence. I told you about the School of the Americas, joder!"

"I know, but"—I tried to reroute my effort—"but what does that mean, exactly? James Bond missions? Censorship?"

"No James Bond for me, rather unsurprisingly. And I'm quite against censorship, truth be told. Gives us nothing to work with. It's boring, too. Like so much to do with literature in this country, alas. Borges, Cortázar— so brainy! None of the Argentine flair for drama. What are you reading these days, Tomás?" he continued without pausing. "Don't say the news! Tell me about that English class you're taking."

"We're—I'm behind on *Moby-Dick*," I answered, feeling somewhat turned around. "I had exams last week, and the old-fashioned language is hard for me."

"Now Ahab, he had a flair for the dramatic. Do you read any contemporary authors? I hear the kids are mad about Lawrence of Arabia. What's that book? *Seven Pillars of Wisdom?*" Recalling Rodolfo's grandiose discussion of it in Isabel's basement, I nodded as nonchalantly as I could. "I think I'll pick up a copy. I like to be up on all the latest trends, you know."

Mercifully, Mercedes returned just then with the dessert, before any tension could settle over us. "Him and his trends—you should see him in a clothing store, Tomás. The way Felipe spends money to be fashionable, my God."

"Such a tyrant, this one," the Colonel replied, scooping up a large, jiggling portion of flan. "Mercedes would impose martial law in this house if she could."

"I imagine we'll be having that countrywide soon enough," I said, regaining some of my nerve amid their banter. "Martial law, I mean."

"Yes, Mercedes will be dictator any day now," the Colonel said.

"Actually, I was being serious," I said.

"So was I. Be careful with these porteña women, Tomás. They're almost as mad as porteño men."

"Don't listen to him," Mercedes said, rolling her eyes. "It's how much personality we have that scares men like him." She fixed her perfectly mascara'd eyes on me. "And what's going on with your extracurricular life, Tomás? Do you have any crushes on anyone?"

"A bad one," I admitted. Smiling, Mercedes made a gesture of zipping her lips, and I decided to follow her lead.

Not long after, I got the expected invitation to stay over. We said good night, and I pretended to get ready for bed.

———

FOR TWO HOURS I KEPT MYSELF AWAKE in the guest bedroom trying to read *Moby-Dick*. It felt incomprehensible—all those nautical terms and rambling paragraphs about whales' heads and spermaceti. I gave up and picked a random Silvina Bullrich novel off the shelf, but that proved no better— the sentences drifted over me like background noise. It'd be my excuse, I decided, my reason for going to the study in the middle of the night; I had to find something to read.

It was almost three in the morning. I got out of bed and made my way to the door. Listened a moment, then quietly turned the knob and stepped barefoot into the shadowy hallway. I tiptoed to the Colonel's study, anxiously going over my explanatory speech if discovered—insomnia, you know how that goes, Colonel, no rest for the wicked. The study door was ajar, and I slipped past. I approached his desk and opened the top drawer as softly as I could.

What I found I glanced at too swiftly to make sense of—unmarked clippings, what looked like leases for rental properties, lists of locations with check marks whose connection I couldn't fathom: BRIGADA DE INVESTIGACIONES DE BANFIELD. PLANTA DE FORD MOTOR ARGENTINA. UNIDAD PENAL NO 9. ESCUELA SUPERIOR DE MECANICA DE LA ARMADA.

It was too dark, too nerve-wracking. I sprang away as if the words had been shouted at me, and hurried back to my room, where I lay short of breath and frantically attuned to every creak down the hall, however minute.

Over breakfast the next morning, the Colonel placidly read the paper without saying anything. But Mercedes kindly inquired if I'd had trouble sleeping.

———

WHEN ISABEL WAS SLOW in calling me back again, I tried to be more sanguine about it. It's just how she is, I reminded myself. Don't worry. (*Don't worry about us, Tomás . . .*)

But then she called and asked me to meet her at an appliance store.

"An appliance store? Why?"

"There've been stories about walls and light switches being bugged in people's homes."

"A café then?"

"Will you just come? I have to buy something anyway."

I had trouble finding the place, and Isabel was outside smoking when I arrived, framed by a display of shiny new washing machines in the window. In her hands was what looked at first like a wide brown box, until I saw the stylus and plastic casing.

"They didn't have what I needed. But look!" she cried, overly enthusiastically. "I bought you a record player! I remembered you said you didn't have one."

"Thanks," I said uncertainly, as I took it from her.

"How did it go with the Colonel?"

"You want to talk about it out here?"

"Safer than a café. Shall we walk?" Isabel said, going ahead. The turntable heavy in my hands, I followed her and started giving my report.

Mostly she just nodded along, giving me occasional taps on the arm when other pedestrians passed so I'd pause or lower my voice. But here and there she added commentary. "Great to know he puts in time at Coordinación Federal," she replied to that detail, and to the anecdote about the T. E. Lawrence, "It's probably about code breaking, he figures we're using the book to send each other messages. Or maybe it's just getting to know the enemy." Neither explanation was especially comforting. "Did he mention anything about international cooperation?" she followed up. "Foreign funding?" Both times I shook my head.

"Those weren't the kinds of things you told me to fish for," I defended myself.

"Of course not, don't worry, Tomás. You're doing great," she said. "Did you stay the night?"

After navigating a construction crew, I relayed what loose phrases I'd gathered, as well as my reluctance to search any harder. "They're light sleepers," I explained.

"Well, what if you asked the Colonel to host a dinner party? That way you could sneak off with the lights on while they're distracted. You could tell him my mother and Ceci want to meet your patron or something—it sounds like the wife would want to have them over, no? And who knows, he might invite someone useful. I could come too, help you look."

"You're not coming," I told her. An instinct told me to keep these worlds separate to whatever extent I still could. That their overlap was dangerous— who knew what Isabel could get up to in the Colonel's presence? Or what might transpire later with her presence in his recollection, this fervent, irrepressible Peronista?

I also must have secretly asked myself: What use would I be to her if I connected her to the Colonel directly?

I felt tired. The sun was strong, the sidewalk wasn't shaded, and my forearms were straining under the weight of the turntable.

"Can't we sit down somewhere?"

"I'm sorry, Tomás, I don't think I have time. Why I had to squeeze you in like this—I have to meet someone."

"Can we at least talk about something else then? Five minutes, Isa. Let's just talk. Get to know each other, like you said we would."

She gave me a puzzled look.

"When I ran into you last year. You said I'd get to know you again if I moved here . . ." I trailed off, for the first time doubting whether she actually had said that. Maybe I had.

"But you are getting to know me, Tomás," she said. "That's what I meant that day in the rain. I warned you you might not like what you see."

I looked at her. Overtly, lingeringly. Including her whole body in the sizing up, so she'd know this wasn't just about the cause for me, or that the cause still had this fleshy underbelly. So she'd know I hadn't forgotten its image—not a single detail. The constellation of little moles across her abdomen swam back to me, along with the diaphanous look of her closed eyelids when she slept. Nothing seemed so intimate as the knowledge of that fine skin, the fact that her eyes didn't always have the hard diamond shine they did now.

"I like what I see," I told her. Either the sunlight cast a particularly rosy hue on her face that instant or she blushed.

"Boludo," she said. She rose to her tiptoes and gave me a hasty kiss good-bye.

—

ARRANGING THE EVENING with the Colonel, I had him invite only Pichuca and Cecilia, who implied they were glad it was a more exclusive affair. "Some young people these days," Cecilia said to me, "you just can't trust to be decent."

The Colonel made his own invitations on top of mine, but I wasn't sure they were the type Isabel had hoped for. Another chess acquaintance, this one from Rosario, and an American businessman with an unexplained tie to the Colonel who had the lispy accent of a Spaniard and spoke of Argentina as if it had been stuck in the nineteenth century and only now, in selling its state-run companies to private international entities and opening its markets to free trade, was starting to catch up. ("I mean, shit, your main export is beef! Your whole economy relies on the fact that bulls don't turn fag!") He worked in cars and went into a fifteen-minute diatribe over cocktails and hors d'oeuvres about a rubber plantation Ford had opened in the Amazon back in the twenties. The town built for its administrators was apparently deemed a "New Detroit"; it had paved sidewalks, he emphasized lustily, and white picket fences!

Aside from that, the night was off to an unexpectedly lovely start. The Colonel put on a great speechifying performance that succeeded in subduing the businessman, and Mercedes put on her own performance to subdue the Colonel. "Felipe, please. Only Tomás and I are willing to listen to your philosophical talk," she said, and proceeded to jest about his need for attention and pupils wherever he could find them. "He's like a beggar in the street asking for listeners. Sometimes I wish we'd had children. Sometimes I thank God their poor ears were spared!" She was impeccably dressed and made up as usual, and attractively perfumed. She smoked from a long vintage cigarette holder and catered to Pichuca and Cecilia as if they were foreign dignitaries. The mood was jolly, effervescent. And the whiskeys the Colonel kept pouring me—Johnnie Walker; it was a special occasion—relaxed me enough to think I might go through with this plan.

After my third, he asked, "Tomás, don't you have friends your own age?"

"Pardon?"

"These ladies are charming, don't get me wrong. But they're rather old, no?"

A prickle of alarm wriggled through my skin.

"They're your age," I said. "I'm friends with you."

"Yes, but I'm a child at heart. My question is, given the times we live in—well, I'd be curious to meet some of these idealistic agents of change."

"What makes you think my friends are agents of change?" I said, trying to keep my tone light. "Here I am with a colonel, an American businessman, and a bunch of upper-middle-class conservatives."

He laughed. "Right you are, Tomasito. You're a regular bourgeois imperialist."

He clapped me on the shoulder, still grinning, then turned back to the others.

For a moment, I didn't move. My legs felt wobbly, and my heart was pumping with adrenaline. I took several deep breaths, ordered myself to stop drinking and go throw some water on my face in the bathroom.

It was occupied. But there was another upstairs and the staircase was just around the corner. After a moment's hesitation, I went up and found myself outside the Colonel's study.

Reassured by the ongoing murmur of the voices below and the fact that I'd heard no additional creak on the stairs, I entered and switched on the desk lamp. This time, not even hidden away in a drawer, but right there in a neat stack, there were papers.

The first few entries on the memo's top page were enough for me to flip the light back off as soon as I'd read them:

RE SUBVERSIVE INFILTRATION SCHEMES

A. On infiltration vis a vis obligatory military
   service [Page 2]
B. On infiltration vis a vis children of officers
   and other familial/social connections [Page 10]
C. On infiltration vis a vis offers of intelligence
   [Page 15]

The list went on, but I stopped there. It could have been a coincidence, but knowing the ever-calculating Colonel, I didn't interpret it as such. To me, the message was his own and clear as day: Be careful, Tomás, he was saying.

When I returned, they were gathering around the dining room table and platters of juicy, smoky-smelling red meat. The topic was today's "young ruffians," and Cecilia was leading the charge, focused on the American businessman and telling him how they frightened her, these kids who wanted to destroy everything.

"Feeling all right, Tomás?" the Colonel asked me in an aside, patting the empty chair next to him to indicate he'd saved it for me.

"I'm all right," I said.

"You're probably just hungry. Here," he said, serving me. "You like yours rare, no? I'm the same. That's the real Argentine way. For us? It's the bloodier the better."

TEN

Without realizing it, I'd been wandering, going door-to-door to find the memories lurking behind each one like I was sleepwalking. Coming to, I found myself in a hallway with many more to go. The Colonel's apartment had ballooned in size, spawned mansionlike passages that branched into other corridors lined with room after room and punctuated by staircases where none had ever been before. Whispers drifted through them all.

More than whispers. The jingle of a cash register, the slap of meat on counters, the belting of orders, quantities. The sounds seemed to be coming from a closet in the guest bedroom. I opened it and saw—the breakdown of space and logic barely registered—the butcher shop on Juncal where I'd gone with the Colonel to get chorizos and morcillas the evening of his party.

"Great sense of humor, no?" he said behind me, the ghost version of himself again. "This place. It puns! In English, even—must be the special treatment you Americans get in Argentina. *Skeletons in the closet*, joder."

Carcasses hung on the far wall, fatty pink sides of ribs and thighs and long ropes of sausage links. I caught the thread of our conversation while we waited in line: "Our American friend does have one thing right," the Colonel was saying. "What to make of a country whose chief resource is big, dumb animals, eh?"

He chuckled beside me now as if newly impressed with his wisdom.

"You seem to be enjoying this," I said.

"Mostly an act, I'm afraid. You could say it's part of my punishment, in fact, having to relive it with you. Come," he said, stepping away from the room on tiptoes, as if our intrusion had been indiscreet. The staircase had relocated right outside and now twisted into a spiral, and I followed him down it.

We emerged back in his garage. It had grown in size too, become a massive underground parking lot. Mostly the cars were Fords, and mostly Ford Falcons. But there were other models as well, many discontinued: The legendary Mercedes 170 V my father grew up riding in; the Chrysler Valiant with the frequently jammed stick in which he gave me my first driving lessons; a neighbor's apple-red Cisitalia Spyder I coveted; and a Hispano-Argentina "Criollo" I had read about in a history textbook detailing the country's futile efforts to develop a domestic auto industry.

Then there was the vehicle the Colonel was evidently taking us to: his classic coconut-colored 1965 Chevrolet Impala. He took out his keys—they were on a huge ring that must have likewise expanded—and searched for the right one.

"Is this all hell is?" I asked, taking in the cars, wondering if each one led to a different recollection. "Just your life again?"

"Unfortunately, it's more complicated than that. Your life—oh, I know you consider yours some terrible tragedy. But most people's, they're relatively okay in the end. Full of pain, but full of joy too. No, Tomás, I'm sorry to say, hell is not merely life a second time. You know what else is here. I told you at the outset, or have you forgotten?"

I hadn't. His description of death in the cemetery: confined to what was and—I said it aloud—"what never had a chance to be . . ."

"Very good, Señor Shore. We're trying to give it that chance. Mind you, we have a ways to go yet. What could have been is the underside of what was, in effect. We have to keep digging through all these layers of the past to get there."

"And once we do?"

"One thing at a time," the Colonel said casually, getting into the car and whistling some scattered bars of an upbeat Gardel. He rolled down the top.

"You don't usually think of things one at a time," I pointed out.

"Well, death does force some adaptation, Tomasito. Even I—I know it doesn't seem like it, I know I must look like a shiny beacon of life to you. But I've changed, Tomás. I've changed terribly."

No, not Gardel—he'd picked up the tune in a light, pacey hum. Fleetwood Mac again? The lyrics were American certainly—I had a flashing glimpse of Nerea and Tito singing along with awful accents in Pichuca's basement, their heads bobbing like figurines. *Sometimes the light's all shinin' on me, / Other times I can barely see . . .*

"Good grief. Grateful Dead? You must be kidding."

"Alas, no," the Colonel said, cringing as we started off. We were quickly submerged in daylight and traffic, the weekday bustle—taxis flying furiously around bends, suited businessmen on Vespas swerving in and out of lanes.

"And where are we headed in the meantime?"

"In the meantime I'll drive you home the way I did after that party. But where home is in this world—that is another question."

"What do you mean?"

The wind sweeping in carried the taste of memory, that peculiar flavor I was growing used to: sharp and random enough to seem new, but emotionally musty, sprinkled with something I can only describe as soul dust or spirit ash—a kind of sandy, aged interior. Familiar, but heightened and mystical.

"Certain places in this world, they keep calling you back the way they did in life. They're not homes per se, more like portals, gateways, that propel you on the way they did in life too. Only problem is, the deeper down you go, the more muddled they get. All those rivers in the Greek underworld? It's more like a delta, I'd say. They all get tangled, mixed up. And eventually dissolve into the ocean, of course."

"That happens here too? Dissolution into the ocean?"

"I think so. I think you keep on dying in a way. Why we still age here too, probably—I don't know. I haven't found any Argentine cavemen, that's certain, so I'm inclined to say ghosts pass on eventually. Everything does, after all."

Suddenly, there it was: the déjà-vu-like hint of—what was it this time? The cigar smoke still clinging to my clothes, the faintly minty scent of the Colonel's cologne. It had made me want to vomit on that jittery, hungover morning. Or maybe it was the monologue itself—the words clattered against my skull like ambulance sirens. After what I'd seen the night before, everything took on an additional layer, a latent warning or possible pitfall.

"I think you said something like that on this ride actually," I recalled painfully.

"Did I? What was it now? Oh, yes, I remember! Waxed scientific, didn't I?" And now he waxed again, and the transition was complete: late March 1976, Gardel back on the radio, aviators on the Colonel's decade-younger face, and the early-autumn breeze in my hair. "People say the military is going to destroy this country. But destruction is progress, Tomasito. It's the only measure of it, in fact. Scientifically, I mean. My father—a chemist, don't forget, and a much better chess player than either of us—he told me the only indication that time has a direction, from past to future, is entropy. And what is entropy, Tomás? Disorder. *Destruction* of order. The direction it increases is the direction time moves. So, something breaks, a country falls apart—that's just what time is."

I waited for time to resume, as if it had been listening to his speech; for the reminiscence to crumble and the present or whatever you'd call it to dive back into its place. But it didn't, not completely; though I could reply like we were back in 1986, nothing else rearranged itself accordingly. Neither the Colonel's appearance, nor, I saw, glimpsing my bare cheeks in the side-view mirror, my own. Even my mental state maintained its pressurized, jumpy quality. Disorder, destruction, things breaking and falling apart—the words rang and rang in my ears.

"This place confirm your view?" I asked, disoriented.

"I suppose, in a way. Despite what I said, things can also stand still here. And it hurts when they do. I will say that: It hurts when they do."

He'd overshot the street of my pensión. He turned left on Avenida Hipólito Yrigoyen, then pulled up on the corner of Jujuy and I saw—remembered—why. The small, unlit neon sign for Parada Norte, the café the Colonel had insisted on our breakfasting at that morning after I made the ill-advised confession that I wasn't going to class.

"Not home, per se," the Colonel repeated, reaching over to unlock the passenger door and the memory beyond. "But it calls us back all the same. Ja!"

———

THE CAFÉ WAS QUIET AND DARK, especially compared to the frenetic glare of the morning outside. The place was empty except for a few men of the

Colonel's generation and older, reading the news over coffee, their expressions vaguely disgruntled; despite the dimness, I could make out the all-caps headlines about the precariousness of the presidency and emergency meetings at the Casa Rosada. We sat and—handshake with the waiter, exuberant introduction of his "prized pupil"—the Colonel ordered us cortados and plates of medialunas and ham-and-cheese tostados to share.

"You've never been here, have you?" he asked, prompting me to take another look around: ashtrays full to the brim at nine a.m., most of the liquor drained from the bottles behind the bar, the air seedy with smoke and secrets. "No, why would you? Most of the regulars have been coming twenty years or more. I'm a young buck here comparatively. It was my father who introduced me to it—he was like one of these fellows here, except studying a chessboard instead of the paper. He'd come every morning, and in the evenings he'd return before dinner. Mostly alone, I think, but I'm sure he also brought lovers here. It was that kind of spot—safe, no one would judge you. It was understood, accepted, for that whole generation. Your grandparents', I believe? Were they in this country then, in the twenties, thirties?"

"My father's parents were," I said uneasily. "Their parents came from Spain."

"Ah yes. One of the ladies you brought last night was saying so—Basque connection? Or was it your mother's side, and I'm conflating things? Regardless, they might have come here, your father's parents. It was a big immigrant café back then—lots of tango types getting nostalgic on the bandoneón, missing their homeland. I've always thought it should be more in our cultural memory, the way it is for the Americans, New World and all that. But somehow we got stuck in the old one. Rather like what I was saying in the car—time has to do its work. Out with the old, in with the new. It's the one point we all seem to agree on. The politicians, the intellectuals, the guerrillas and gorillas alike. Gorillas—a good name for my military colleagues, I admit. You kids coined it, no? Oh, excuse me," he corrected himself halfheartedly, "I forgot you wished to be considered older and wiser than your juvenile peers."

I couldn't tell if this was the particular slyness of the night before or if it was the same slyness as always and it simply felt more barbed in the night's aftermath. I wasn't even sure if he was trying to trap me or save me, only that he was enjoying the cat-and-mouse nature of it either way.

"At any rate, I like it here. The kind of place you can be yourself in. Not many in Buenos Aires like that. As you know, for me it's mostly the tourist sites, which tells you something. Plaza San Martín, my beloved Recoleta Cemetery. But this city is hard in that respect—the whole country is. It's one of the vainest in the world. So many of our problems stem from that. Have to be better than the Brazilians, have to be pretty, have to be European. I mean joder, I say *joder*, for God's sake! My father's parents would disown me if they knew I was still saying Spanishisms. For much more than that too, I'm sure. Some of the things I do—they'd be rolling in their graves if they knew."

The plates of food came out. They were bready and bland-looking in the extreme, but a glimpse of them was enough to exacerbate my queasiness.

"Do you know what else Americans have mastered? The art of the hangover breakfast. Bacon, eggs. We're stuck with croissants, meanwhile."

He plucked one out and examined it between two pinched fingers, buttery flakes gliding off them to the table.

"Listen to me blabbing on. Anything you'd like to say?"

"About what?" I asked, as if I'd lost the gist. It was the one relief his constant sidebars allowed.

"I don't know. About being yourself, Tomasito! That's the point of this place. You can say whatever you want here, and for a change no one will blackmail you or put you in prison."

I grabbed a tostado, drew it slowly to my mouth—my hand was unsteady, likely as much because of my hangover as my nerves—and discovered that it tasted fine, that I could stomach another bite. I even managed a third before I answered.

"American breakfast does sound good," I told him.

He laughed. "You have no idea, Señor Shore. Because let me tell you: If you're having breakfast in America, odds are you woke up there."

"Please, Colonel," I said, welcoming the opportunity to jest, to slip out of the conversation through this jokey crevice. "Whatever you say to the contrary, you're as Argentine as Gardel himself."

He laughed again, more heartily. "Don't you know? Even Gardel had his secret identity: he was French-born and applied for Uruguayan citizenship. Look it up if you don't believe me! He was hardly the pure-blooded Argentine we have made him out to be. Another defining attribute of our country—our god isn't even ours. But listen, Tomasito," he added more seriously. "All I'm saying is you can come to me. Whatever it is. You need never be afraid with me."

———

I GAVE UP MY ABORTIVE FORM of espionage after that. I called Isabel and, when Pichuca picked up, asked her to pass on a message.

"Can you tell her the party was a failure?"

"The party at the Colonel's?" Pichuca said. "But it wasn't a failure."

"It's a joke," I said. "Isa will know what it means. You can tell her I'm done throwing parties altogether."

I tried to focus on school, to meet classmates and stay busy. I even asked my lab partner—a nice, freckly girl from Mendoza who reminded me of my ex—if she wanted to go on a date sometime.

I never followed up. Instead I kept waiting for Isabel to call. I thought she'd try to enlist my help again or want to hear more about the Colonel's party at least. But there was no word from her.

A study group from my organic chemistry class was convening in Palermo on Saturday, and since I couldn't tolerate the idea of another fruitless phone call, I decided to go and drop by Pichuca's afterward rather than wait for a summons.

Isabel wasn't there. And Nerea, who'd answered the door, didn't know where she was. "It's Isabel—you know how she is," she said, and I admitted regretfully that I did. "Anyway, what'd you expect? Like I said when you first got here, you do it to yourself."

"Do what, Nerea?" I asked with aggravation, like she was my annoying little sister as much as Isabel's.

"Do this. Follow her around."

"You always followed her around too."

"She was my big sister. My idol, the one who took care of me growing up, who put her arm around me whenever I needed it. Of course I followed her."

"I don't remember her putting her arm around you very much," I said pettily.

"Well," she replied, "you may not remember a lot then."

I didn't stay, convinced despite whatever Nerea claimed that Isabel must be avoiding her too. Maybe another of their activist friends, someone more devoted to the movement, had more insight. The only one whose number I had was Rodolfo, and when I got back, I called him to ask if he'd seen Isabel recently.

"No," he answered curtly.

"Well, do you know what she might be up to?"

"No, why would I?"

"Because you're friends?"

"We're not friends," Rodolfo said. "Listen, Tomás, I'm not involved with her type anymore, okay? My advice, you shouldn't be either."

"What about all that Mao Zedong shit you used to spout?"

"Fuck you, Tomás," he said. "Don't call me again." And he hung up the phone.

—

I WAS STILL TOSSING AND TURNING around two in the morning, trying to make sense of his behavior, when I received a call. It was Isabel.

"Tomás, can you come over?"

"Right now?"

"Yes, as soon as you can."

"Is something the matter?"

"Please," she said. "Just come as soon as you can."

Flustered and exhausted, I didn't ask why. I told myself she was drunk and feeling remorseful and got ready as fast as I could, throwing on deodorant and patting my hair down with a wet towel. The bus would take too long so I called a cab, but it was still forty-five minutes before I got there. I didn't ring the doorbell; it was so late, I figured Isabel wanted the visit to remain stealthy. Correctly, it appeared; she was waiting for me in the entryway and didn't turn on the light when I entered.

"Isa—"

"Shh. In the basement," she said, leading me down. "Careful," she added, in a harsh, distinctly unseductive whisper. "The stairs might be slippery."

It wasn't raining. Why would the stairs be slippery?

The basement light was on. Seated on one of the metal chairs, his foot resting on a second chair, was a man holding a bloody towel to his thigh.

The sight of him didn't summon any pity in me. Only intimidation, a reptilian sense of rivalry. For one thing, he hardly seemed in pain. A smile—*suave* was the descriptor—creased his flushed, swarthy face. Long-framed and dark-featured, with flowing black hair glistening with sweat and a five-o'clock shadow that placed him five years older than me and would have won my envy under any circumstances. Aside from the blue eyes that matched Isabel's and contrasted with my muddy brown ones, he seemed the picture-perfect definition of tall, dark, and handsome. He even had a leather jacket draped over the back of his chair.

"He's a major," Isabel said to me.

"In the military?"

"No. Not in the military."

Of course he wasn't in the military.

Later I learned that the Montoneros used the titles to give themselves a sense of legitimacy. To give the whole so-called war that sense.

I looked at that red, drenched towel.

"I'm not sure I can do this," I said.

"He can't go to the hospital, Tomás."

The police would be monitoring the emergency rooms if they knew they'd wounded him. And if he gave his name and address, they wouldn't have to hunt for him at hospitals. They could just wait for him at home.

My first question was what this man had done to earn a bullet in his thigh. But it was quickly superseded by another: What was Isabel doing with him when the shots came?

"It's all right, Isa," the man said. "He's afraid."

"He's not, Gusti, not the way you think. Are you, Tomás?"

"A limp could do me good," he intervened again. "Give me some credibility against these milicos."

"It could be more than a limp these milicos give you, Gusti," Isabel said. I noted the pejorative: it wasn't just the police who were after them, it was the military. I also noted the familiarity: she called this "major" of hers Gusti, rather than Gustavo. "Tomás isn't afraid to help, he's afraid he won't be able to—"

"Stop fucking speaking for me, Isa!"

She opened her mouth and closed it. I pulled her aside.

"You lied to me," I told her. We'd gone only a few strides away and I don't know if my voice was even lowered.

"The phones could have been tapped. Also, I never lied."

"Whatever you want to call it, Isa."

"I can't help what you hear, Tomás," she said.

I looked away and caught sight of the sofa, where we'd had our moment of passion. The cushions were in disarray again, one of them back on the floor.

"He won't be able to leave here for a few days," I said, changing tacks. "Doesn't your mother employ a cleaning lady?"

"Nelly? She'd probably want to help. But that's all right, I'll hide him."

"And nurse him?"

"I'll do whatever has to be done."

"Because he's your major?"

She rolled her eyes at me. "Are you going to let a good man die because you're jealous, Tomás?"

I said nothing. What could I say but that a part of me very much wanted to?

"I'm not asking you to fight," she continued. "I'd never ask you to do that."

"Of course you would," I said. She smiled. Laughed, and then I did too. I even heard faint laughter from Gustavo.

"Well," she said, "I'm not asking you that right now . . ."

I recalled what she was asking me. Did everything I could to recall my minimal medical training, which seemed incredibly far away.

"If it hit the bone—"

"I don't think it did," Isabel said. "Positioning his leg, I thought I saw an exit wound. Thank God they wanted us alive—otherwise they wouldn't have gone for the leg."

I was not thanking God for this. For any of it.

"Sewing kit. Scissors. Alcohol—vodka if you have it, no wine," I directed Isabel, as I turned at last toward the man in the chair. "More towels—as many as you can carry. We'll have to apply pressure to stop the bleeding."

"Tourniquet?" Gustavo asked.

I shook my head. "If the blood flow stops altogether, you could lose the leg entirely." (*Right?* I asked myself privately, poring through mental images of textbooks and hazy conversations with doctors at the hospital where I'd volunteered the previous summer. *Tourniquet, tourniquet*—it was like a missing entry in an index.) "Is Nerea here?"

"Tito's," Isabel said. "Luckily—she'd have panicked."

While Isabel went upstairs, I removed Gustavo's towel and tried to inspect the wound. With his pants on it was difficult, I'd have to cut them off.

"I should know how to do this myself," he said, wincing at my every touch.

"I should too," I told him.

"Fuck," he said, and I couldn't tell if it was from the pain or his worry over who'd be attending to his wound.

Isabel came back with what I'd asked for. Using the scissors, I worked past the fabric and sticky towel threads for a better look. The red, seeping hole was hideous, and I felt a wave of nausea. But Isabel's guess as to the bullet's exit seemed right: it had passed through the meaty outer part of his thigh, missing the artery as well as the bone.

"You're going to need to get antibiotics—penicillin probably," I told her. "However we sew this up won't matter if it gets infected."

"It won't get infected," Isabel said. "You and I won't let it."

I took one of the towels. Handed it to the man and indicated his mouth. "Sorry in advance," I said.

"Me too," he answered, and after a deep breath that revealed his own fright, bit down on it.

I asked Isabel to take over applying pressure with another fresh towel, showing her how before I proceeded to disinfect the needle. "Ready?" I asked them stupidly. No one answered.

———

THE NAME HE WENT BY—I never learned if it was an alias—was Gustavo Morales. Apparently being a Che Guevara–like warrior wasn't enough, he also had to have morality itself etched into his identity. It was as if Isabel had fallen prey to the same trick I had at twelve, when I'd lined up the names Orilla and Nerea and made a pretty, aquatic myth of them.

When I checked in by phone over the next few days, Isabel was surprisingly available. She sounded as chipper and carefree as someone on vacation. "Yes, yes, I got the medication," she said, as if I were her nagging mother. "Yes, I've been changing the bandages and cleaning the wound like you showed me. Don't *worry* so much, Tomás."

The fact that I did worry was its own mystery. Was I genuinely concerned for the healing of this pseudo-major? Or was I worried she would forget who his healer was—would forget my whole existence, if I didn't thrust it back in front of her as often as I could?

Eventually I resolved to visit Pichuca's again. Again Nerea came to the door. She took me down to the basement, where she and Tito were alone.

"Where's Isa?" I asked.

Nerea shrugged, but with evident satisfaction, as if glad that my conception of our old Pinamar triangle had at last openly collapsed. "With her new boyfriend, I think? Gusti? Mr. Morales? Isa must have told you about him. She talks about him even more than the resistance."

And that, I thought, with the kind of finality I have a devastating inclination toward, was that.

"What do you think of him?" I asked Nerea after an interval.

Another shrug. "He's not afraid of her," she said. "For Isa, that's something."

—

MARCH 24 WAS THE COUP. The newspapers declared it with welcoming fervor, suggesting it was necessary for stability to return to the country. My mother was more cynical, but not the way ensuing history might make one think: her view was that it'd be no better or worse than the twelve previous military governments we'd had since Uriburu back in 1930. (But that it was better than a Peronist government—of that she, typical of her generation, was certain.)

I wasn't exactly anxious myself. How much worse could things get, really? We'd had the Ezeiza massacre back in '73, the death squads had been operative since '75. What had been our de facto reality had merely become an officially recognized one. And I'd grown relatively numb to it, or believed I had. Repression is sneaky that way: you get used to a little, and chances are you'll get used to more.

—

ON THE FIRST OF APRIL, with no warning or preamble, Isabel called and asked me to go on a walk with her in the Bosques. And devoted puppy that I was, I went.

"I have a favor to ask," she told me after a few banal, hurried exchanges about the news. We were under trees at that point, patchwork sunshine overhead.

"Of course you do," I said. "You wouldn't have called me otherwise."

"Tomás . . . ," she scolded.

"Isa . . ."

"I was trying to protect you."

"Whereas now?"

"Now there's been a coup."

"There was always going to be a coup. This is Argentina."

"It's different this time," Isabel said. "What they're doing, it's more than just a coup. We found out they have illegal detention centers—one is the ESMA, right here in the middle of the city. They're taking journalists, unionists, people who volunteer in villas like we did—it's not just Montoneros or other guerrilla bands anymore. It's anyone they want."

The ESMA. It was an abbreviation for Escuela Superior de Mecánica de la Armada—a phrase I'd glimpsed on one of the Colonel's papers that night I stayed over. Those other places I'd seen named—I remembered the American businessman lisping poetically at dinner about Ford, the fact that "Ford Motors Argentina" had also made it onto that list—they must have been illegal detention centers too.

"You found this out how?"

"That's sort of the favor I have to ask," Isabel said. "We have people in the military, working with them, who help us. Give us information."

I recalled entries on another, subsequent memorandum: *On infiltration vis a vis obligatory military service. On infiltration vis a vis offers of intelligence . . .*

"I tried to give you information from the Colonel," I said.

"I know. No one said you did a bad job. There's just another way you can try, is all. If you still want to."

Maybe it was the knowledge of those detention centers. Maybe the unspoken fact that I'd unwittingly discovered some myself and, in passing their names to Isabel, helped the higher-ups map out the full scope of the regime's strategy. Maybe the frightening snowballing of that repressive strategy, and the bravery and importance implied by what Isabel was doing—what she was asking *me* to do.

All these factors contributed to my decision, I'm sure. But the most compelling must have been that Isabel was asking. What were danger and caution compared to that?

"I still want to," I said.

Lighting a cigarette, she relayed her plan. It seemed completely insane from the start, but I didn't want to say it—I didn't want to say I was useless to her. So I simply listened. Listened and nodded and said, over and over again, yes.

They'd gathered intelligence—her word now—that one of the bases of the self-styled war against subversion in Buenos Aires was at the ESMA; in English that abbreviation would refer to the Higher School of Navy Mechanics. Young people worked there, non-navy types too, according to Isabel, and seemingly in every capacity: as guards and messengers, helping forge documents, even as doctors' aides. Her proposal centered on the last: I could go to the Colonel and tell him what I'd heard, tell him that I could use the money, that I needed it for rent or for my mother or whatever lie I felt like trying, and see if he'd look into a job for me. (An imagined memorandum entry flashed through my mind: *Infiltration vis a vis offers of labor . . .*) I could even add a personal touch, she said: "You can tell him you always wanted to know what went on behind those beautiful white pillars on Avenida Libertador, that it seemed like a small paradise to you from the outside. That you used to walk by when you were little and foolish and think, 'There, there must be a training ground for something that matters.'"

I grew up in La Plata; I never walked by the ESMA when I was little. Had Isabel?

"It doesn't matter really," she continued. "Just plant the seed. Knowing what you've said of the Colonel, he'll want it to grow."

I DIDN'T WAIT VERY LONG. Better to get it over with, I thought. Especially as—I kept landing on these additional, half-baked justifications—it might provide a buffer for any suspicions the Colonel had formed since the party. Clearly I couldn't be spying or involved with those idealist kids if I wanted to work at the ESMA, could I?

On April 3, I made two calls: the first to the Colonel, asking to meet for a coffee later that day at Parada Norte. It would have to wait till tomorrow, he told me—"Who knew there'd be so many logistical complications to taking over a government? I barely thought Argentina had one to begin with"—but he was very glad I'd seen the charms of that particular locale.

The second was to my mother; she'd been trying to reach me since the coup, and I'd put off the task of calling back to ease her worries. But I decided to use my meeting to help in this regard as well: "Don't worry," I told her. "I'm seeing the Colonel tomorrow and I'm going to get his advice, make sure I'm staying safe."

"Make sure he's keeping an eye on you too," she said, only moderately relieved.

"I don't think we need to worry about that, Mami. The Colonel's always keeping an eye on me."

"But you know what I mean. Make sure he puts in a word with the right people about you. Tell him to do it for me, to ease a mother's fears. The number of arrests the last few days—there were six high schoolers here in La Plata who were taken. High schoolers, Tomás!"

"I'm not in high school, Mami."

"And the other night, Alba Quiroga was woken by a moving crew next door at two in the morning. At least she thought it was a moving crew at first—loud thumps, the scraping of furniture, you know. But then she saw the time and how fat the rugs were when they carried them out."

"Sounds like one of Alba Quiroga's stories to me. After all, a rug would never be fat enough for her."

"Tomás, don't you—" She cut herself off, forgoing her reproach. "I love you," she said instead, and I muttered the words back before hanging up.

———

THE DINGY INTERIOR OF PARADA NORTE seemed much the same when the Colonel and I met the following afternoon. The newspapers had been replaced, but it was impossible to tell about the men, what with their identical comb-overs and buttoned-up shirts, the outlines of crosses or military tags visible under their collars.

I started by passing on my mother's request. It'd smooth the ground for the main one, I figured, make it seem like just another in a handful.

"It's embarrassing to ask, especially since I don't quite know what I'm asking," I said, "but could you help put her mind at ease?"

"Embarrassing! Not at all, Tomasito. Didn't I tell you right here you could always come to me?" He gave a proud, cartoonishly wide smile, and I nodded. "Tell your mother you're very much under my protection. You can also remind her what I said when she asked me about your moving to our lovely capital in the first place: I told her I personally believe things are safer for students in Buenos Aires than in La Plata. Such an intellectual city, La Plata—it's not a great time for intellectuals. For Thomas Shore types. Better to be one of this country's big dumb animals."

"You're not exactly that," I said.

"No," he laughed. "Some of us, if we're clever enough, we can slip past their defenses. But tell me, Tomás—is there anything else I can do for you?"

Haltingly, allowing for pauses as I sipped on my cortado and nibbled on the tostados the Colonel had ordered again, I made my second request as Isabel had instructed.

"Tomás, my dear," the Colonel said when I finished, "if you're short on money, you can just ask."

"I don't just want money, I want work."

"If you want work, you can do anything. You can be a waiter here at the café," he said, gesturing to one at random.

"There's not much . . . esteem for waiters at cafés, Colonel," I said cautiously.

"I'm not sure there is esteem to be found at the ESMA either, Tomás," he said. I felt him measuring my reaction, like a parent delivering disappointing news to a child. At length, he sighed. "But that's because I'm an army man, not a navy man. If it's the ESMA in particular you want, I can't help you. Other places, perhaps. I know other places you might be interested in working, though I can't speak to the status they might grant you among your friends, or whether your friends would even have heard of them. In fact, to be candid, I don't believe they ever *should* hear of them. Is that the kind of place you want to work, Tomás?"

It was horrible to relive. To experience at once the convoluted logic of the instant itself and, at the same time, all the intricate knowledge of the months and years to come. So many repercussions, so many if-thens rippling endlessly—if I could have just reached into that idiot version of me from the past and altered his response, who knew how the rest would have changed? Might Isabel have lived? Might others have died? Though I'd been over it again and again, explored every hypothetical, serpentine tunnel in that speculative labyrinth trying to solve the brutal calculus of one life's value against another's, I still didn't know what the answer was, or should have been. I only knew what answer I gave.

"If you don't think it's a good idea—"

The Colonel brushed me off with a casual wave. "When I was your age,

I certainly didn't have only good ideas," he said, and smiled, closing off one whole future of mine if not more.

He paid despite my protests and told me to go ahead, he had to stop by the bathroom. But I didn't go ahead. I stared out the window until he got back, wearing his phantasmal form again.

"That won't be the same outside anymore, will it?" I asked him.

"The same outside?"

"Avenida Jujuy. That'll be Venancio Flores now, won't it?"

He gave me one of his supremely nonchalant looks. "Why? Something scary about Venancio Flores?"

I suspected he was toying with me. So I went to the door without bothering to answer that it wasn't the street I feared but what was on it, five minutes from the train station. The so-called Garden—Automotores Orletti, the way it was ten years ago.

ELEVEN

There were other conversations with Claire about my nightmares. They provided a kind of shorthand, a neat excuse for my being so closed off, emotionally unavailable. A crutch, in other words, though it was a genuinely comforting one at the beginning of our relationship, when at the mere mention of my nightmares Claire would put her arms around me like none of it—none of what I'd become—was my fault.

Then my troubled dreams became the sort of thing Claire tried to fix, or help me fix—by getting me to look head-on at the past and confront it, to "deal with my issues." After I proved no better at adopting even passive strategies like "moving on" and "letting go," my muteness around my nightmares took on a different cast, became the type of characteristic that contributed to Claire's calling me a slab of stone.

"They're never about the torture itself?" she asked me once while encouraging me to talk about my dreams. The details I'd given previously—the train, the garage—must have seemed odd to her, tangential to what she imagined was the real horror of my experience.

"Sometimes I'm asked to keep someone alive," I told her. I guess it scared her off, since she didn't ask me to elaborate.

The main feature of those nightmares was the sound of the radio. I would have preferred to hear screaming. Since screaming meant the person behind the door was alive. It was when the screaming ceased that I grew terrified. Both because the person might have lost their life and, worse, because I might get called in to determine if they'd get it back. That is, to decide if they'd have the chance. If this life was worth coming back for.

———

IT HAD BEEN MADE EXPLICIT when I was hired that this would be one of my duties. Aníbal Gordon told me outright, in what was by far the strangest job interview of my life. It was later that April, and the Colonel had driven me down. Among other warning signs, on the way over he'd told me, laughing, that prior to working for the intelligence agency SIDE, Aníbal had been accused of murdering Silvio Frondizi, brother to the former president Arturo Frondizi. But, the Colonel added, I shouldn't let that intimidate me.

Aníbal belonged to that mythologized class of Argentine power-mongers best represented by Admiral Emilio Massera of the junta, who was rumored to help enact kidnappings himself, and José López Rega, the infamous "Warlock" of the Triple A (the Argentine Anticommunist Alliance). Whatever the Colonel contended, their chief purpose was large-scale intimidation via political eradication. Aníbal had worked with the Triple A death squads as well as his own gangs and, according to the Gringo, who would later relay this list admiringly, had been suspected of armed robbery, racketeering, and the stealing and selling of fuel from commercial planes. Though his alias was Black, no one made use of it, perhaps because his real name was more frightening or because no one dared report him, in any case.

Aníbal had thick, muscular features, including a bulbous nose and large, fleshy ears, and often visibly perspired through the suits he wore to work. When I met him in his office—the heart of the place was kept hidden from me at first—he said my proficiency in English and ability to communicate with his American friends made me an appealing prospect. But the real reason he was open to the Colonel's idea was that none of his men knew a thing about medicine—which was very much in keeping with the disorganized, "unprofessional" nature of Automotores, he said. He added that recently one of the guards, trying to determine whether a prisoner's heart was still beating, had stuck it with a fucking syringe and watched for movement in it. Suffice it to say, there was none.

The point was, a medical student was good enough for him. If I could do CPR, operate a defibrillator, and use the syringe only for fucking vaccinations, that was all I needed.

———

BUT AS THE CULTURAL REFRAIN about that time went: I knew, but I didn't *know*. I didn't truly know what my job would entail until the moment I heard the sizzle of static pouring from the radio beyond the torture room door.

At lunchtime on my first day, I met several of the other men, sitting in the kitchen around a nicely set table with sandwiches and empanadas. Neither Aníbal nor the Priest was there—the Priest offered his services elsewhere occasionally, when they thought they could extract information through an actual confession, and Aníbal checked in from time to time at Coordinación Federal. (It turned out it was a detention center as well as a federal police headquarters, and an appropriately named one at that: what good was getting all this information if they didn't coordinate how to use it?) Rubio's lunch break was brief; he'd been at it with a "squealer" since the night before and wanted to get back to it. When I finished—I barely touched my meal, and spoke almost exclusively with the Gringo, since Triste showed no interest in speaking to anyone—I went to the prisoners' side of the floor to patrol the hall and be near the torture room in case I was needed.

I could tell by the raspy pitch that it was an older man inside, and by the volume that he was new. After a week or more, people tried to stay quiet if they could, I'd been informed during my tour with the Gringo, and they rarely allowed themselves to plead. This man did; he shouted at the top of his lungs for help, screamed he was innocent, said he didn't know, he was just a psychiatrist, it wasn't his fault his patients—and then he said nothing.

Czzzzshhkk. Krrrrzzzzccshhkkk.

Radio static. I was nauseous and scared to be seen throwing up and had the awful thought: The sooner Rubio calls me in, the better.

Finally the bolt loosened and Rubio revealed himself, adjusting his glistening blond hair and wiping his brow. "Verde," he summoned, and I went.

Czzzzshhkk. Krrrrzzzzccshhkkk.

The man on the table—the parrilla, or grill, as the Gringo called it, to the Priest's distaste—looked to be what my father's age would have been. He was naked, and the indignity of that moved me, more than it should have. He'd been tortured, possibly to death; what did it matter if he was naked on top of that?

Rubio stood aside, and I got the defibrillator from where it was kept in the corner. I'm sure I moved quickly, but it felt slow, routine. Without urgency. Rubio took a toothpick from his pocket and went to work on his teeth while he waited, like he had all the time in the world.

The man was already shirtless, so all I had to do was feel his pulse, make sure the use was appropriate, then place the pads and push the button. I didn't hesitate on the first try. But at the convulsion in the man's body—it was my first time using the defibrillator on someone in need of it—I paused and reckoned with what I was about to do. It had only been one morning, but that was enough to comprehend what the rest of a prisoner's days were likely to be at Automotores.

I applied the defibrillator again. Again the convulsion, and nothing more. Again I pondered the momentousness of what I was doing, as if the stakes got higher the further from life the man seemed. I looked at the squiggly white chest hairs surrounding the defibrillator pads and wondered: How much longer could he have anyway?

I used it again. Again that dramatic tremor of the body and—that was all. Maybe the problem was adding more electricity to a heart stopped by electricity?

I glanced at Rubio. He waited, toothpick in his pristine white teeth.

Again. Again. Ag— I'm not sure how I knew. But there it was, in his throat, running feebly through his veins—breath. Life.

Rubio thanked me, and I went back out.

After all that, the man died a few weeks later; his heart stopped again, only this time on one of my days off. I took fewer after that.

—

WHEN I GOT HOME THAT FIRST NIGHT, I called Isabel. Pichuca said she was out. I tried again an hour later—she still wasn't there. Neither was Nerea—she was probably off with Tito, Pichuca said, complaining that her daughters never told her anything. I considered asking more pointed questions but realized it could open me up to questions in turn, and I worried about my ability to handle them in my state.

Anger doesn't do it justice. Not even betrayal. I felt used and abandoned, thrown away. When I went to work the next day, the impact of every sensation was amplified: the muffled screams; the grimy stray car parts strewn around the garage to give the appearance that the place was still operating in that capacity; the broken lightbulbs hanging in the air—they all seemed analogues to the pain induced by Isabel.

Maybe if she loved me, if I could tell myself it was for love of her—if I could inject the experience with that kind of sacrificial spirit and heroism—it might feel worth it, endurable. But as it was? With Isabel absconded away with Gustavo, fucking in the throes of revolutionary passion? I had no idea how I'd find the strength for this. I had no idea—the thoughts spiraled from rage to terror to sudden, chest-thumping panic as I listened to the violent Liszt concerto playing inside the torture room—how I'd *survive* this. One wrong word or revealing hesitation—that'd be enough to put me on the table.

All that made me show up again was the danger of not doing so. I couldn't go to the Colonel after a mere two days and say I wasn't up for it. I couldn't ask him to protect me either, after what I'd witnessed. How would he even be able to protect himself, if the likes of Aníbal Gordon believed he'd put a Montonero spy in their midst?

Two days. This could last two years—more, even. That was what might have tormented me most: Isabel must have known that if she got me in there, I'd have no way of getting out.

———

IT WAS ONE OF THE LONGEST WEEKS OF MY LIFE, that first one at Automotores. The sounds and sights that broke the murky dankness of the place hadn't blurred together yet, grown numbing. Each was still its own startling horror, even the minute ones like the unintelligible sound of Portuguese between two Brazilian guards, the roar of the rusty garage door when it opened or closed. The stink of engine oil, of infection. The flickering of the lights when the picana was being used at high voltages, and the terrible care with which prisoners drank soup, to avoid the blows they got when they spilled. The request one made that I tighten his blindfold, because he might be punished if a guard thought he could see.

The conversations, the laughter among those guards. Rubio and the Gringo making fun of Triste's grumpiness, chatting about soccer or a girl one of them was seeing. Aníbal and the Priest going over "evidence" taken during a kidnapping, choosing among stolen watches or cigarette lighters while making remarks about moneygrubbing Jews, their commenting on humiliating entries in a journal or calendar. ("What the fuck you think this lady's chest appointment is, eh, boludo?") Aníbal giving the Priest a hard time for driving to work when it was all of fifteen minutes away from home, and in his own personal car to boot. (The Priest responded, smirking, that it was God's duty to protect him, since He was the one who made him lazy.) One of the visiting SIDE officers complaining about lawyers' pesky writs of habeas corpus—if only they could be more like the notaries who happily signed over detainees' assets, no questions asked; another telling stories about other centers' methods and congratulating us on not using "the submarine," a vat of water filled with shit and piss they'd dunk prisoners' heads in—it wasn't good, someone had drunk the dirty water trying to kill herself, he explained with amusement.

The endless hours after my second and third days, unable to eat, unwilling to sleep because morning would come too soon if I did. The additional attempts to reach Isabel to no avail, and the time I spent lying on my bed afterward, listening to my records or the samba that came from Beatriz's room and plying myself with her weed and a bottle of Chivas Regal the Colonel had bought me. ("Verde's a party animal!" the men often exclaimed when I entered, because I stank of booze. "A party *monster!*")

Every call I got from the torture room too, of course. There were tasks Aníbal hadn't mentioned in our interview, like helping bind prisoners to the table before a session and throwing water on them to reduce the electrical resistance of their skin. Or, on occasions we knew they wouldn't sing and the goal was solely to make them suffer, putting a rubber truncheon in their mouth to prevent them from destroying their tongue.

And then there were the "vaccinations." These were actually injections of sodium pentothal, a knockout tranquilizer used for surgeries. On transfer days, as I learned that Wednesday, when the truck arrived and Aníbal called me to his office to give me the list of prisoners—five that first time, no names, only numbers—Triste would get them from their cells and line them up and, in the role of "doctor," I'd inject each one so they could be taken more easily. Where, no one told me explicitly, but I knew. The prisoners, I could tell from the tears gradually wetting their blindfolds or escaping down their cheeks as they waited for my syringe, must have known too. After all, their clothes were left behind, their possessions.

They weren't allowed to speak. But one, a boy near my age, asked me in a whisper if it was poison. I told him it wasn't.

———

I'D WORKED THREE WEEKDAY SHIFTS. On Thursday, Aníbal told me he'd be switching up the schedule: I'd take most weekends and get days off during the week. "The men don't want you giving up your education, Verde," he said. "And they don't want to give up their weekends, the lazy shits."

My fear remained just as intense. With each hour came another risk of failure to dissemble, to convincingly trade barbs with the men or hide a grimace at a spasm on the table. I kept waiting for them to notice, to say something. The only one who did, later that morning after I helped him with a session, was the Priest.

"Not the easiest work in the world, is it?" he said warmly, a smile creasing his bald, amiably round head.

"No," I admitted.

"And not the likeliest type of work for a man of the cloth either, I suspect you're thinking."

"It does seem"—I groped uneasily after the right word—"specialized."

The Priest laughed. "I suppose you could say that," he said generously, as if I could say anything in his presence. "I was a chaplain in my youth. And, actually, I found myself disillusioned with the army at a certain point and left. Perón with all his young women after Evita died, all those internal squabbles among the armed forces. Everything seemed so *petty*. But then," he continued, shifting tone with the practiced cadence of an orator, "with Castro in Cuba, and Allende in Chile, and the communists defeating the Americans in Vietnam, and all these terrorists attacking officers. Suddenly the fight felt so much larger to me. Argentina was threatened. Democracy was threatened, Western values. Christianity—since the Second World War, it's been in retreat. And, well, here we are." He breathed deeply, taking in the torture room with pride. "It's important to keep the bigger picture in mind, my son. Our work here—these are small battles in a larger war, you see? And the war is what you have to consider. Meanwhile," he went on, gently taking my arm and leading me to a closet in the hall; he opened it and indicated a mop and bucket, "would you mind, Verde? I like this place to conform to certain norms. We may dirty our hands here, but what we do—it is *clean*."

———

THAT DAY, ISABEL FINALLY CALLED. Or rather, left a message for me at the pensión in the middle of the afternoon when she likely knew I wouldn't be there to answer. The message: Meet at the entrance to the Japanese Gardens at 18:00 on Friday. Nothing more.

She was late. I couldn't believe that on top of everything else she was late.

When she arrived, she was already raising her hand to stop me from whatever tirade she expected me to go on. Something else I could scarcely believe: I heeded her.

We circled the pond until Isabel directed us to a bench by its side. It was getting cold, and few others were about—probably why she was more willing to meet in parks now than in places like appliance stores. As soon as we sat, paying no attention to the picturesque flowers, the bonsai trees, or the charming red footbridge, I started in: "You knew what they were doing, didn't you? You knew and you asked me to work there. How could you do that to me, Isa?"

"Do *that*? To *you*? What about what they're doing to *them*, Tomás? It's not about you, none of this is about you. This is war."

"It's not war. It's annihilation."

"And what, you're afraid to be annihilated? Can't you think about anyone else?"

"Can't you? If it's so fucking honorable to help this way, why didn't you just ask me outright? Don't pretend this is about other people, this is about your misery and purposelessness and finally having an antidote to them. You're happy, I can see you're happy, Isa."

She shook her head like she pitied me. Maybe she did.

"I'm happy because I'm trying to help people, Tomás. Fighting for them. Fine, I used you—betrayed you, even, if you want. Are you going to betray *them*?"

What I wanted right then was to betray *her*. I'd only gotten involved in the first place for her, not for those other people. That my selfishness could have gotten so tied up in some greater good didn't seem fair. Nor that Isabel's could.

And yet. And yet and yet and yet—the phrase thudded through me perniciously. Let me go, I pleaded to whatever part of my brain wouldn't, that kept beating that drum. Let me go.

It didn't.

"What do you want from me, Isa? The names of the people they've taken? The names those people give?"

Isabel nodded. Then added: "And anything you can do to ease their pain."

———

THERE WASN'T MUCH I COULD DO. Especially since I was afraid to be caught doing anything outside my job description that wasn't vicious or cruel. Even when I found out that other guards occasionally gave prisoners snacks or other small treats, my trepidation persisted, as I didn't compensate for such indulgences the way they did in the torture room. I couldn't necessarily rely on the prisoners to keep any kindness of mine a secret either; they could turn on each other with stunning rapidity—some even became "markers" who went on kidnapping raids to earn better treatment. Which meant I was too scared to bring them anything but their standard food rations. Too scared to ease or briefly take off their blindfolds as well. Too scared to give the women tampons, since those were certain to be discovered. I couldn't even offer the tiny caresses I'd seen some prisoners give each other stealthily in their common cell or when they were made, on Rubio's lazier days, to torture each other in a two-birds-one-stone way.

All I felt I could do was take advantage of the Priest's morbid fantasy of bringing the place up to the standards of a hospital and clean. Clean the bathroom. Clean the utensils the prisoners ate with. Clean their clothes every once in a while and hang them on the balcony to dry. More often I cleaned and dried the towels the guards used to wipe their sweat—anything to provide an excuse for me to get that needed breath of fresh air. The balcony was one of the few solitary sites at Automotores, since the Priest, who could withstand the rot of prisoners but not the smell of cigarettes, didn't permit the men to smoke even out there.

Clean the garage. Clean the kitchen. Clean the blood off the floors so the men wouldn't dirty their shoes and the prisoners didn't walk through it barefoot. (Even when they weren't beaten, they still often bled from the lacerations the straps made when their limbs were thrashing.) Clean the guard quarters. Don't clean the prisoners' cells but do clean their wounds to avoid infection. (That at least was part of my job—keeping them alive.)

I wasn't naturally a clean person—it wasn't a compulsion I had in any other sphere. An unintended benefit was that it gave me the reputation as a hard worker. Not all the men liked it—"What are you sucking up for?" Rubio asked me when I stayed late washing dishes. "There's no report card here, Verde"—but those who mattered more did. The Priest cooed with pride at my mopping, and after one of my shifts, Aníbal told me, "Little did I know the Colonel would give me such a committed employee. When you see him next, tell him I'm impressed. You may not do the dirty work, but you sure as shit do the rest, Verde."

———

AT THE END OF MAY, my mother insisted on visiting. I tried to put her off, but I'd been doing so for two months already and hadn't gone home for Easter, and she threatened to stop paying for my room at the pensión. "You either see me there or you see me here, Tomás," she said with unusual authority, and I told her I'd see her here.

Among the complications it raised was that I knew she'd also want to see the Colonel. I hadn't seen him myself since starting at Automotores. Partly I was avoiding it, afraid of revealing my state or making a slip in conversation. But partly it was his doing. No calls or invitations, only a postcard from Rio de Janeiro of the open-armed Christ Redeemer statue overlooking the city that read: *Churchman beating freethinker here too, alas.* It was dated May 24, and I hadn't heard from him since.

But when I phoned, Mercedes picked up like nothing was the matter, saying simply that it'd been too long since I'd been in touch and going to get the Colonel.

"Why, if it isn't Señor Shore," he said. "And here I feared you'd died."

"You feared I'd—"

"Kidding, Tomasito!" he exclaimed. "Joder. To what do I owe the pleasure?"

"My mother's coming to town," I answered stiffly.

"Well, why so grim about that? We'd love to host her, of course."

"She's going to stay at a hotel—she insists," I added honestly. My mother wasn't the type to impose, except occasionally upon me. "We'll make a dinner date. It's just that she—she doesn't know about what I'm doing, my job," I faltered. "I'd appreciate it if—"

"Of course, Tomasito. You know I don't like to worry your mother. Your secret's safe with me." He said it with such ease it threw me, and before I could thank him and hang up, he added, "How is it working out for you, by the way? That secret."

I looked around the common area. A business student from Lima sat at the dining table, engrossed in a textbook. A kettle was whistling loudly from the kitchen.

"Aníbal said to tell you he was impressed with me."

"Oh, did he? How nice. Especially for Aníbal. And do you feel you're getting what you wanted out of it?"

"Getting what I . . . ?"

"You know, learning, worldly experience and the like. Didn't you say you wanted more than money out of it?"

I breathed. Switched the receiver to the other ear to give myself more time, but I still couldn't answer. If the Colonel knew why I'd wanted to work at Automotores, I assured myself, he wouldn't have gotten me the job.

"Of course, we don't have to talk about it if you don't want," he said at length. "Especially not on the phone! I should know better, shouldn't I? I'll let you be off. Just don't forget, if you change your mind: I can always keep your secrets safe, Tomás."

———

ANOTHER ISSUE WITH MY MOTHER COMING was that I had to ask Aníbal for that Saturday off—a change in my schedule. And by a strange turn in logic, figuring I should tell him any truth I could so that he wouldn't suspect my lying in other realms, I explained my mother was the reason.

I braced myself for invective or worse. We were in the hallway outside the torture room, Elvis playing loudly within. Aníbal was going through the prisoner's wallet and barely raised his eyes at me. "Look at the fucking beak on this Jew, eh," he said, dumping an ID card on the floor. Next he flicked a photo of the prisoner's children after it. "Ugly Russian brats. Anyway, Verde, sure—whatever you need for your old lady. We're all family men here."

———

I WAS TENSE AND SURLY throughout my mother's stay. Blaming schoolwork and stomach problems—I'd had diarrhea on and off since beginning at Automotores—I refused to join the meals I'd set up at the Colonel's and Pichuca's. Both seemed too stressful to me, and I knew Isabel would find her own excuses not to show up at the latter.

I took my mother to a Mahler symphony the Colonel got us tickets to (I fell asleep during the second movement), and I introduced her to Beatriz, pretending we were much closer than we were, since she was desperate to meet friends of mine. But most of my mother's trip I made her sit silently across from me at cafés while I read, or brought her on walks in which I said little and showed her nothing of interest. ("That's my local confitería. . . . This is Avenida Santa Fe. . . . No, I don't know what that monument is.")

"What's wrong with you, Tomás?" she asked me at last, when I wordlessly picked her up at her hotel on Sunday evening. "In La Plata we got along fine."

"Nothing's wrong with me," I said.

"Is it Isabel's influence? Pichuca says she's worried about her, Nerea too. They're never at home, they're—"

"Goddamn it, why do you have to pry all the time, Mami? Don't you know that's why I left, to get you out of my hair?"

She gave me a confused, heartbroken look. "That's not why you said you left."

"Well, I'm saying it now. Mind your own business."

She was supposed to drive back Monday morning. But she wound up leaving that night, after I spent another dinner shoving uneaten pasta aimlessly around my plate.

───

I RETURNED TO WORK ON TUESDAY. It was lunchtime when I arrived, and the entire group was eating together in the kitchen—a rarity.

"Your visit with mami go okay?" Rubio asked, snickering.

"What's wrong with a visit from his mami?" The Gringo came to my defense. "I want more visits from my mami."

"You and the merchandise probably have that in common, Carlitos," Aníbal said with a laugh.

"Now, now," the Priest replied. "You know they don't have mothers, Aníbal. Not here, not with us. The prisoners, when they are in our possession, should have no identities. They are no one."

Silence, as the men contemplated this grand concept. I started to clear their plates.

"Your mother must be very proud, Verde," the Priest said as I went to the sink.

"She's the one who taught me to clean," I said, making myself nod.

—

IT TURNED OUT most of the names I got at Automotores weren't even likely to be of use to Isabel. As part of Operation Condor, our targets were suspected socialists, Marxists, communists, and their specific Argentine offshoots, particularly the ERP, the People's Revolutionary Army. They were the equivalents of Montoneros, but for a different cause: they didn't want Perón in Argentina; they essentially wanted Castro in Argentina. Indeed, the possibility that Cuban-style communism would spread to Latin America was the one that concerned the United States and its proxies most. No matter that the People's Revolutionary Army's actual army had been routed in Tucumán the year before, we were to eliminate every last trace of the ERP. Along with their supporters, which typically meant unionists and laborers and anyone else who had agitated for better wages or conditions. Recalling that American businessman in love with Ford's venture in the Amazon, I formed the hunch that the dictatorship had backing from more than the military sector alone.

Montoneros were technically beyond our scope. And though it hardly stopped us whenever we landed on one, there were few in Automotores' possession. Most of our prisoners were involved with labor movements, and those who weren't often weren't even Argentine but foreign exiles who had fled other Latin American countries after military coups and were to be handed back to the Uruguayans and the like. ("We're behind the times!" the Gringo exclaimed to me, delineating the nuances of our purview. "Chile and Uruguay have a three-year head start on us. And Brazil, la puta madre—they got a fucking decade.")

My next meeting with Isabel was in the Barrancas de Belgrano. Per her instructions, I got off and on the subway at least twice to see if anyone was following me—should someone else get off and on, I was to head home. I arrived without incident, but the Barrancas was so little different from the Bosques that it was hard to feel we were fooling anybody. The elaborateness of the arrangements seemed silly, as futile as collecting names of abducted Montoneros. And when I joined Isabel on the shaded bench where she sat, I immediately started pleading the uselessness of my position to her.

"It doesn't matter if Automotores isn't after Montoneros," she answered. "We're all in this together now. We're all fighting the same fight, the same bad guys."

That was its own issue, though—those bad guys. I coexisted with them, bullshitted with them. I even slipped into the "we" when relaying their activities. How could I explain that the blurring of those battle lines might have been what was getting to me most?

When Isabel asked for the names of those we had, I gave them. And when she expanded her inquiry, asking for details about our organizational structure, I tried to give those too.

"Coordinación Federal," she said, buttoning up her coat. (I wore only a sweater and was shivering.) "The bosses all stop in there, no? The Colonel does—we know that already. What about Aníbal and the rest of them?"

"I don't know," I said. Information was shockingly hard to hang on to under the circumstances, so easily overwhelmed by all the terrible sensory input. (Although, sickeningly, my ability to retain the details of organ diagrams and the fetal pig corpses we dissected in my biology labs had improved; the sterilizing of life and death could have a narcotic effect on my psyche when I let it.)

"But copies of all the interrogations and confessions go there, don't they? Like a library? Isn't that how they cross-check?"

"Aníbal goes," I told her. "I don't know why—he's always boasting about this big communications antenna in his office, and how Coordinación has a matching one, like a radio. They're very fast—the Americans made it," I added, as if that were key.

"So Coordinación is sort of telling Aníbal who to go after—does that sound about right? On this radio?"

"It's an antenna. I don't know, Isa. I don't hear any of that stuff. Only—" I almost said the radio, but stopped myself, seeing the confusion that could cause. "I'm sorry, I don't . . ."

"Don't be sorry, Tomás." Isabel reached out and raised my chin with her index finger, the way men did to damsels in distress in movies. "There's nothing to be sorry about. You don't know how much you're helping us— how much you're helping *them*." She'd taken to emphasizing that word, as if it aggrandized the whole concept of other people to her, obscured the misanthropy she could fall victim to when considering individuals. "Every name you give, you could be saving someone else's life. You see that, don't you?"

I didn't. But Isabel looked so pleased, her blue eyes so bright with belief, I didn't want to say so. Instead I just sat there dumbly, until I felt the dutiful, speedy peck of her lips on my cheek.

"I have to go, I'm running late for an appointment. I know, I know," she said, as if I'd been on the verge of teasing her for the tendency. "Really, you don't know what this means to me. I wish you did, Tomás."

I wished I did too. "I'm afraid it's going to break me, Isa," I told her.

She stood over me, and despite my trembling, she said, "I think you're unbreakable, Tomás. Maybe it's all the shitty things I've done to you, I don't know. You just—you're like me. We're not scared of pain, remember?" She gave me another, longer kiss on the forehead, her hands on my ears as if she could block out every other sound. "Just don't drink so much," she added with a sly smile, standing upright. "We wouldn't want another of those blacked-out calls to my house, would we?"

Somehow I also found myself smiling. "I'll try to ease up."

"Ease up on yourself, Tomás," Isabel said. "That's one thing I agree with my mother about. I wish you treated yourself better."

All I did was nod. I shared that wish, too.

TWELVE

On the second of July, the Montoneros set off a bomb in Coordinación Federal. If Isabel had played a part in it, or if the information I gave her did, I was never informed.

They killed some twenty officers. It wasn't much compared to the numbers of their own felled by the enemy—and the building continued to stand tall, along with its detention center—but it was the most damage they'd done in a single attack to date.

The retaliation was ferocious. That Montoneros weren't in our jurisdiction didn't matter; kidnappings increased, as did transfers. Tortures grew worse—the picana started to be applied while hanging someone from the rafters by the arms or legs instead of using the wire bed. The infamous "submarine" method made its first appearance, when we brought in the man who'd infiltrated the Federal Police and helped set the bomb: Ricardo Alberto Gayá, of the Workers' Revolutionary Party. How he got hooked up with the Montoneros, I had no idea, except that, as Isabel had pointed out, they were all fighting the same fight now.

Rubio and Aníbal himself dunked Ricardo Alberto Gayá in a two-hundred-liter vat of I don't know what and, after he sang, drowned him in it. They left his corpse in the vat afterward, sealed it with cement, and transferred him out that way, throwing him into the Luján River.

My nightmares, which had been as erratic as my sleep since joining Automotores, grew more consistent. Nightly I'd find myself caught in some new way, the Colonel concernedly uncovering links to Ricardo Alberto Gayá I didn't know I had, Rubio making me stare into the toxic brown pool of the submarine. In one, my mother even gave Aníbal my teenage correspondence with Isabel, convicting me herself.

Reality was hardly better. The Gringo's claims over lunch that the Montonero conspiracy among our ranks was vast, the expletive-filled lecture Aníbal gave to staff one morning, insisting that no one in his shop would be so fucking stupid and we shouldn't worry about it. The Priest's more sedate assurance that there were many higher-ups already looking at the matter closely.

No one looked suspiciously at me yet, that I could tell. For now, the men focused their hatred on the detainees. The ones we had, and the ones we gained. The new "packages."

One morning, Rubio called me in to resuscitate a young blond girl they'd gotten the previous night. The skin around her blindfold was purple, her bottom lip large and puffy, and other bruises were quickly forming along her breasts and torso despite the mandate to use the machine to avoid physical traces. Blood stained the inside of her thighs.

I retched, working every muscle in my throat to swallow the stomach acid back down and conceal my reaction from Rubio.

"Well?" he said. When I still didn't do anything, he laughed. "You know if you want a shot with her too, you'll have to bring her back."

I did. I brought her back.

—

SHE WAS AMERICAN, I found out the next day. I was in the garage, where there was a fresh array of bullet holes in the floor—Aníbal and the Priest discouraged warning shots, but sometimes the men couldn't resist. I heard a crash, and I rushed upstairs to see what had happened. Aníbal was speaking to Rubio outside the torture room. The crash was the radio, which Rubio had knocked off its chair in anger at the discovery. He'd been told about a blond Montonera hiding in a hotel in San Telmo and, with nothing more to go on than the physical description, had picked up the wrong person. No one had bothered looking at her papers until after his session with her yesterday.

It was as humiliating for him as it was potentially endangering. Americans were our allies. They funded our operations and had once even sent one of their own to conduct a session with two acquired Cuban diplomats. I had been alerted that my English might be called into service, but as it happened, the interrogator spoke Spanish and, though his gringo accent made the Gringo Carlitos seem as Argentine as the first-ever gaucho, he didn't end up needing me.

It was the Gringo who best explained our nations' relationship to me. Biting into a cheeseburger over a recent lunch, he'd said, "You know this Kissinger guy in their Casa Blanca, Verde? Got us eighty million dollars! If he wasn't such good pals with Pinochet over in Chile too, the church would name him patron saint of Argentina, I swear ..."

Rubio must have known he was in a pickle. Kidnapping an American—much less raping and torturing one—was not politically ideal. When he caught me staring at him from the end of the hall, he spat and rushed off, shoving past me furiously.

Aníbal picked up the radio, which had a bent antenna and a dent in its side and no longer worked. "Fucking shit," he said, and rattled off a few more choice oaths: hijo de puta, concha de su madre. He handed me the radio. "See if we have any electricians in the cells. Guerrillas are supposed to be good with machinery."

———

IT SHOULD HAVE BEEN an easier task than most. But I knew who we had in the cells by name and profession—we had a "merchandise" closet where we kept their things, including IDs, which was how I got the names I'd give to Isabel—and there were no electricians. I didn't imagine any of the prisoners would open themselves up to the additional torture that would come with admitting they'd worked on machinery for guerrillas either. We were in the middle of a relatively busy neighborhood in Buenos Aires—the better to instill fear in its residents, however obscure—and I could have gone to a local electrician in Floresta, but Aníbal hadn't said to do that, and an unwritten rule was that you always did what Aníbal said. There was also the psychological divide between what went on inside Automotores and what went on outside. We rarely bridged those worlds. Not even for a radio.

I couldn't figure out what to do. So I went to Triste. It wasn't that he was particularly friendly toward me; the Priest and the Gringo were more so. But Triste wasn't friendly with anyone, and that made him a kind of indirect ally to me. Skulking around, ignoring the Gringo's jokes about his skulking around, limiting his interactions with the other guards to work and really treating it like that—a job he clocked in and out of. His lack of interest in any broader goals around what we did was palpable.

Triste did have other interests, though, more extensive human interactions. They were with the prisoners.

The majority we kept in the common cell that fit about twenty people— the Uruguayans and other foreigners had a separate cell downstairs—but we had three isolated cells for individuals we wanted to protect (or, depending, to torture using the method borrowed from the ESMA—capuchita). Some guards, like Rubio, paid visits to the women, for predictable reasons. Others, like the Gringo, stopped in to bring them things: leftover cakes or slices of steak from family occasions, a supplement to their usual diet of canned soup, cornmeal, and stale bread. He also brought toilet paper he bought himself so they wouldn't have to use the newspapers Aníbal kept stocked in the bathroom, which were coarse enough to make the prisoners bleed. As far as I could tell, the Gringo never questioned the strangeness of showing care for their bodies in one instant and torturing them the next.

Triste's attentions to the prisoners were arguably even stranger. He didn't bring treats and, unlike Rubio, he never visited a woman in her cell—whether because he had a wife and daughter or a conscience, I don't know. The only thing he seemed to bring was conversation. He'd sit with some of them for hours when he was off duty, and if you passed you'd hear murmurs inside, maybe catch a name from the news or the score of a soc- cer game, as if they were just chatting, catching up on the goings-on of the outside world.

The outside world—what could be a bigger treat to them than that?

I imagined Triste would know which of the prisoners could help, and that afternoon I showed him the radio. "What of it?" he replied tersely, taking off his glasses to mop his face with a rag. I told him it was broken. "Again," Triste said. "What of it?"

"Aníbal wants one of the prisoners to fix it," I explained.

Glasses went back on; sour, usually averted eyes glanced at me. With- out saying anything, he directed me down the hall to the isolation cell where he spent the most time.

THE PRISONER INSIDE they called Gordo—Fatty. The appellation was ironic; he was skinny and droopy as spaghetti. But there was a steadfastness to him, a degree of control: he walked without stumbling even in his blindfold, and he turned at corners on his way to the bathroom or torture room before the guard accompanying him had a chance to tug him in that direction. He was an old-timer, relatively speaking: probably in his forties—a good fifteen years older than the average prisoner—with a creased brow and splashes of gray in his reddish-brown beard. That he'd survived at all when another prisoner his age had died of a heart attack after a few weeks already commanded respect. But it went deeper than that. He wore his dignity like a physical feature. Even with his shrunken, fragile frame, you got the impression that little could break him, and that his silence, when he kept it, was of his own choosing.

Turning on the cell light, I laid the radio and some tools from the garage at his feet. Gordo ran his hands over them as I figured a blind man would, mentally recording the exact shapes and details.

"I'm sorry," he said earnestly, as if he really were sorry about it. "I need you to take my blindfold off to do this."

"You don't seem to need it walking around the place," I observed.

"I count my steps," he answered. "It's different."

After weighing my options, I went over and lowered his blindfold.

The way he looked around called to mind someone on a scaffold whose noose had been taken off. His first few blinks were slow and mesmerizing, his control over his eyelids as uncertain as an infant's.

I saw prisoners' eyes only when they were dead or soon to die; these were the only occasions when their blindfolds were allowed off, since there was no risk to it then. But it meant that there was little sense of humanity to it then either; what life could those eyes reveal, taking in the world just before being pushed into the transfer truck?

This was different. When we made eye contact, we held it. No more than a few seconds, but there was as much communication between us in that time as has ever been carried in people's words, I think.

His eyes were hazel. I know they weren't special. But at that moment, they seemed the most dizzyingly unique and complicated shade I'd ever seen.

He lowered them and got to work. Neither of us spoke for a while.

"Where'd you learn to do things like this?" I asked eventually, and when I saw the wary look on his face, clarified, "I'm not asking if you're in the movement. Just if you were—I don't know, a mechanic."

He continued working meticulously, and I got the impression his mind was too, calculating if this was a trap, if he really could speak candidly. When he answered, it was without raising his eyes, as if the magnitude of their meeting mine again would be more overwhelming than he could bear. "My father taught me. Worked in a garage—probably not too different from what this place used to be."

"And you?"

"Professor. Engineering."

"University of Buenos Aires? I don't recognize you." I'm not sure how I would have—there were hundreds of professors across different buildings. But I could have, and as an engineering student Isabel certainly could have—I tried in vain to recall her reaction when I'd given his name. The truth was, you'd stretch any connection you could in that place to bring it closer to home.

"I've been in custody since March, just after classes started," he said. "Why I've made it so long, I don't know. Maybe for this, to fix things like radios."

"I thought it was for Triste," I said, with accidental boldness. It was just so good and freeing to speak openly about the people here with someone who knew them.

Gordo must have felt the same: "There's no fixing him," he said, before glancing up to catch my own wary look and adding hastily, "What? He'd say so himself. Has, in fact."

"He tells you he's broken?"

"He tells me he's like me. Another victim of circumstance. Loves talking about his shoes."

"His shoes?"

"They're two sizes too big, apparently," Gordo said. This was another frequent target of the Gringo's jests, but I'd forgotten. "He told me that in training they stole your shoes. One or two people's, and if you showed up at roll call without them, they gave you a beating or threw you in a cell like this. Only way out was to steal another soldier's shoes. Triste got used to his being too large."

I didn't know what to do with this. In myself, I mean: What happened to you when you started seeing the humanity in monsters? To your humanity? Your own monstrosity?

No one had told me how Triste came to be stationed at Automotores. For all I knew, he had just kept at it after his obligatory military service, decided to make a career of it. Not that it would absolve him, but it made you wonder. Made me wonder, anyway.

"And what was your circumstance?" I asked Gordo.

"My father," he said, with pride that shouldn't have been audible—less so visible, in those luminous hazel eyes. "He taught me socialism too."

———

THE RADIO RETURNED TO ITS PLACE. Normalcy, insofar as it could be called that, resumed. The rhythm of Automotores and my minimal life outside it chugged along, from hangover to hangover, vaccination to vaccination.

Regarding that minimal life: Automotores had shrunk it, the way it did everything, skinned it of all but the bones. I stopped seeing what few school acquaintances I'd made. I stopped going to classes. (No one seemed to notice except Beatriz, who remarked sporadically on some crazy fact I'd missed in physics when selling me more pot.) I also stopped calling my mother. Since her visit, our every conversation had devolved into a rote exchange about how hard I was working ("Very," was my brusque, unremitting reply), and except on the rare occasions when she called me, I hardly spoke to her at all.

I stopped visiting the Colonel as well, to the extent that I could. It remained a precarious balance: I didn't want him to see the state I was in, but if I didn't see him at all, I feared he would guess it more easily. So I did my best to include Mercedes in our plans, and confined our moments alone to activities like chess. Oddly, the Colonel didn't seem to mind. Nor did he broach the subject of my job again. If he was playing a waiting game with me, I was content to let him.

I stopped sleeping. My insomnia—already bad like my mother's—got to the point where I'd take overnight shifts and fall asleep on the short train ride to Floresta, leaning my head against a window or pole until it knocked forward with a start and an otherwise innocuous sight—the soccer stadium at Ferrocarril Oeste or the greenery of Plaza Pueyrredón—reminded me of my destination.

I stopped almost everything except my drinking and smoking and listening to records from bed. Even music barely broke through the fog.

I also didn't stop taking walks, despite the onset of winter. I took long ones during my days off, when I was supposed to be in class, and shorter ones in the evening, after I finished work. They helped me put off lying in bed and smoking and drinking and listening to records for as long as I could.

I don't care what Isabel or the Colonel would later say; I was as much a ghost then as I ever would be.

———

IT WAS A NIGHT LIKE ANY OTHER during this period. I lay on my bed smoking, too lazy or numb to bother putting on a record. After I finished the joint, I didn't get up or under the covers or move at all. Just lay there, like a corpse.

Noises sounded downstairs. Harmless ones—doorbell, greeting, the shuffle of feet and small talk. It wasn't uncommon to have late-night visitors at the pensión. What was uncommon was that the visitor and the subsequent knock on the door would be for me.

I sat up, alert.

"Tomás?" the voice outside asked. A woman's. Soft, quiet. Not Beatriz's or the landlady's.

Isabel.

I let her in, and she brushed hurriedly past me. Took in the tiny room in a frenzy, as if her eyes needed more to land on; they skittered like birds unable to find a perch.

"What is it, Isa?" I asked. "Why'd you come?"

"No idea," Isabel said.

She sat on my twin bed. Removed her coat and threw it down beside her so haphazardly, it immediately slid to the floor. She was drunk.

"Do you want a drink?" I asked.

"Yes," she said.

I got my bottle of Old Smuggler from off the dresser. It was cheaper than Chivas, and since starting at Automotores, I'd been replacing it weekly. Usually on Thursdays, after putting myself in a stupor the night before.

I owned tumblers Mercedes had bought me, but the prospect of having to wash them in the kitchen, when I didn't want to see or speak to anyone, had grown so tiring that I'd switched to styrofoam cups. I poured us each one and sat down beside her. We drank.

"Orphans, no?" she said.

"What?"

"That's what we used to say we were. You don't remember?"

"I remember saying we were cousins."

She waved that off with a smile.

"Orphans, Tomás. That was our link. Did I ever tell you my father died last year in a car accident? On the LIE—that was the name of the highway. My mom kept emphasizing that it spelled 'lie' in English, and the whole thing felt like one. The sadness at his death, but I mean the sadness before too. All of it."

"You didn't tell me," I said.

"You never asked. You used to ask about such things, all the time. We both did."

"You stopped asking before me," I told her. It seemed so petty: *I know you are, but what am I?* "Why are you telling me now?"

"No idea," she said again. Then, quickly, rushing out the words as if they'd be caught and gagged if she didn't, "You've always been so good to me, Tomás. I don't deserve you."

"Maybe not," I said, and she laughed before we both went quiet. We drank more—timid but consistent gulps. I could hear her every swallow.

"I've killed, you know," Isabel said. "Ended a person's life."

"Is that what this is about? Coordinación Federal?"

She shook her head. Shrugged. "Not the way you mean it. It's not about guilt or anything. Elba Hilda Gaudio can go to hell."

"Who's Elba Hilda G—"

"You didn't read the news? Secretary who died a week later. Gusti was all torn up about it. I pointed out that civilians are killed all the time by the milicos, but—shit. You think I'm bad, you should hear him when he's up on his soapbox. All that holier-than-thou shit. There's nobody more arrogant, I swear."

"You've been fighting with Gustavo?"

"He thinks I'm cruel. Not that he's wrong. I just thought he accepted me for who I was, you know? Didn't need me to tell any more lies."

"I do," I said. "Accept you."

"You should run, Tomás. You know that, don't you? You should get as far from me as you can."

There was no hesitation on my part. "You know I'm not going to," I said.

She nodded. Stared into her cup.

"You should drink out of glass," she said. "Something you can break."

"It'd be too dangerous. I'd be walking on shards all the time."

She smiled. Then gradually opened her hand and watched the cup drop out of it, as if she wanted to pinpoint the exact moment in which her fingers no longer clasped it. It fell without bouncing.

"Tomás," she said, but by then I'd thrown my own cup aside and leaned toward her. Brought her closer with a hand on her neck and kissed her before I knew what I was doing. Isabel kissed me back.

In some ways, it was less like the time in the basement and more like when we were teenagers: those flashes of uncertainty, the delicate pauses that followed bursts of hunger and tearing at clothes. The pain at the core of it, the sorrow and solace we found in burying ourselves in each other's flesh.

But it was also wholly, radically new. Rawer, more violent—like we were clawing at the world as well as each other, trying desperately to fling ourselves past it. If as a boy I'd wanted nothing more than to submerge myself in such a moment with Isabel, now it was like I wanted the moment to submerge everything else, to blot it all out. And it did. In a sense, it has continued to ever since. I've been playing that night back to myself for years.

THIRTEEN

Loud thumping on the door. Terror at the sound of my name. They'd learned; they knew. I sat up in a sweat, awaiting the machine gun that would be pressed within seconds into my nose.

"Wake up, boludo!" Beatriz shouted. "A call for you! You think you're the only one skipping physics to sleep in today? La puta que lo parió ..."

I glanced about my room, blinking, trying to ground my recollections. Old Smuggler. Two styrofoam cups. An open condom wrapper with a weird sheen in the glaring light of day—it must have been well after noon already. Where was the other condom? I remembered we'd done it twice, without speaking in between. Absurdly, I got out of bed to search underneath, and only dressed once I found my evidence and could confirm that it had all been real.

I went downstairs. Usually I avoided my housemates' looks, but now I met their gaze. I didn't know what they thought of me, and I didn't care.

I picked up the phone. "Hello?"

"I'm sorry," Isabel said immediately. "It was wrong. A bad idea."

"It can't be both, can it?"

I meant her reason, the issue. Whatever prevented her from being with me. Either it was wrong or a bad idea—it seemed to me it had to be one or the other.

But Isabel answered, "Yes, it can."

I looked for a rejoinder, a counterargument, proof that we should be together.

I didn't have any.

"But don't you think—"

"We shouldn't even be talking right now," Isabel said. And again: "I'm sorry."

Then she hung up.

When I called back, the line was busy. I went to the bathroom before trying again, and when I returned, someone else was on the phone. He stayed on it nearly an hour, and by the time I got through, Pichuca informed me Isabel had gone out.

"Is everything okay?" she asked me. "She seemed upset."

I told her I didn't know. It was already late afternoon, and I had a night shift. Soon enough, it'd be time to go to work.

———

NO DECISION HAD BEEN REACHED about the American girl. Which meant she was treated mostly like any other prisoner, except she got her own cell. And though such treatment should have galled me for anyone, in her case it seemed particularly vile. She was innocent. Not that being a socialist like Gordo, whose only crimes against the government probably consisted of voting a certain way and attending a few meetings, wasn't. But her innocence was different. It wasn't about the cruelty of this country or these men so much as the cruelty of the universe: Why did it make her blond and put her in this hotel when Rubio went hunting for his mark? How could it be so stupidly inconsiderate?

Or—I don't know. I don't know if it was really different from Gordo, despite what I'd told myself. Sometimes I even have the appalling thought—I deny it to myself, always—that she was just an attractive girl around my age whom I discovered in the wake of the worst rejection I'd ever known. That that's all the extra innocence she really had for me.

Her name was Elizabeth. Elizabeth Brady-Watson, as American a name as you could conjure. Especially if she went by Lizzie: Lizzie Brady-Watson. The day after my conversation with Gordo, I went to the "merchandise" closet and snuck a look through her wallet—the only confiscated possession of hers they'd kept. Any jewelry she wore had probably been sold or given to girlfriends or wives—possibly her clothes as well, if they'd been fashionable.

She was a student at Columbia, one ID card told me. Another suggested she might be from New York originally, or at least had a permanent address there: 218 West 108th St. That piece of identification also told me her birth date: February 9, 1955. She was twenty-one. More than around my age—a mere eleven days older.

That was one of the reasons I gave myself for deciding to visit her cell—we were peers. Another was the fact that I spoke English and would be able to communicate with her, to explain, to the extent that it could be explained, what was happening. But again, maybe it was simpler. Maybe it was just that I knew I could visit her now. Could maybe have the kind of relationship Triste had with Gordo, the ability to say to someone: I'm broken too.

Her breakdown was much more palpable. The stench rose to my nostrils as soon as I entered her cell. I sat opposite her on the ground to signal some sort of equality between us, but she cowered in the corner all the same. Even in the dark—hers was one of the cells without a hanging bulb, and I had only a flashlight on me, which I positioned awkwardly against my leg and shone toward the ceiling—I could see her wounds and bruises hadn't healed. The only other discernible change at first was the dirtiness—of her blindfold, her cheeks. The latter from sleeping on the floor.

"You don't speak Spanish?" I asked in English. She shook her head. "Here as a tourist?" She nodded. "Friends?" Nodded again. It was like speaking to a scared child. "They're probably looking for you." Again. "It isn't fair," I said, as if to mix it up and get another shake of the head. It came. "Will you speak to me, please?" It was the most pathetic question I have ever asked.

"What do you want me to say?" she asked timidly.

"Anything but what they've been asking you to," I said. "You're from New York? I saw it on your driver's license. I always wanted to go to New York. I have this dream, this image of my life where—" I broke off idiotically. "Please, Lizzie," I said, and even with the blindfold on, I could see it in her face, in those cracked lips and tight jaw: disgust. How many times in this place had she said the word *please*?

"My name's Elizabeth," she said.

—

THE RHYTHM IN AUTOMOTORES. Time cycled differently there. With rare exceptions—the bombing of Coordinación, or Isabel's coming to my pensión—outside events no longer marked time for me. Instead of a change in season or a new exam period in school, the months were clocked by the arrival or departure of a prisoner, or a torture method. The man who died of a heart attack back in May; the Uruguayan family picked up in June (the whole house cleared out, including furniture, children, and dog; the mutt scampered around for days until it disappeared with the children, supposedly given up for adoption alongside them); Ricardo Alberto Gayá's death by submarine in July; Elizabeth's kidnapping in August—which coincided with the introduction of capuchita and my new task of tying prisoners' hoods before leaving them in the dark. Weeks were simpler; they always started and ended on Wednesdays now.

On the following Wednesday, five days after Isabel's call, Aníbal gave me my list. Gordo's number was on it: seventeen.

He'd been one of Automotores' earliest prisoners—we were into the two hundreds by then. For some reason that made it even harder, more unjust. Gordo had survived this long—didn't that earn him survival generally?

"He fixed the radio, sir," I reminded Aníbal; that was the only bit of moral logic I felt he'd understand.

"Right. He fixed it," Aníbal said, as if I were the one lacking understanding. "You think I'm going to let Rubio break it twice? He's taking up space, Verde. A private cell, what's more, thanks to Triste. But we just picked up a kid from a copy place in Retiro with ERP credentials who's ready to sing, and I want to make him feel special, well treated. He's trying to sell us his services like he's a fucking mercenary, I swear. To think—a fucking mercenary, here, in the Garden!" He laughed boisterously. Then calmed himself and clarified, as if in an effort to console me: "Besides, Verde. We can always get a new radio if we need."

⎯⎯

GORDO WAS ONE OF SEVEN Triste lined up for me—wordlessly, with typical stoicism—on the garage level. The blindfold was back on, so we couldn't make eye contact at first. I was glad we couldn't.

I gave my speech: They would become legal detainees and be handed over to the jurisdiction of the executive government to be processed in federal court; for their transfer to the federal prison in Devoto they had to be vaccinated to avoid the spread of disease after being kept in these conditions. Why I had to go to the trouble when the narrative wasn't fooling anybody, I'm not sure. I didn't look at Gordo until it was his turn, and even then I tried to keep my gaze on the limbs that pertained to me, as if he were just a collection of body parts. I raised his right arm and injected him in the armpit. I removed his blindfold. He didn't look at me either. He didn't move or say a word. I half hoped he'd have the fortitude or forgiveness in his heart to whisper that I was a victim of circumstance too, but he didn't. He didn't acknowledge me at all.

When I was done, he walked off and got into the truck on his own. He wouldn't have needed to, but I wondered if he'd counted the steps of those who preceded him anyway.

———

THAT NIGHT, after most of the other men had left, I went to clean the torture room.

By now it had become my first response to almost anything. A new arrival—go clean. Hear Elizabeth's screams—go clean. Transfer Gordo—go clean.

So I took the deodorizer, the mop, whatever I could lay my hands on. I went at the floor like it was marble in someone's mansion; scrub, scrub, scrub again. I took the flowers—yellow tulips—to the bathroom to water them and brought them back. I adjusted the defibrillator's position in the corner ever so slightly, the same with the picana, as if they were picture frames or objets d'art. I was contemplating yet another adjustment when I heard a voice. The Priest's.

"Aníbal told me you didn't like transferring Gordito." Aníbal had a jarring fondness for diminutives. The words could even seem cute and harmless in his mouth—asadito, mojadito—unless you knew their meanings. An asadito, a "little barbecue," was a reference to sessions with the picana on the so-called grill; mojadito was a "little wet one," a transfer who would be thrown in the sea. There was capuchita too, of course, and affectionate-sounding nicknames for many of the camps: el campito, la casita, la escuelita. The last had apparently been an actual school in Tucumán before the military took it over.

The Priest's ball-like head had been leaning over the threshold as if it needed permission to enter, and he ambled in with a small smile that implied he was grateful I'd granted him admission.

"You must remember that even the worst sinner is human," he said. "Which is not to say you must forget the sin. But that sometimes you must forget the humanity."

Despite myself, I actually glimpsed some wisdom in that statement. In the Priest more broadly as well. Like the Colonel perhaps, you could hate him, but you couldn't help but listen to him. The roundness of his head, as if he were open to the world, without the sharpness of prejudice, the hunch in his back that aided his feigned air of humility—he filled the role I needed filled there.

"Can I ask you, Father," I began. Father was what we called him to his face, and I always stumbled on it. "What about forgiveness? Doesn't the church teach—"

"*You* are forgiven, hijito." *Little son.* I wondered whether Aníbal had actually picked up the diminutives from him. Maybe their propensities fed off each other the way their anti-Semitism did. "That is what is important. They may be forgiven as well and, if so, will meet our savior in the world above. But in our battle for *this* world, for a righteous, stable Argentina, we must eradicate the sin even if it means eradicating the sinner. The tree of evil must be pulled out, root and branch, even if the seeds seem innocent."

That compelling voice of his. So soft and sage. So *priestly.*

"As for Gordo himself," he continued, "he was not so innocent, I promise you. I know, his family's from Boedo, right by me. Went to the church off Avenida Chiclana, where I take confession from time to time. His friends worried about him, thought he was using his technical expertise to build bombs."

"His friends told you this?"

"I took confession, Verdecito!" He laughed. "Mothers do it too, when they can't reach their children. It's their duty to tell me. And mine to absolve them for doing so."

Hearing this, grasping what it meant, caused me almost as much pain as the physical kind I watched him inflict, and occasionally was forced to contribute to. *Che, Verdecito. You're a medical student, no? My patient may need your help . . .*

The Priest looked around, inhaled the smell of deodorizer like it was incense.

"This place is looking gorgeous, Verde. One of the smartest things Aníbal ever did, bringing you around." He wished me good night and clapped me on the back encouragingly on his way out.

I went to the balcony, as I often did when I needed a safe-haven cleaning couldn't satisfy. I looked down at the street and noticed the taillights of a parked car blinking on. Why I had a pen on me, I have no idea. But that I had paper—that I can explain: It was the list Aníbal had given me of the day's transfers. I wrote the Priest's license plate number down on the back of it, right beneath Gordo's name.

———

I CALLED ISABEL THE NEXT MORNING, and I kept calling until I reached her. "I need to see you. Not like that," I added hastily when I heard her intake of breath, the pained preparation. I heard her relief, too.

"Okay," she said after a moment, and we proceeded to make the arrangements. We had to be more careful since the bombing of Coordinación and the discovery of Ricardo Alberto Gayá. Mix up our meeting places, the way we actually met. This time we each took a starting corner on Calle 25 de Mayo, six blocks apart, then walked in opposite directions until we "bumped into" each other in front of a university building. We even went through the charade of exclaiming at its being so long, how we should go "catch up" in Plaza Roma. Isabel was a good actor—well-tossed grins and megaphoned references to long-lost school friends ("Can you believe Francisco's started to go by Frankie? . . . Paz is trying to get into Argentine *Playboy*, I kid you not!"). Unsurprisingly, I was not as convincing.

We didn't stop in the plaza, as Isabel had announced we would for any eavesdroppers, but continued toward the abandoned harbor of Puerto Madero. Where once there might have been bustling docks, with steaming industrial barges and puffy white sails, now there were only large, empty warehouses and fenced-off tracts of undeveloped land. Forsaken cars were in the weeds here and there. The nearest was missing its tires and windows and had rust on the bumpers, but the hood was clean enough for us to sit on. The only sign of the river basin was the smell—a rotten sweetness, like spoiled food.

"It's no Pinamar, eh?" Isabel said wistfully. "I wish I'd been cut out for it. All that prettiness and happiness. But I wasn't. Do you know what I mean?"

"No," I said. All those conversations I'd spent dissecting her every sentence for meaning, and now I barely listened.

"It could never work. It's like this port," she went on, in what struck me as a dithery irrelevance. "You know the history, no? It was going to bring Argentina into the twentieth century. And now look. It was an illusion, a fiction. Reality is darker, often crueler. I'm crueler, you know?"

"No," I said again. I had tears in my eyes, I noted without interest.

"Tomás," Isabel said, her hand taking mine, "what I'm saying is I—"

"I can't ease their pain, Isa. I can't—I—"

I couldn't ease my own, may have been what I was trying to say. But I couldn't manage that either; bent over, my head in my hands, I'd started fully crying.

Isabel slid closer. Hugged me with one arm and pressed her face near my cheek while I heaved and sobbed. "It's okay, Tomás," she whispered. "It's okay. You can ease their parents' pain, their friends'. Just tell me what you can—whomever you can. It'll be enough, Tomás, I promise you. It'll be enough . . ."

I sat up. Rubbed my eyes and wiped away the snot that had dribbled onto my upper lip. Then I went through the routine, to the best of my abilities. New prisoners included Samanta Gelman, the daughter of the poet. Enrique Rodríguez Larreta, the Uruguayan journalist. Eduardo and Nelly Vicente—the Priest would often torture the husband and wife together. Gonzalo Piera. Ana Vidaillac. Silvestre Salvadora. The list went on. I also told her about the kid from the copy place in Retiro whom Aníbal was excited about—Rubén Wilkinson was his name; relating it made it harder to hold his betrayal against him somehow—and she noted everything accordingly.

She asked for other details—more about the tortures themselves, the daily goings-on. She was sorry for doing so, she said, but they'd made connections at a couple newspapers—*La Opinión*, which sounded like something grander than the struggling operation it was, and an English-language paper I'd never heard of—that still operated with some freedom and might be able to publish the information. If not, they could use it for pamphlets, she continued, and I thought: *Pamphlets?* That's what you have to fight them?

Still, I gave her what she asked for. And when I was done, and my sniffling and breathing were back under control, I said, "I want to do more than ease people's pain."

She looked at me without understanding. "What do you want to do?"

I wasn't trying to impress her or to join the ranks of her and Gustavo. This I wanted for myself.

"It's war, you said," I reminded her, and thought again of the Priest's words:

You must remember that even the worst sinner is human. Which is not to say you must forget the sin. But that sometimes you must forget the humanity . . .

I reached into my pocket, removed the list of transfers, and handed it to her, back side up. "The Priest's license plate. Lives in Boedo, takes confession at a church somewhere off Avenida Chiclana. Can you . . . or someone . . . ?"

Isabel nodded. "It'll ease their pain in the afterlife, Tomás," she assured me.

Now I couldn't help but wonder if it did.

FOURTEEN

I'd put my head back in my hands at some point, and when I removed them, I found that Isabel was gone from my side, and the Colonel's ghost stood before me instead, pouting in commiseration.

"Well," I said to him, my voice hoarse, as if my sobbing had been more than a memory. "Did it?"

"Did it what?"

"Ease anybody's pain."

"Some, perhaps. Hard to say. Knowledge here is a tricky thing. You begin to lose it quickly. But when you gain any ... Ahhh!" He sighed elaborately, as if the port air were made of roses. "Like a fine whiskey. Or those clean sheets of mine. Now," he continued more contemplatively, "if your question is, was it worth it? For that you need not consult the dead, I think."

"Then whom should I consult?"

"Yourself, boludo. Whom else? That's the whole point of this."

"I thought the point was to get Isabel."

"It's the same thing, really."

"How can that be the same thing?" I didn't conceal my irritation. I felt unwell, like I hadn't fully returned from that moment with Isabel—sleep-deprived and astonishingly fatigued, my eyes dry and straining.

"Was it worth it? That's the question you'll have to ask about her. That's the question this place is always forcing you to ask. Over and over and over, rather monotonously, truth be told. Was it worth it? Would you do it differently, given the chance? What would you change? It's like a nagging mother, this place, taunting you with what you could have done better, what choices you should have made. Come, Tomasito," he said, tacking suddenly, heading into the weedy field. "We're deep enough now that I can give you a peek at this nagging mother of souls."

I followed him. Through a clipped opening in a barbed-wire fence and past a blocky brown factory with smokestacks emitting trails of black smoke. Then across a road and into another small lot just off it.

There was only one car in this one—another Chevrolet—and some-one was packing the trunk with towels, umbrella, a bag of plastic shovels and buckets and other beach equipment. A tall, skinny man in his bathing suit, with a young girl at his side. Her hair was dark and wet, with a strand stuck to her broad forehead, and she was tugging on his arm, trying to tell him all she'd accomplished. "It had two moats, and there was a tunnel too, Papi, and I made towers so—"

"Come here, love," the man interrupted her. He knelt and wiped the sand off her legs and feet.

She continued, her brown eyes big with excitement. They reminded me of Claire's: the youthful eagerness, the hunger for small, silly pleasures.

"Papi, do you think we could make a dragon? I could draw scales into its side, but the wings—the wings would be hard. Maybe—"

"Yes, love," the skinny man said. "Dragons, monsters, anything you like."

He straightened and I recognized him: the Colonel. Not quite the version from a decade before, or the one beside me. But from some point in between, maybe five years younger. He took the girl around to the passenger's side, strapped her in, then took the driver's seat and turned on the engine, removing the rest of their sweet, arresting dialogue from earshot.

"That was you," I said to my version of him after they'd driven off.

"It wasn't, actually. But could it have been? More important, *should* it have been? We're nearing the delta, to use my earlier analogy. Soon you may not be able to tell one person's hell from another. Or even if you're in hell at all."

I looked around. A majestically beautiful sunset, with a bloodred sky and unnaturally vibrant pink and purple clouds. I couldn't tell if it was due to the magic of the place or the pollution, the fumes of the factory towers behind us, or the exhaust from a plane in the distance. I could even hear waves now, murmuring softly somewhere over the dunes.

"Doesn't seem like anybody's hell," I said.

"No indeed," the Colonel said. "It's deceitful, the maze of possibility."

"The maze of . . . ?"

"You know: contingency, if-thens. If this didn't happen, then that would have. If Gardel didn't come to Argentina, we'd be as much a backwater as Chile; if you didn't meet me and learn English, you'd be in as much a backwater as Chile. Et cetera. It's a vast, tragic labyrinth, what with all those dead ends . . ." He trailed off sadly.

"Are you saying Mercedes miscarried?"

"I'm more inclined to say I did," the Colonel answered.

I thought again of Claire. Having children was perhaps the one topic in our relationship in which I'd provided any resistance. I'd even moved in and proposed at her suggestion: "It just makes sense, doesn't it?" she'd said in the lead-up to both, and I'd basically agreed. When Claire cared to, she always made sense, and she did with regard to children too. But I dug in my heels, at least as much as someone like me could. Sometimes her entreaties took the form of a picture she painted, of our happy, stable, very

American marriage completed by "a pooting, chortling little Tom or Claire Jr." Sometimes she took a more philosophical tack: she'd tell me she understood why I was scared of bringing a person into this world, having seen all the terrible things people can do, and I'd have to explain that it had nothing to do with other people, that it had to do with me, and shrug when she told me I wasn't a bad person.

Most of our arguments petered out like that. Despite a decade living and translating in New York, I still didn't like having them in English, especially not when pitted against Claire's lawyerly mind. "Do you know what it was like having those conversations and then going to work and seeing someone cheerful and open, who had dreams about a life with you, who wanted a family with you?" she'd said, telling me about her affair. Responses of varying degrees of bitterness and candor had gone through my head: "I don't; I work at home." "I don't; I barely see anyone but you." "I don't; I don't know what it's like to have dreams." But in the end, I didn't say anything except that I'd be sleeping on the couch that night.

"And here I always thought you wanted to have children but weren't able to," I said to the Colonel. He shook his head, disappointed with his bumbling pupil.

"You were always rather a stupid kind of intelligent, Tomás," he said, taking off toward the water. "Good at chess, bad at nearly everything else."

IT WAS THE BEACH IN PINAMAR. Its most romanticized manifestation— rose-hued twilight, pines casting long shadows over the dunes and filling the breeze with their scent. It was as if the place had snatched a picture from my imagination and plopped me down to testify to its accuracy. All that seemed to be missing was an image of a young Nerea, dancing dolphinlike about the water and sand before I met her sister and my heart ceded her place.

Isabel I never fantasized about in quite the same way. No glistening perfection, no painted clouds above a picturesque landscape. I daydreamed scenarios, increasingly sexual ones as puberty plodded its way through my body. These scenes were always grittier, beholden less to fairy tales than to tales of sacrifice and adversity and—what else could I call it?—reality. The kind I'd believed my love for her would battle through. The kind I must still believe it would battle through, to come here. Reality has a way of never letting even the direst of expectations catch up with it.

Even though I knew this wasn't really the site of my reveries, I still looked for signs of Isabel. The fragments of a broken Quilmes bottle, footprints made by her wide feet. A silhouette skirting the tide with that slightly lumbering stride I found enchanting.

Nothing, though. Aside from the Colonel and me, the beach was empty. Aside from that plane too. Objects were falling from it now, catapulting toward the water like birds with broken wings.

The most common way to dispose of transfers, the Gringo had told me: drug them with an injection of sodium pentothal a fake doctor like me said was a vaccination, then drop them into the depths of the Río de la Plata.

One at a time they fell. I couldn't hear the splash or, if there was any, the cry.

"Come on," the Colonel said. I felt the shakiness of his fingers as they reached for my elbow, scrambled along it like a squirrel trying to grasp a slim branch. "It's not time for this yet."

"Time for what?"

"For them. For others. This is my hell as much as anybody else's, as I said."

I looked at the water. Waited for some indication of movement underneath, the surge of bound hands or the silhouette of a head. But the waves passed quietly, and there were no cries on the wind.

"These others. They're not like you?"

"Some, depends," the Colonel said. "People die as differently as they lived. I would suggest keeping your distance, regardless."

Unconsciously, I'd taken a step or two forward, as if there'd been an instinct in my legs to dive to a drowning person's aid. The sand was oddly soft beneath my shoes—less like sand than something else. Mud? Tar? I glanced down and saw there was foam around my heels, and it was tacky, suctionlike. I could tell, with dreamlike certainty, that it wanted to draw me in. Down. *Under.*

I pulled my foot free and took a step back.

"They're so lonely, Tomás. We are, I mean. Staring all day into rooms we never got to be in, reliving memories we can't actually live, or can but don't want to. Cloistered away with thousands of others we love and hate, yet equally far from them all, so stuck within ourselves you can't imagine. Sometimes we get jealous, want company. We won't want you to leave."

I turned to him. His face was as mournful as I'd ever seen it.

"Is that the real reason you brought me?" I asked.

"Ja. We'll see. I may have guilt enough to make up for it regardless, don't forget."

I looked again at the waves, listened to their sleepy tumble.

The Colonel continued: "If I told you you'd get stuck here going much deeper, Tomás, would you? Would you keep going?"

I recalled the pull I'd felt moments ago, the sucking of the sand beneath me and the hypnotizing swell of the tide. I thought of Claire too, crying in the shower the night before I left.

Then I thought of Isabel. That smile when I handed her the bottle of Old Smuggler to throw at the general's statue.

"Yes," I said.

"What if it wasn't just that you got stuck here, but that you'd been here all along, since 1976? Never met your wife, had those ten years? What if the place didn't just show you how things could be different but gave you the opportunity to change them?"

"*Will* it give me the opportunity to change them?" I asked. *Abuela said you'd get a do-over,* I remembered Pichuca's granddaughter telling me at Hospital Alemán. *Like in a game.*

The Colonel smiled. "You always did want to be a martyr, Tomasito, didn't you? Well, let me tell you, this is less a case of heroic altruism than it might seem."

"It doesn't feel very heroic to me," I said, but he pressed on, heedless.

"Fleeing your life, abandoning your marriage. Venturing to the underworld of the disappeared to pluck a sexy, lovey one out, disturbing all those who grieve here just to heal your itty-bitty little bit of emptiness. Heroism—ja!"

"You think my emptiness is little?"

The Colonel grunted disdainfully. "Hmph. You living think you grieve. You are chipper little tweety birds with your sadness. You especially, Tomás—I can hear your happy birdsong all the way down here."

"You didn't seem to think that when you invited me along. What did I have to lose, you asked me."

"And by the end of this expedition, you'll be forced to answer."

"What does that mean?"

"You'll see what it means. Your emptiness is like an empty stomach, no more. Hunger. Hunger! Ja. Can you imagine? I haven't been hungry in centuries."

"You only died a couple years ago."

"Millennia ago. Millennia I was dead before I was born, and millennia I will be dead after I lived, and what the shit did I have in between? Sixty years? Watch me count them. Poof!" He blew so quickly and intensely, spit smacked my forehead. "That's about as long as that nonsense lasts."

"All right, I get it," I said, wiping my face. "I'm sorry."

"No, I am. I'm beating a dead horse. Or the devil is beating a dead me—ja!" His wicked chuckle was quickly becoming less amusing. "I'm sorry, Tomasito. As I said, we still get jealous sometimes."

"I understand."

"You don't. But it's all right, I forgive you. Like I said, you're not so adept in some areas."

Another plane roared overhead. Bodies fell like fat drops of rain.

The Colonel grabbed my arm. "Shall we mosey, Señor Shore?"

We did. Back to the original lot where I'd sat with Isabel, and then to the bus that took me home. At some point, as I drifted into my foggy 1976 state, completely inattentive to the muddled press of passengers getting on and off, I must have missed the Colonel sneaking out. When I returned to my pensión, I was alone again, and there was no trace of him, unless you counted the new bottle of whiskey I'd bought after finishing the one Isabel and I had together. I opened it and drank myself to sleep.

FIFTEEN

I never found out how they killed the Priest—shoot-out, car bomb, something more macabre. I learned about it only when he stopped coming to work and the Gringo started raging about the terrorists he'd punish in revenge. The net result, in that sense, did not necessarily seem a gain.

I did find out who killed him, or at least who must have been involved: Isabel and Gustavo, Nerea and Tito. Two days afterward, Pichuca called to tell me the four of them had gone into hiding. Separately, she made clear, her voice a frantic mix of relief and apprehension: Nerea with Tito, and Isabel with Gustavo.

She was living with him. Fenced off, beyond my reach. Pichuca had no way of contacting them, she said; they'd contacted her only to alleviate her worst fears, any more and they'd be putting us in danger. For the time being, we just had to wait for them to make contact again.

⸻

THEY DIDN'T. Not with me, anyway. My stranding felt complete. Not only because it destroyed the idea that I still had people looking out for me, however outnumbered; but because with no one to confirm that I was on the other side, it became frighteningly easy to feel I was on *theirs*—the military's, Automotores'. If I was no longer in that evil place for some greater good, who was to say my role, through sheer complicity, hadn't tumbled across that murky divide into evil itself?

That evil—it seemed to balloon as well. The Gringo wasn't the only one affected by the news; all of Automotores had been. It was like after the bombing in Coordinación Federal, but tenser, more foreboding; you had the palpable feeling that other, bigger bombs were soon to go off. The halls were perpetually smoky now that Rubio and the Gringo could have and toss cigarettes wherever they pleased, adding to the doomy, haunted-house atmosphere as well.

The most noticeable reaction besides the Gringo's was Triste's. Without saying good-bye to anyone, he simply stopped showing up for work after the first week in September. The Gringo told me he'd sought a transfer to another army division, Campo de Mayo, which had a unit linked to ours under different oversight.

The effects on the rest of the men were subtler. They spoke less over meals and more often in hushed voices—once I came into the kitchen to find Aníbal and Rubio awkwardly silent, as if they'd cut themselves off at my entrance. The joy some of them took in the torture room also diminished; it seemed fueled less by power, the pleasure young boys got plucking wings off flies, than by anger. It was profoundly disturbing, to find myself wishing for fiercer screams or to see the Gringo emerging as he used to, with a big, fat grin plastered on his childlike face.

In Rubio I sensed the greatest transformation. Paranoia may have been part of it, my mental filter translating cold glances into piercing, knowing stares. But every time I fell into Rubio's field of vision, I felt his eyes probing me like searchlights. No one had ever looked at me with such loathing. His attractiveness accentuated it, finding such ugly desire buried beneath such a handsome face. When we bumped shoulders in the hall, I felt the tension in his muscles, as if he were holding himself back. And whenever he called me into the torture room for some task, it was with the contempt reserved for a shifty, unreliable servant. Once, when I stayed to clean a pool of blood he'd left behind, he returned to gawk at me while I worked. "Puta madre," he eventually said. "The Priest is dead. He's the only one who gave a shit about keeping this place clean."

"I give a shit about it," I heard myself say.

"Do you?" Rubio said. He gave my bucket of water a kick, and it slid across the floor several feet before spilling over. "Now you have more cleaning to do."

Truthfully, I was grateful. I was always grateful when I had more cleaning to do.

———

I COULDN'T SAY IF THAT WAS THE MOMENT that motivated Rubio to speak to Aníbal about me. I couldn't even definitively say he did, no matter how many times I replayed that interaction or the one in the kitchen, trying to capture the exact expressions in his and Aníbal's eyes when they landed on me. But that Wednesday, when I went to retrieve my list, Aníbal said something that put me on guard.

"Twelve today," he instructed, handing me the slip of paper. "Not too many for you, Verde, is it?"

"No, sir," I managed.

"Good. Because after Gordito, some of us worried. The Priest, God rest his soul, he was worried as fuck about you, like a lamb in his flock. But me and Rubio, we were worried too."

"I'm fine," I told him.

"But that's what we're worried about, Verde!" he exclaimed, as if intervening with an alcoholic relative. "Gordito goes, the world caves in. The Priest goes, and you're fine. You see why we're concerned?"

The experience was an out-of-body one. Some fight-or-flight mechanism switched on, and it was like I was observing myself from afar, evaluating if it was over or not, if I'd reached the end.

"Well? Alleviate our worries, Verdecito."

"I can't," I told him.

"You . . . can't?"

I shook my head. Swallowed. The moment at the Colonel's dinner party when I feared I'd been caught came back to me. Numbly, preposterously, I thought: I went up the stairs. At the Colonel's party, I saw the stairs, and I went up them.

"You're right," I said. "I'm not really fine. Since the Priest was killed, I've been cleaning twice as much as usual."

"You've been . . . ? La puta madre, but the Priest was killed, Verde!"

"I know. Rubio said the same. But I was a lamb of his flock, like you said. I can't help thinking he'd want me to."

Aníbal assessed me for what felt like centuries. Then pulled out the garbage bin from under his desk, shook his head, and spat.

"Fucking sentimental types," he said. And since he didn't say anything else, I assumed I was dismissed. I went off with twisted relief to vaccinate the twelve names on my list.

———

ELIZABETH WASN'T ON IT. That relieved me too. I needed to speak to someone, anyone, and she was the only person there with whom I believed I could.

Not that I planned to tell her what had happened with Aníbal. But to sit with her, to feel, in some way, recognized—I still clung to that possibility, even if it had proved unattainable so far. I hadn't made many more visits to her cell since the first, but enough that they'd become enmeshed in my rhythm, grown dependable. Perversely, it had helped with my credibility too; the perception that I was having my way with a prisoner and indulging my own animalistic desires put me more on their level.

They'd moved her into Gordo's cell after his transfer, and as I remembered well from watching him fix the radio, there was a functional bulb in it, meaning I could see her more clearly. The old bruises had blossomed into purples and blues, the newer injuries were still raw and red. Her limbs and face were bonier, her sharpened chin especially. It was as if Automotores had eaten the meat off her.

The conversation was as one-sided and start-and-stop as usual. I resisted the urge to tell her that if she knew what was good for her, she'd be more talkative.

Instead I wound up asking her, as I always did, if there was anything I could do. Typically she didn't answer, but now she said, "Can you put me back in my old cell? There was a hole in the corner in that one."

I didn't understand. "A hole in the corner?"

"I have to call a guard to take me to the bathroom now. That gives them a reason to come in. Sometimes they don't leave. Sometimes they take me and lie about where the toilet is and laugh. Or they don't give me toilet paper and laugh. Then I have to leave it on myself. It smells just as bad on me as in the hole in the corner."

They'd picked up a high-level ERP operative named Juan Miguel Pereyra a few days earlier—high enough that the men had celebrated after his capture, uncorking a bottle of champagne in the kitchen; apparently he had ties to the ERP's treasury and was quite the soldier to boot—and he inhabited Elizabeth's old cell now. At least when he wasn't hanging from the rafters—it was almost exclusively the way the picana was applied these days. They'd leave someone up there for hours, returning as the mood struck to continue the session. With Pereyra, whom they called negro de mierda because of his indigenous descent, the mood struck frequently and powerfully.

"I can't get you your old cell," I told Elizabeth. "But I can try to get you a shower."

"I don't want a shower," she said. I didn't ask her to explain.

⎯

WHEN I GOT HOME THAT NIGHT, I called the Colonel. I asked if I could stop by the next day. Tomorrow was no good, he told me, and my heart snapped a little. Would the next day work? I said I guessed it would have to. He must have detected my desperation, since he muffled the receiver a moment to check with Mercedes, and then returned to say that dinner tomorrow was actually dandy. "Never a better day in all of 1976, Tomasito."

I wasn't sure what I'd do when I saw him. It was an instinctual urge, as simple an equation as: I needed help; the Colonel could help me.

I had the full day off. To kill time before dinner, I walked. It was humid and muggy for Buenos Aires in October, and I arrived sweaty.

"You don't look good, Tomasito," the Colonel said on seeing me. "You're all white. You need some blood in those veins. Good thing Mercedes is already working on the meat."

She gave me a kiss on the cheek before returning to the kitchen, apologizing that it was the housekeeper's day off. Without asking, the Colonel poured me a Johnnie Walker with ice. I tasted little difference between that and his usual Chivas, but the Colonel treated it like it was far more refined. I supposed it was the English sound of the name, the elegant top-hatted man with the cane.

He set up a game of chess without asking if I wanted that either. Taking black to give me the advantage, he grumbled disparagingly when I played the queen's pawn opening—he preferred the freer, wilder board that came out of king's pawn. "Joder, Tomasito," he said. "You play it so safe."

I looked up. When I did, he was a ghost again and I was ... whatever I was now.

"Do I?" I asked him.

"I concede the point," he said. "Perhaps you overcompensate sometimes."

The grandfather clock that had been ticking tiredly was suddenly silent, and the curtain at the open window no longer fluttered in the breeze.

"Hell freezes over," the Colonel said. "Another good one, no?"

On that I didn't comment. "We're nearing the end, aren't we?"

"Depends how you look at it. You could also say you're nearing the beginning, no? Of the rest of your life?"

"It doesn't feel like it," I said.

"No. The *cross of the matter*, as they say in your language. Will what happens shortly be the end or the beginning of Señor Tomasito Shore? Wait—is it *cross*? Or *crux*? At any rate, you understand."

Tick ... tock. Tick ... tock. The clock slowly started back up, as if yawning itself awake.

"I'm afraid," I told him.

"That's just the memory talking." The Colonel laughed. "Don't worry, Tomasito. Sometimes you overcompensate, as discussed."

He nodded to the board, and when I glanced back down, we were our 1976 incarnations again, the spring air drifting past our necks once more.

We resumed playing, and soon he was poking holes in my defenses. My wall of pawns began to leak, and he sacrificed a knight I took without thinking.

"You're distracted," he said.

"I'm sorry."

"Please, Tomás, what could you be sorry about? I'm winning!"

The Colonel was always winning. I'd come close over the years but had never beaten him. A few moves later, I discerned from the position I wouldn't win this game either, and I knocked over my king in resignation.

The Colonel was already resetting the board. "Is Aníbal taking care of you?" he asked suddenly.

It was the opening I'd come seeking, but I was still surprised to get it. Barely anyone even asked me how I was anymore.

"He says he worries about me," I answered.

"Well, that's good, better than his not worrying about you, no? I'll give him a call, though. Say it seems he's working you too hard."

"You probably shouldn't," I said. Best case: like Rubio, Aníbal would conclude I was soft. Worst case: he'd conclude I was scared and wonder why.

"Please, Tomás, are you concerned about my lack of subtlety? The beauty of not having any is that no one notices when you lack it. The truth is, I didn't know it would be such a hard place to work. Don't get me wrong! I knew it wouldn't be easy. But I didn't know they'd wear you so thin. I'll give Aníbal a call, make sure he's treating you well."

I didn't want Aníbal to treat me well. I didn't want him to treat me at all. I almost said so; variations of the statement knocked about my mind: *I just want out, Colonel. I just need to get away—from Automotores, Argentina, everything. I just need your help.*

But I said nothing. I don't know why. Not even by reliving it, in the excruciating manner that I relived our conversation in Parada Norte, could I figure it out. Mercedes came, true, called us to the dining room a few minutes later and put an end to the exchange. But before that, in some covert chamber of my unconscious, it had already been decided: I was going nowhere. I would not ask for help. I've relitigated the moment many times since, turning over possible explanations—I still clung to Isabel, to my role in the fight against oppression, to my worries over the repercussions, to my fear more generally, to the country, to my gnarled roots and home in it, to something beyond all this, to fate or purpose or some more numinous force I lack conception of—and the only satisfactory answer I could pluck out of that messy heap of contingency was that the opportunity had already slipped.

We sat down to dinner. The steak was wonderful, but I couldn't eat. The wine was full-bodied and almost too flavorful for my palate as well. I longed for the burn of the Johnnie Walker.

"Your mother must miss you, Tomás," Mercedes said at one point. She couldn't tell me to eat my food, but I caught her glancing at it as if she wished she could—have a son to scold and fuss over, I mean. "Do you call her enough?"

"No," I admitted.

"That's the problem these days. Family has gone by the wayside."

"Everything has gone by the wayside," the Colonel said.

She rolled her eyes at him for me to see. "He likes putting on a show for you. We both do, truth be told. But call your mother more, Tomás. She must be worried sick. I know I would be."

I RETURNED TO WORK THE NEXT DAY. Avoided Aníbal in case the Colonel had called him, and stuck to the cells and the torture room. I hadn't lied when I told him I was cleaning twice as much as usual since the Priest was killed.

Rubio spotted me at it again late that morning. I gave my soap bucket an anxious glance before turning to him.

"Aníbal wants you to make him a sandwich," Rubio informed me.

"What?"

"You're so good at the womanly stuff. Figures you can make him a pretty good sandwich too."

"Where's the Gringo?" The Gringo was the closest thing we had to a cook in the place, often bringing leftovers or making snacks for the rest of us to pick at.

"Having his own lunch," Rubio said. "Look, Aníbal asked for you to make him a sandwich. Are you going to or not?"

I didn't bother confirming that I would. I just went to the kitchen, to have my moment of panic there.

Aníbal had never asked me to make him a sandwich. For that reason alone, the request seemed ominous. The routine at Automotores, grim as it was, could be relied upon. You could steel yourself for certain guards' sessions, for night shifts, for Wednesdays. But this was a Saturday at noon, and a departure. Again and again I kept thinking: Aníbal has never asked me to make him a sandwich.

I surveyed the kitchen, my memory as well. I recalled Aníbal saying there was an art to mayo, the proportions—or had that been the Gringo? Best to trust my instincts, not doubt myself. I tremblingly pulled the refrigerator door open and took out the jar. Scrounged for cheese—there were some cheddar slices I could use—and ham. Cured would be better, but the only kind in there had been cooked and saran-wrapped. It appeared pink and soggy when I removed it.

Bread. Baguette would be ideal, but of course we didn't have any of that either, and I cursed the ever-munching Gringo under my breath. Swung open a cabinet—there was American Wonder Bread, it would have to do. We had no toaster. How could Automotores not have a fucking toaster?

Shaking, smelling the whiskey in my pores, and barely able to steady my butter knife, I tried to coat the bread with a fine layer of mayo. But I lost control and slathered so much on I had to get a napkin and—looking over my shoulder to make sure Rubio wasn't spying, ready to pounce on my tremors—dab it clean and try again. The ham followed, then the cheese. Everything felt so wet and gummy and wrong. Artificial, like rubber. How would Aníbal eat this? He'd throw it back at me and say I wasn't good for anything, I couldn't even do my job without tattling to the Colonel about it. Or worse, without tattling to the Montoneros.

I put the sandwich on a plate. Considered cutting it into two rectangles and opted for two triangles instead. Prepared to take it to Aníbal's office before remembering I should bring a napkin too. I got another and, staring at the sad, sodden meal in my hands, breathed and headed down the hall.

Aníbal didn't look up when I entered. Didn't speak either, at first. I set his lunch on the desk and made to leave, when he said, "Did you suck the Colonel's cock, Verde?"

"Excuse me?"

He picked up one half of the sandwich and turned it in his hand, inspecting it as if to make sure it wasn't poisoned. He bit into it and chewed.

"When he asked me to give you a job, he asked me not to give you certain kinds. And now we're down two men, and I'm asking myself how to make up for it."

I didn't answer. Don't until you know if the Colonel called him, I ordered myself. Prepare excuses: You didn't ask him to, you don't feel overworked. You're willing to do whatever's needed.

"You wouldn't be willing to pick up the slack, would you, Verde? Put in some hours with the picana?"

I swallowed the way I did so often in his presence. Like my conscience was creeping up my throat, a kind of moral acid I felt an urge to puke out. Wrong answers were in it too, so many wrong, impossible answers.

The right one was stuck as well, though: *I'm willing to do whatever's needed.*

"I'm sorry, sir, I don't think so," I said. "I'd understand if you needed to fire me."

"*Fire* you! La puta que lo parió, we're down two men, Verde. And you don't just get a fucking severance package from this kind of work, you know what I mean?"

"I do," I told him. And again, before I could catch myself, "I'm sorry."

He finished the first half of his sandwich, picked up the other. Examined it as before, but with repugnance on his face.

"You know why I trusted you, Verde?" Aníbal said. I shook my head as casually as I could. "The Colonel's vouching for you, sure. But truthfully, I'd trust just about anyone who worked here, who saw what went on. Do you know what I mean?"

I told him I did; I knew what he meant.

He took another bite and licked his lips.

"Fire you," he repeated, with his booming, full-bellied laugh. "No, Verdecito. In fact, you get a promotion. Congratulations. On top of your other responsibilities, you're Automotores' new chef."

MY DREAMS THE NEXT FEW NIGHTS all played on the theme of my new position: In one I was stooped over a bubbling cauldron, stirring soaked, steaming blindfolds; I wasn't sure whether I was cleaning them or preparing them to eat or—this seemed likeliest, based on the internal logic of the nightmare—both. In another, I was in Gordo's old cell, with him handing me the battered radio parts and a toolbox saying he didn't know the recipe, and I, feeling guilty and dismayed, had to confess I didn't either.

In the last and most horrid, I was a waiter at Parada Norte, serving a table at which sat the Colonel, Isabel, and my mother. I kept getting their orders wrong, and despite their low voices when I turned my back, catching snatches about my incompetence, my failures.

On the way to the kitchen, I passed the Priest. He was playing the bandoneón, a yellow tulip in place of the classic red rose on the breast of his cassock, and singing, his whispery, feminine voice serenely beautiful. It was Gardel. In "La Canción de Buenos Aires," he prayed for the cry of the bandoneón to play at the end of his life, and in "Silencio" he intoned again and again about silence in the night. Worst of all, in the chipper ditty of "Caminito," he chimed: *Una sombra ya pronto serás, una sombra lo mismo que yo.*

A shadow you'll soon be, a shadow just like me.

SIXTEEN

I woke from the last of these dreams in a twin bed I thought must be mine at the pensión. But in the moonlight from the window I realized the room was much bigger. Empty, well-made beds with crisp, tightly tucked-in sheets lined the walls. It had to be a military barracks.

I went out to the hallway. The Colonel was standing several doors down, gazing into a room. His office, I gathered, judging from the framed commendations and the bar with his Chivas and Johnnie Walker. But it was unornamented for his taste, had a characterless feel: the blank walls, the cushionless chairs, the solitary jade plant on the windowsill and the lack of a bookshelf. The younger version of him was sitting on the desk, legs dangling freely before an officer who was younger still. His cheeks were clean, his hair longish and slightly glistening, as if he'd recently showered. They were laughing over whiskeys that hovered by their lips.

"Ah," my version of the Colonel said, like he'd just taken a delectable sip of the liquor himself. "Beautiful, no?"

"Did this happen?" I asked.

"It could have."

I recalled my belief that the Colonel went to the men's club in La Plata mainly for the chess. Also those words of Aníbal's: *Did you suck the Colonel's cock, Verde?*

"Why didn't it?"

The two specters clinked glasses, ice tinkling, and the Colonel's bushy mustache crawled up over the most earnest smile I'd ever seen on him. "To subversion," he toasted.

"Because of that," his ghost told me. "My position, the army, all those Catholic farts around it. The definition of subversive got pretty bad, you remember."

The younger officer leaned in to kiss the Colonel's ear, his cheek reddening. "To love, boludo," he replied.

"That too," the Colonel said to me. "Mercedes and I. We really did love each other, in our way."

"Did she know?"

"She looked away. Same as with everything else in our marriage—she looked away until she didn't. And when she stopped, it wasn't because of any handsome young stallion, I can assure you. It was my other faults as a husband. As a person, I mean."

"And him?" I asked. "What happened?"

"No idea. We only ever flirted. Then there was a bit of a reshuffle in the army in '77, and, well. Let's just say I hope he still only ever flirted." The Colonel gave me an elbow tap to signify we were moving on, and led me down a nearby staircase. "You can try to return the favor someday and sort out all my might-have-beens if you want. But right now, Señor Shore, we're trying to sort out yours."

We emerged in the yard of a base that could have been the ESMA's gargantuan older brother: neoclassical white buildings separated by large, well-groomed pastures, a webby network of runways filled with jets and helicopters. The sky above was cloudless and peppered with stars, and the big, lush palms were moist enough to send shimmers of reflections back like ponds.

The scene's splendor was marred only by the thick, smelly air, reminiscent of my chemistry labs, where steam rose and objects caught fire. Fabric in this case? Hair maybe? It stung my nostrils, whatever it was.

"Nearly as beautiful," the Colonel said. "I didn't stay many nights here, but when I did—ah! Those stars. Everything else, war and the rest, it all seemed so small by comparison."

"The School of the Americas?" I asked, because of those large, tropical palms, that heavy air suggestive of the Caribbean. Though it had been located in Panama, not Argentina, the American base certainly had a history hellish enough to belong here; it had trained not only the Colonel in the CIA's preferred techniques for quashing subversion, I knew from the Gringo, but some of the bloodiest rulers across all of South and Central America.

"No, alas," the Colonel said. "This is an ugly desert compared to the School of the Americas. The school was like a resort, a resort in the jungle on a beautiful lake. If you didn't mind the mosquitoes or the rather long torture manuals they made you read, it was as nice as any American university, or so I believed. Stanford was the one I compared it to in my imagination—ever been there? I heard when I was up above that they'd moved the School of the Americas to Fort Benning, in Georgia. A shame, but probably still nice, no?"

He sounded disillusioned.

"No, alas," he repeated, when I failed to answer. "This is Campo de Mayo. I oversaw operations here for a time." He sniffed with regained delight. "Ah, the smell of hellfire . . ."

"That's bodies burning," I told him. The chemicals and hair—suddenly the source of that acrid odor had become clear to me.

"Yes, well, I never understood why it was supposed to smell like sulfur, but I wasn't a good Catholic boy, so what do I know?"

The only other animate being on the grounds was a dog. Muscled and rangy, some kind of pit-bull mix. It was sitting just off the runway, chewing a long, dirty bone, and as we neared, I was able to discern what kind: a human femur.

"We loved these beasts," the Colonel said. "We really did. The treats we gave them! Real treats, I mean, not . . . this. We played Frisbee with them too. Isn't that amazing? We'd feed them corpses, then throw the Frisbee with them."

I watched the dog work the bone. "Amazing," I said.

"Does it seem like a contradiction to you, that we could be so good to dogs and so bad to people?"

"You could be good to people and bad to them too," I said.

"It's true. Like I was with you. But do you know what I think? Usually we speak of people doing good to make up for the bad—we talked about ourselves doing just that. But what if we have it reversed? I wonder if I didn't do some of the good I did, with you and others, my wife, for example, for the sake of the bad. To store up a kind of moral credit, as it were, before I returned to work. Take my identity off like a suit, put it in the closet for a time, and recharge before wearing it again. Does that make any sense?"

It did, but I said no.

The Colonel smiled. "Señor Shore, do not pretend to be so sure of yourself. You have several suits in that closet yourself."

"I don't own any suits," I said.

"So literal. Your translations must be tedious."

"The texts themselves are tedious."

"In any case," the Colonel continued, and we did too, strolling the base like a park, taking in the sights, "what I guess I'm really saying is I'm not all that bad. I did enjoy badness sometimes, I admit. But sometimes it got tiring."

"The mere fact that you know what you did was bad would suggest you aren't."

"Would it, though? That's giving humans a lot of credit, I think. I saw it in my men, sometimes they loved doing a thing even more because they knew it was bad. Sure, some told themselves the woman they raped in detention deserved it. But most, even if they told themselves that, they weren't raping out of a sense of justice, I can assure you. Not even brute animal savagery. You remember how it was."

"I do," I said.

"Take Triste. We overlapped here—I got him his transfer out of Automotores. A sweetheart really, Triste. And not the only one under my supervision either. Some of the worst, most terrible torturers—they were actually the most fragile of men. So insecure. Little arms, many of them, little skinny arms like mine. Outside of a detention center, I wonder if they could have killed a fly. But inside—something was set free in them. In all of us. No one remained innocent in the orbit of such a place."

As we neared the end of the runway, I realized we were in fact in something of a park—an amusement park. The tops of rides poked out of a valley below like skyscrapers in a madcap city. One—a Ferris wheel—rose up to where the pavement and moonlight stopped and the earth broke off like a cliff. The highest cart was level with us, its door open.

I smiled fondly, despite everything.

"You don't strike me much as the roller coaster type, Tomás," the Colonel said.

"I'm not—scared of heights. But Isabel—I remember her telling me in Pinamar about the rides in Coney Island, how much she loved them. That moment right at the top, before the plunge. She wasn't scared of anything."

"Hmm," the Colonel murmured. "Rather naive, don't you think, Señor Shore?"

"You mean everyone's scared of something?"

"I mean *she* was scared. Her love of roller coasters and gunfights and all that flailing after a meaningful life? Who cares about that if not for the fear that it'll end? Oh, I'm sure you've drawn comfort over the years from the idea that she wasn't, that she was ready for her death. Made it easier for you to swallow, no? If it was her choice what happened, if she wouldn't have had it any other way? But there always are. Other ways, other choices. Other suits in a person's closet, if you like."

I didn't like it. Hadn't he said just the reverse when we started out on this journey, in the cemetery? Why did it feel like he—like everything—was going in circles? I gazed at the Ferris wheel, as if it were there solely to emphasize that fact.

"You're saying I didn't know her really?"

"I'm saying the maze is complicated. This or that, either or—it's not that simple, with life or with people."

Big red swervy letters on the door of the cart read ITALPARK. A misleading name: it was an attraction in Buenos Aires, not in Italy, and if it meant anything to Isabel, she'd never told me about it.

"Do you know what this was to her?" I asked.

"I know what it is to you. How'd you say she put it? The moment at the top, before the plunge?"

"Plunge into what?"

"Let me tell you something, Señor Shore. For thousands of years human beings have been trying to come and go from the underworld. Usually it's to bring back the dead. Gilgamesh, Orpheus, who knows how many others. Sure, the landscape would have been different for them, the symbols, they'd probably have squinted through proper hellish gates instead of Argentine steakhouses and seen three-headed dogs and better demons than the likes of me and Aníbal Gordon. But the quest? The outcome? The same, I'm sure. They'd come back with ghosts or wisdom or nothing at all. The flimsy stuff of loopholes, in any case, the wispy sort of phantoms we all come back as. Life is where you save lives, Tomás. With death, it's more of a give-and-take."

"Plunge into what, Colonel?" I repeated, tired of all his dancing around.

"I told you. What could have been is the underside of what was. What happened and what might have happened—flip sides of the same coin. I've been taking you through each of your tosses, as it were. Most you don't really wish landed differently. But there's at least one I know you've dreamed for ten years of throwing again . . ."

I shook my head in annoyance. Stepped into the cart and waited for him to follow.

He didn't.

"Aren't you coming? We have to get to the underside of whatever the fuck."

The Colonel sighed regretfully. "You have to *go your own way*, Tomasito. My proverbial coin—you have to toss it yourself."

"You and your proverbs," I said. "That's all you have to offer, isn't it?"

"Not all," he answered. "I gave you my revolver too."

My hand went instinctively to my lower back. The gun was tucked into my belt, the way I'd worn it during the few periods when I did.

"Tom, why do you have this?" I suddenly recalled Claire asking me, dangling the revolver from her pinkie like she was afraid to get fingerprints on it. She'd come over to help me pack my things before I moved into her apartment, and had been digging through bags stuffed with miscellany like a giddy child digging for treasure.

"The Colonel gave it to me in '76," I told her, "for protection."

"And do you still feel you need protection?" she asked. She'd worked so hard to convince me I had a future. It was like a personal project for her, outlining all those shimmery years it supposedly had in store for me. "Do you need *this* kind of protection?" When I didn't answer, she carefully put the revolver down on the linoleum floor and said, "I won't have you killing yourself in my apartment, Tom."

I didn't pack it after that. Instead I took it to the Hudson that evening before going to her apartment, and threw it in. I told Claire afterward, and tried to tell myself the same, more or less: I was done with regret, with doubt. With death. As Claire frequently put it: I'd survived; what did the rest matter?

Grasping the cold metal handle again reminded me how reassuring it felt. Like a safety net—or better, an escape hatch. Knowing it was in my closet had meant I could always escape again.

"You've held on to it in a way," the Colonel said to me. "All this time, you've been deciding. And now you get to. End of the road, my Dantecito."

"Dantecito?"

"Well, we *are* more Virgil and Dante than Orpheus or Odysseus or any of the others, don't you think?"

I smiled. How could I help it?

"She's more Persephone than Eurydice," I said. "Isabel."

The Colonel nodded approvingly. "Queen of the underworld. Half the time she's spring, no?"

"Still married to the place, though. Even when she leaves."

"Well," he said, "let's hope Argentine hell isn't as Catholic as Argentina."

"What do you mean?"

"Divorce, Tomás. We better hope she can get a divorce."

I wanted to laugh. But the Colonel had already closed the cart door, wistfully as a parent sending a child off to school. I glanced into the murky ravine below. In the starlight I could make out more rides—a water slide and a Chair-O-Planes, its seats hanging limply in the air—as well as a motley assortment of jarringly out-of-place structures: a glassy office building;

an airport tower; three rows of long, industrial barns, from which the faint but frenetic hum of clucking rose to my ears. I remembered Isabel's story about Gustavo working at a chicken farm, and what the Colonel had said about a delta, all those rivers in the underworld mixing and dissolving into the ocean.

"What will you do?" I asked him.

"You mean while you're down there?"

"No," I said. "I don't mean that."

He shrugged. "Little, Tomás. Over time, I expect I will do less and less. And hopefully, eventually, I will do nothing except look at the stars." He looked briefly up at the sky, then back at me. "Are you ready, Tomasito?"

I wasn't. But I sat down and closed my eyes, knowing I'd feel nauseous if I didn't. When the wheel started turning, it felt as if it had been all along.

SEVENTEEN

This time I did wake in the pensión. More knocking, another disgruntled shout from Beatriz or somebody telling me about a call. I rose lethargically to get it.

Slowly, perhaps delusionally, my paranoia had decreased over the previous days. Nothing had happened to me, and I told myself that every additional day nothing did suggested nothing would. Every meal I survived, every platter of shitty sandwiches or plain pasta, increased the likelihood I'd survive in general. (Though somewhere in the back of my mind was an adage the Colonel had once told me about chickens: they know the farmer comes every morning with corn until the morning he comes with a butcher knife.)

It also helped that a week after cooking was added to my duties, the suspicion whirling about Automotores was redirected at the Uruguayans. Their country had done such a good job eliminating its communist threat that it could no longer pretend to need American funding and was cut off. The result was the Uruguayans took the twelve prisoners they had in custody at Automotores back to Uruguay and used them to stage a terrorist attack, claiming that guerrillas were still afoot and they needed money for the ongoing defense of capitalism. It was quite a publicity stunt. But the last thing Aníbal and the rest of the crew at Automotores wanted was publicity; tensions flared, but not at me, and when the remaining foreign operatives were kicked out, I, as a fellow Argentine, was treated more as part of the team.

Then that morning, Pichuca called to let me know how to reach Isabel and Gustavo.

We were to telephone a man at a locutorio—a new kind of communications shop. I was to give my alias and that of the party I wanted to contact, and the man would deliver the message I left with him when the other party called. Isabel's alias was Señora Amarga, "Mrs. Bitter," which I found endearing. Gustavo's was El Profe, short for "the professor," which I found less so. My own, Pichuca informed me, was Pingüino.

"Why am I a penguin?"

"I don't know," Pichuca said. "It's Gustavo's system. Maybe he chose it."

Still, it felt like a life preserver, getting news of this system. More so when I tested it out: I called the enigmatic message man at the locutorio and told him to tell Señora Amarga that Pingüino wanted her to come with him tomorrow at 15:00 to see his brothers and sisters at the zoo.

The next day, she was there, waiting for me at the entrance, and on time to boot.

"Your message was terrible," she said. "Lucky I found you—you think there are penguins in this zoo?"

I managed a smile, and we went in. There were no penguins, but where we sat we could hear the chirps of exotic birds, which gave our meeting an uneven, alien cadence. After asking for updates on Automotores—I related the Uruguayan "scandal," as the Gringo called it, and the names of the most recent pickups—she gave me her own about the Priest, the search for his murderers.

The milicos had no idea who it was, she asserted confidently; I was safe. The devil used to stop in at other centers too, she reminded me, and he had his share of enemies at his church in Boedo—so many people had wanted him dead, they'd have no reason to point the finger at me.

I could have answered that they didn't typically need a reason to point a finger at someone, but I didn't. Isabel was trying to comfort me, and I wanted to let her.

She also told me we couldn't meet in public like this anymore, it was too dangerous; from now on, if I needed to see her, I'd have to leave a message saying what time to pick me up for the asado, and one of them would come get me by car.

"One of you?" I asked, realizing this meant I'd mostly see her in Gustavo's presence going forward.

"Our house is pretty," she answered. "I think you'd like it."

I didn't. But I didn't say that either.

—

TWO WEEKS LATER, I received another call at the pensión when I happened to be there.

"Thank God," the voice on the line said when I picked up. Pichuca again.

"What is it, Pichu?"

"This is the third Tuesday in a row I haven't heard from Nerea. Our arrangement was for her to leave me a message every Tuesday morning, and I can't reach her. I can't reach Tito or Isabel either, I can't reach anyone, I thought you were all, all—"

"We're fine, Pichu."

"Nerea's not fine. It's not like her, you know it's not like her."

"She's in hiding, Pichu. You know that—you're the one who told me."

"Hiding! It's not like they went to Australia, Tomás. I know Isa and Gustavo are in Villa Ballester. I just want to speak to her, Tomás. Will you help me speak to Isa?"

I was quiet a moment. Not because of her request but the phrase preceding it. *Villa Ballester.* I didn't know Isabel and Gustavo were in Villa Ballester.

"Isa doesn't leave you a message every Tuesday?" I asked.

"Of course she doesn't. You know her."

"I do. Which is why, Pichu, I don't think I can—"

"You're afraid of Isa? You think she got that personality on her own? I'm her mother, Tomás! And I'm looking for one of my daughters!"

"I know, Pichu," I said. "I understand. But Pichu, I can't—"

"Stop saying my fucking name, Tomás, and say you'll help me speak to Isabel. Say you'll help me find her," she said, and started to cry. "Say you'll help me find my Nerea . . ."

I listened to her sobs. Waited for them to stop so I could tell her I would, but they never did.

———

I CALLED THE MAN at the locutorio afterward, leaving a message for Señora Amarga that Pingüino would be waiting for her to pick him up for the asado at 15:00 on Thursday, my next day off. I added—thinking fast, trying to figure out how to do this in code—that I knew the, uh, the *ninfa* might not be joining us, and I wanted to talk to her about that. The ninfa's, uh, her—*fuck it*—her mother was upset, and I wanted to talk to her about that too. What should I tell her?

It was too long and cumbersome a message, and I hung up feeling defeated.

But when I called some hours later asking for my own messages, the man told me, from Señora Amarga, that the Profe would pick me up when I'd asked. Nothing was added about the ninfa or her mother.

Still, I relayed the arrangement to Pichuca, taking pains to explain it should be safe—the military had names and addresses for targets only, maybe an old school photo or vague physical description, little that would give away Gustavo on the drive, assuming he had fake documents. Pichuca answered curtly that she was aware of the thinking; she'd been to see Nerea twice. And Nerea had contended it was safe too.

―

BY OCTOBER, Automotores had grown quieter. Without the foreigners, Triste, or the Priest, our numbers were considerably reduced. We had a few new recruits—the SIDE agent designated Red and those two thugs of Aníbal's, Goat and Nose, who looked like mobster twins in their nearly matching Puma tracksuits—but they had other posts and inconsistent shifts. Depressingly I reflected that, if only the thirty-odd prisoners we had knew they outnumbered us about six to one, they'd have a decent chance at escaping.

Instead, as I learned that Wednesday, the result was a higher turnover of transfers.

I kept worrying Elizabeth would be on the list. She wasn't, not yet. And though I wouldn't say she seemed worried exactly, it was clear when I visited her that she was aware of her predicament. Not long after I entered, with a can of bean soup that I presented as if it were a delicacy, she said, "You have no reason to keep me alive, do you?"

It was worse than that, I believed. There might be reason to make sure she didn't stay alive. The United States was in the midst of a presidential election and might vote in Jimmy Carter, who was certain to have a less favorable view of the regime. If word of Elizabeth's abduction were to reach the US government, international concern could be aroused. Uruguayans and Brazilians carrying tales of torture posed comparatively minute risk. But a pretty, young American?

If Rubio didn't like to toy with her, and if the rest of the men didn't think I did, they probably would have punched her ticket already.

Still I told her, "I do. Have reasons."

"Do they?"

I didn't know how to keep it going. I felt like such a liar just by speaking to her that the idea of actually lying—I couldn't stomach it.

"Not good ones," I admitted.

There was nothing like the silence of an isolation cell in Automotores when the torture room was quiet and the train outside wasn't passing. In Elizabeth's cell, not even the tittering of mice or the sound of a leak in the walls came through.

"Maybe it's for the best," she said.

"What is?"

"I don't want to stay alive for those reasons."

I looked at the soup on the floor; she hadn't touched it. Was she trying to kill herself before they could? It felt like a crueler injustice than any, somehow, that she couldn't even get her way in this.

Yet I picked up the soup can and held it out to her.

"There are other reasons to stay alive," I said. I felt like I was pleading with her.

"Are there," she said. She didn't take the can from me. "I don't remember them anymore."

⁓

ON THE DAY OF OUR MAKE-BELIEVE ASADO, Pichuca met me downstairs at my pensión. We didn't speak of Nerea or much at all. I got the sense quickly—after a dumb icebreaker referring to the sign outside the building for the hardly grand "Gran Atlántico" fell flat—that opening her mouth risked uncorking everything else inside her, and she was already struggling to keep it tamped down.

I didn't know what car Gustavo drove and was surprised when a little turquoise Fiat pulled up at the curb—not exactly the guerrilla-mobile I'd envisaged for him. He rolled down the window, and I could see his expression change—an uncomfortable swallow, his protrusive Adam's apple rising and dipping—when he realized two of us were there.

"Well, this . . . this is a surprise," he stammered. "Tomás, we weren't expecting—"

"Nerea's missing," I told him.

"Nerea's pregnant," Pichuca said.

Gustavo sucked down more saliva. Then he leaned over and opened the car's front door for Pichuca, calling her señora like he was trying to impress. I got in the back.

He instructed us, with apologies—at least to the señora, who he must not have realized had experience already—that we'd have to look down the whole way, that it was safer for everybody if we had no idea where we were headed. "Or close your eyes, pretend to sleep. But head down, if you don't mind. I know it's hard on the neck"—he offered a consolatory chuckle—"but you'd be surprised how they can blink open right at the wrong time, catch a street sign."

"Shouldn't you just give us blindfolds?" I asked.

"Right, because that's not conspicuous. Two passengers in my car with blindfolds on you can see through the windows."

I didn't like his tone—especially compared to the tone he employed with Pichuca. "The milicos do it," I insisted.

"The milicos don't need to be inconspicuous. They put blindfolds on you and then they throw you in the trunk. Do you want to be thrown in the trunk, Tomás?"

I didn't like that either. But I was out of rejoinders, and I stared at my feet as we drove off.

———

SOME SUBURBS OF BUENOS AIRES were suburbs in the American sense: big green lawns and lovely fences, glimmering pools, and housecleaning help. Villa Ballester was not a suburb in the American sense. I'd never been, but my understanding was that in economic terms it rivaled the suburbs between Buenos Aires and La Plata, and those I had enough familiarity with to avoid. It made sense that Isabel and Gustavo had ended up there—what kinds of jobs could they hold down with fake documents and without bachelor's degrees?—but it was unsettling. This was not the upper-middle-class Palermo where Isabel had grown up.

I'm not sure if it would have unsettled me more or less had I been able to look out the window and take in the neighborhood. It was enough that when we pulled into the long driveway—it was the type of house common in such neighborhoods, tucked behind another, usually the landlord's—I accidentally looked up and took in the series of bolts on the door and the thick bars on the windows.

Isabel greeted us with fierce hugs, her mother especially. Under the pretense of giving her a tour and wanting to start with the garden, she took her out back. Leaving me alone with Gustavo.

His limp was still significant, and he'd sat down right after entering. Declining his offers of *mate* and a seat at the table—it gave me a tenuous sense of superiority to stand over him—I surveyed their home. It was small: a front room that served as kitchen, living room, and dining room, and a bedroom just off it. Furniture was scant, as were decorations. Few of the books Isabel had discussed with me in the past were on the shelves.

No T. E. Lawrence or Che, Rodolfo Walsh or Eduardo Galeano—all too dangerous in the event of a raid. I told myself it was nothing to be jealous of, this tiny barren house of theirs. But the barrenness actually had the opposite effect, solidified the sense that all they needed here was each other.

Gustavo and I were silent, watching Isabel and her mother through the garden door. Isabel had lit a cigarette but barely taken a drag. Pichuca was crying again, intermittently yelling, while Isabel rubbed her back. Scattered exchanges snapped in and out of earshot: "Don't you see? Your sister's dead because of your stupid cause." "We don't know she's dead, only taken." "What difference does it make, what difference . . . ?" Soon they were out of range, at the far end of the yard, but I could see Pichuca gradually calming down. Whatever Isabel's words of comfort were, I imagined they must be both as good and as ineffectual as they'd been with me.

"Women make the best guerrillas, did you know?" Gustavo said to me then.

"I didn't," I answered.

"Men are good for one thing: shooting bullets. Women can sew clothes, fix shoes, nurse wounds, trick guards. And they can shoot bullets too."

"Sewing clothes and fixing shoes doesn't seem very useful."

Gustavo laughed. "You're right. That was more useful in Cuba. Where I got my training—there and the mountains of Tucumán. Always in rural guerrilla warfare anyway. Urban is different."

"Did they acknowledge that in your *training*?" I asked, braiding the word with condescension.

"In Cuba? They did what they could. Couldn't exactly send us to Havana to set off bombs and disrupt their own rule, could they? With urban warfare, you pretty much have to learn on the job. Most of us do, anyway. Isa, though—I swear sometimes I think she learned it in the womb."

I grimaced. "That's unpleasant."

"Is it? I think it's beautiful. Shows purpose, no? Destiny? If only the rest of us were so lucky."

"You don't think it's your destiny?"

"I got into it during the Cordobazo in '69. Going on strike, protesting. Demanding change. I was nineteen, I didn't know what I was getting into till the police started beating us and killed someone I knew. Then I wanted to kill too. But that part never came naturally for me, not like the change part. Not like it was for her." We looked at her in the garden, admiring her in our different ways. "You'd know better than me, though," he said.

I continued looking at her. Searching for the young girl at the beach in Pinamar who stepped on a piece of glass. Then I remembered she'd stepped on it on purpose.

"I'm not sure I would," I said.

When they returned, Isabel told Gustavo to open a bottle of wine, fix her mother something. Then she turned to me. "Want to see something beautiful?"

"Isa—" Gustavo tried to intercede.

"It's Tomás, Gusti. He doesn't even talk to his mother!"

"His mother wouldn't torture him," Gustavo said.

"You never know." Isabel laughed, and proceeded despite his objections. I followed, glancing quickly at Pichuca. She sat at the table with her head down, wine untouched.

As soon as we stepped outside, something luscious hit my nostrils. "You have a linden tree," I said. It was petite and more the neighbors' than theirs, but enough of it branched over the yard to suffuse me with its delicious fragrance. Isabel knew I loved them—as a platense, I practically had to;

they adorned so many big squares in La Plata that it was known as la ciudad de los tilos—the city of lindens. A name that, as my mother had pointed out in a recent call complaining about her sleepless nights, sounded a lot like la ciudad de los tiros. The city of gunshots.

Isabel nodded inattentively. "Gusti's grown to love them too," she told me, continuing across the garden toward their shed. "When we first checked out the neighborhood, and I caught a whiff of it, I screamed 'Tilos!' so loud, Gusti actually shoved me to the pavement in fear that somebody was shooting at us. We cried laughing. Who knows what the landlady thought?"

I knew what I thought. "You seem happy," I said.

"You always say that, Tomás."

"You seem happy, and meanwhile Nerea—"

"I haven't given up on Nerea. We still say her name at every one of our roll calls."

"Your roll calls," I repeated, in disbelief.

"We do them at all our meetings. Say we're present. We say Nerea's present too. Since she's still in the fight."

Isabel started working the combination lock on the door. She turned it in one direction, then the other, then shook her head and started over, the quick little clicks like a clock being wound.

"You say Nerea is present at roll calls."

"She'd want me to," Isabel said. And to what must have been my skeptical look, "She'd made it to sergeant, Tomás. Can you believe it? My little sister a sergeant."

"She probably isn't one anymore," I said.

"Fuck, Tomás!" she yelled, giving the lock an anticlimactic shove into the shed door; it barely thudded as it hit the wood. "We all have our ways of coping. Okay?"

"Okay," I said.

"Do you think it's easy for me? We just have to keep looking forward—we have to. We can't let it all have been for nothing. Nerea wouldn't want us to."

"Okay," I said again. Isabel bent back over the lock. This time it sighed loose and she breathed deeply, as if in imitation of it.

Inside, the shed was crammed tight with stacked crates of Bond cigarettes, a whole shelf on the far wall stuffed with cartons of them.

"We won't be storing guns here forever," Isabel said. "Nor smuggling bullets in cigarette packs either. No, we have bigger plans."

She explained that the owner of Papel Prensa, the country's biggest supplier of newsprint, who had Montonero links and stakes in free presses like *La Opinión*, had been disappeared, his father and brother imprisoned, and his widow coerced to sell the company to Argentina's two biggest newspapers, *Clarín* and *La Nación*, for all of $7,000. That meant there were no major independent newsprint producers left, and therefore no major independent newspapers either. The real battle—here was Isabel's point—wasn't with guns but with information. Well, granted it'd be comparatively modest, but just think—if enough Montoneros set up things like this, and word spread of what was going on throughout this country—well. She kept saying "well," laughing it off like she recognized the child's instinct in her to over-aspire.

"It was Nerea's idea originally—journalism student, you remember. She wanted me to call it Guti—for Gutenberg," she said, giving the cigarette-packed shelf a heave.

Behind it was a wall of guns and ammunition belts and, underneath, as if the weaponry were merely ornaments for the main attraction, a homemade printing press.

It was small, obviously, to fit in the back of a shed. But it wasn't a toy; the wheels, the weights, the wooden boards that formed the base, the intricate mechanism itself. With embarrassment, I recognized how little thought I'd given to Isabel's expertise in engineering. Stroking one of the panels as a sculptor might, she gave the lever a pull and showed me how it worked—how it would work, soon.

"And if we get caught," she said, "we'll blame it on that bitch of a fascist landlady and say we had no idea!"

It was about as harebrained and dangerous as her plan to send me to the front lines of the ESMA. And in hindsight, as representative of the foibles of the young, disorganized movement that was the Montoneros as well. Ultimately they were just idealistic, ambitious kids scrambling over-excitedly toward the future until they fell over its precipice.

Still, it moved me. Inspired me, even. The grandeur of the hope, the astonishing amount of work Isabel was willing to put toward its realization. I'm inclined to think I would have fallen in love with her then and there if I hadn't already.

"Good, no?" she said, pushing the rolling shelf back into position.

"Absolutely perfect," I said, and she gave me one of her quick, cousin-like kisses on the cheek.

⎯

NO ONE DRANK THE WINE, and whatever cheeriness Isabel had tried to set in motion flagged quickly. Soon it was growing dark, and Pichuca and I were back in the Fiat, with Isabel—because their partnership was equal and they shared the risks—behind the wheel.

Just after pulling out of the driveway she stopped again, and though I was gazing at my shoes as instructed, I realized their house must be on the corner. On instinct, I glanced up to confirm it—and not only saw that my assumption was right but in the dimness caught the street sign: Río Negro. Realizing my mistake, I rapidly looked away—away, not down, and it was too late: I'd glimpsed the half-faded number riding down the white door of the outer house: 2166.

After that, I curled my neck like a heron and studied the bits of garbage on the car floor as intently as I could.

———

ISABEL DROPPED PICHUCA OFF FIRST. She'd been crying softly on the ride, and they hugged good-bye inaudibly. I remained in the backseat, as if afraid to move.

Driving again, Isabel said, "You can look up now, Tomás. Open your eyes."

They were already open, but I straightened my stiff neck. I could see Isabel's face in the rearview mirror, but she was looking at the road, not at me.

"Sounds almost metaphorical," I said.

"What does?"

"Opening my eyes. Seeing you and Gusti. Maybe just seeing you." Still not even a glance in the mirror. It broke my heart. "I love you, Isa," I said. It was the first time I'd ever told her so. "I wouldn't be doing any of this if not for you."

"I know, Tomás. I'm sorry."

"Are you?" I asked.

"Yes. Doesn't mean I'd do anything differently, but yes, I'm sorry about what it does to you."

"I'm not sure it means anything then," I said.

"I'm not either. It's a little too simple a concept maybe, being sorry."

Remembering it—hearing it—I remembered and heard what the Colonel had said when I met him in the cemetery. *Much too simple a notion, your regret. Do something, don't do something—as if actions could be reduced to such measly forks in the road.*

"I'm not sure how long I can keep doing this," I said.

"I'm more sure of that," Isabel said, finally peeking back at me in the mirror. "You're braver and better than you realize. It's not just about me, Tomás, not actually."

Through the window, the night seemed peaceful. No sense of violence or danger, no speeding cars or sirens or green Ford Falcons. Where was this war we all kept talking about, this revolution? Why did it seem, ridiculously, as if in this car there was so much more pain?

"We'll see," I said.

"We will, I guess." She pulled the car to a stop. We were a few blocks from my pensión. "Take care of yourself, will you?"

I got out and, uncertain what I meant, I told her I would.

———

IT WASN'T THE SAME NIGHT—I know because I went back to the pensión to get the Colonel's revolver—but I've always recalled it as if it was. As if, instead of going home, I walked immediately to Estación Once and, staring down the shady youths who might have made me nervous before I saw far worse at Automotores, took the train to Floresta for an overnight shift.

Similarly, it couldn't have been the first thing I did when I arrived, but in reexperiencing it, nothing else filled the gap. I went to the torture room and found it empty. Then I headed for Elizabeth's cell.

I opened the door so hard it slammed against the wall. "Let's go! Now!" I yelled, slurring my voice to seem drunk. I grabbed her by the arm and dragged her up, then pulled her, stumbling, to the end of the hall.

She didn't make a sound.

"Time to sing," I told her loudly, practically singing myself. I opened the torture room door and shoved her inside.

Taking her by the wrists, I bound them to the rope hanging from the rafters and prepared to raise it.

"I tied it loosely," I said then. In a whisper, straight into her ear. "In five minutes, you untie it. Take off your blindfold and go to the last cell on your left. The last on your left, you hear me? All you have to do is open it, that's all."

She gave a tremble of a nod. Whimpered, maybe. But said nothing in response.

I left without saying anything more either.

I went to the merchandise closet; we didn't keep just prisoners' booty in there, but weapons too. I took out a rifle, the first I laid my hands on. Then I closed the door and continued down the hall until I reached the last cell on the left.

I opened it and closed the door behind me, more quietly this time. The bloody, half-broken man on the ground started, pressed himself into the corner instinctually. I knelt in front of him, took his blindfold off. Though it was almost pitch-black inside, I could make out the shock on his face when he saw mine.

"Another prisoner will open the door for you in three minutes," I told Juan Miguel Pereyra. "She goes first, you go behind her with this." I held out the rifle; he stared at its outline. "Don't take the wooden staircase down to the garage—continue through the kitchen and take the other one; you'll know it's right if it's marble at the top. I'll be on the balcony when you get outside, shooting to miss. You do the same with me, you understand? With the others, I don't care."

He continued staring. I wondered if he was trying to figure out if it was a hallucination or a trick, or if he was actually deciding whether to follow my instructions and shoot to miss with me. Was that a flicker of temptation in his eyes, or were they merely trying to adjust to the light?

"You ERP?" he asked.

I shook my head. "Montonero." He still hadn't taken the rifle. I dropped it at his feet. "Three minutes," I reminded him. "No more."

Then I rose and closed the cell door behind me without locking it.

I WENT TO THE OFFICER QUARTERS, lay down on a mattress left unoccupied by the Uruguayans; a nap, I planned to say, I took a nap. She must have loosened the rope she was bound with—I'd tied it drunkenly, I'd admit, angry she resisted me—and found the weapons and Pereyra by chance. That she was the main device of the ploy would make it more plausible, I told myself, since he was the flight risk and she the bystander. Or better, the victim of circumstance.

Rubio was working in Aníbal's office, my defense would continue, and there was the guard downstairs in the booth. We couldn't have known to be any more cautious; three or four men overnight was all we'd ever needed.

I removed the revolver from my belt and gripped it in my lap tightly.

Three minutes passed. Then five. Seven, ten, what felt like a hundred, a thousand. Nothing, no signs of any disturbance in the hallways beyond. It was as silent as a cell.

And then—shots. Loud, popping, indubitably a rifle's. A first, a second. A brief pause as an automatic flurried in response, and then a third. I rushed out of the room, revolver in hand. Rubio met me outside, machine gun in his hands, suspicious eyes wildly alert. "What the—"

Another.

"You go downstairs, I'll go to the balcony," I told him. To think he could have easily said that first or simply opted not to, deciding instead that I go downstairs and he take the balcony. But as luck would have it, he didn't.

By the time I got outside, they were already fleeing down Venancio Flores. I fired several meters off the mark—I'd never shot a gun before, and the tug in my wrist and hand was remarkable. Elizabeth continued sprinting toward the intersection, but Pereyra turned, raised his rifle in my direction; I was sure when he pulled the trigger it would leave a giant hole in my chest.

It didn't—didn't even graze me. He fired another two shots at my feet, piercing the concrete, and then turned—Rubio had made it downstairs. Instead of engaging him, Pereyra took off running.

I watched Rubio fire into the night. But it was empty; by then, both Pereyra and Elizabeth had vanished and, in what was surely the greatest moment of empathy in Rubio's life, rather than give chase, he returned to the dying man in the guard booth. In what might have been a hopeful omen to someone else, but struck me as the opposite, a dreadful portent about the rest of our fates, it turned out to be too late for him, too.

PART III
THE DELTA

EIGHTEEN

When I came to—it was like I'd blacked out reliving that frenzy, gone blank sometime after pressing my fingertips to the guard's neck in search of a pulse—I found myself standing in the main corridor at Automotores, the so-called Avenue of Happiness. Deep purplish light was filtering in from the terrace, confirming the time if not the year, and I stared at the open torture room door, deciding if I should enter.

The actual night of the escape, I'd stayed clear. I thought it would look suspicious if I went in given what had happened, like I was trying to rid the scene of evidence. Rubio and I had carried the guard into the garage—Juan Ramírez was his name; he was far enough removed from the detainees not to need an alias. He was in his fifties, waiting for his pension. Whenever I used to pass him in the booth, he'd salute and mention the previous day's soccer game or venture to other sports when that failed—Guillermo Vilas at the US Open; a polo match I knew nothing about. Still, he had been friendly to me, and I felt bad about his fate. Rubio and I looked at his dead body a minute, breathing loudly, as if we'd never seen one before. Then Rubio clasped my shoulder, as if to say, Well, there was nothing we could do, you shouldn't blame yourself. He called Aníbal to let him know what had happened, while I went upstairs, purportedly to patrol the halls in case other prisoners got any ideas after hearing the gunshots.

As I stood there now, Rubio was nowhere to be seen. One of several discrepancies from Automotores as I remembered it then: the upgraded fluorescents on the ceiling, the industrial locks built into the cell doors in place of padlocks. The hallway seemed some twenty or thirty feet longer too. I raised a hand to my beard, and though I touched only the patchy, unshaven fuzz that was all I could grow at twenty-one, it reminded me of the ten years I'd safely survived since that night, and the journey that had brought me back to it.

I felt a pull toward the far room. It was like the entrancing draw of the waves on the phantom shore of Pinamar, that insidious undertow. Only now, I acquiesced to it.

The wire mesh table was in the middle, but no ropes hung from the rafters. An undented radio lay on the shelf at the far end. A small vase of wilting yellow tulips sat next to it on one side and, on the other, equidistant, a picana. It was neatly wrapped in the wire that connected it to the control box, which was plugged into the socket. On the wall above were two more innovations: a swastika and a sign that read:

WELCOME TO THE OLYMPUS OF THE GODS
~THE CENTURIONS

The Olimpo. The detention center founded sometime after Automotores' closing, where the Gringo said they watched the World Cup with the prisoners. It must have been a product of the Colonel's metaphorical delta—the muddling of different people's memories and hells, the tangled maze of possibility. Which begged the question of whose hell I was in now.

"Excuse me?" someone said behind me, as if in direct response to my musing. The voice was soft and polite, instantly recognizable. No one except the Priest would pretend to need permission to enter that room.

I should have known from the flowers it was his domain. Also from the aesthetic, the newness of the appliances, the cleanliness. This wasn't a clumsily appropriated workshop like Automotores, but a room constructed specifically with its vile function in mind. Even if the Priest hadn't lived to see the Olimpo, it made nightmarishly perfect sense that he'd somehow find it in death.

He wore a surgical gown over his cassock, a pristine white that matched his collar and his milky-bald head. He'd aged badly, grown so pasty he appeared to be decomposing, what with his bloated belly, his gouty-looking knuckles. The latter I glimpsed only fleetingly, before he snapped a pair of latex gloves onto his fingers with a sigh of pleasure.

"Ahhhh, Verde," he cooed, like I was a former lover. "You always did try to have it both ways, play both sides. Who knew it'd be the living and the dead?"

His tone was silky as ever, smoothed and sinisterly inflected for false comfort. Rumor had it that prisoners who never saw his face called him el diablo materno. The motherly devil.

"That is what you want, is it not? To have your life and to have your Montonera's?"

I didn't answer or move, even as he circled around me toward the shelf with the radio and the picana.

"How do I know this, you wonder? When there are souls here that do not even know their own names anymore? There are moments I don't either, I'll tell you. But something has held for me still, all this time. My role as confessor perhaps, as redeemer. Though we're all one another's judges to an extent here, all press our dirty fingertips on the scales that weigh one another's hearts, from time to time I find myself entrusted with more of a say. And you, Verdecito, are such a case."

"Maybe because I had you killed," I told him.

"Maybe," the Priest said, with disturbing amicableness. He began fidgeting with the knob on the radio, springing to life a snatch of electric guitar and then an interval of garbled static, a bit of nationalist, late-1976 news, and then more static. "Maybe. It is one of those age-old rules, no, the connection between the murdered and the murderer? But in my own opinion," he went on philosophically, "it may be simpler. A matter of convenience. Who else would take an interest in you? In administering your judgment?"

"Are you going to torture me, Father?" I asked, as if I had no choice about it, no way out despite the open door behind me.

He appeared momentarily confused. "Well. Not with the picana anyway," he said. He had found the opera station, which was playing Figaro's frenetic, upbeat aria from *The Barber of Seville*. "Pity, but that'll have to do. Anyway, I'm sorry, Verdecito. Felipe gave you a more benign impression of the quest, did he? Sneak like Orpheus into the underworld, steal back one of its souls? Very like him, to be so deceitful. But you must have known it wouldn't work that way. Another old rule, no? A soul for a soul? The balance must always be kept."

The baritone skipped along, all those cluttered Italian syllables clattering through the pause: *Qua la sanguigna . . . Presto il biglietto . . . Figaro! Figaro! Figaaaaaro!*

"I don't understand," I said, though I was starting to. The Colonel's plunge and proverbial coin toss, his talk of other choices and life being where you saved lives. *With death, it's more of a give-and-take.*

"You get to do this part over, in effect," the Priest said. "Not quite as it took place then, of course, things will no doubt be messier, more *customized*, if you will, for your edification. But you will get the chance you want, or claimed you did. You will get the chance to give the Montonera back to life, staying behind in her place."

Figaro qua, Figaro là, Figaro su, Figaro giù ...

"Doesn't seem very like this place, no? Second chances, do-overs. But death is not so different from life in that way, Verdecito. Despite what many believe, in both worlds, the greatest curse you can sometimes face is freedom."

"The Colonel told me it didn't work that way," I said.

"What way?"

"It didn't come down to single choices."

Hadn't he claimed that? It had grown confused again, like so much else, gotten lost in all those mixed metaphors. Ceaselessly forking roads and mazes, Ferris wheels that kept on spinning.

"Well," the Priest said, "did you believe him?"

No matter what anyone ever said to me, there was little I believed in less.

"Why this part?" I asked.

"Well," he said again, thoughtfully, "I suppose to an extent you've been doing it all over again. But what came before this—you don't really regret it, do you? Having me killed—not a whiff of compunction there. And saving Pereyra and the American girl—despite causing another man's death, you still think it a good thing you did, no?"

I did, or tried to anyway. Two people were set free, and a few days after the incident, falling on the heels of the Uruguayan scandal, they wound up shutting Automotores down.

But among the lessons of this place was the oldest and most hackneyed: the road to hell was indeed paved with good intentions. When Automotores shuttered, the remaining prisoners were presumably shipped to other centers, and the Olimpo, this twisted garage ten minutes away, wound up taking its place. Perhaps they got a brief reprieve while Aníbal was reprimanded by his supervisors at SIDE, but afterward their treatment likely worsened.

"How you met your wife too, no?" the Priest said. It was true. When I left Rome for New York, it was to find Elizabeth. I wanted—needed—proof that I'd done some good, that my life might by extension serve some good. Elizabeth would be evidence of a kind, her gratitude and whatever life she was leading that she wouldn't have had without me.

One of the Argentine exiles I met in Rome had made connections at the UN, trying to raise international awareness of the country's situation. Though I had little interest in helping his effort, I did ask him to look into living arrangements for me in New York, which was how I wound up in Parkway Village. Unable to figure out which buses to take and afraid to ask, I walked almost three hours along Queens Boulevard before I got a subway that dropped me on the Upper West Side.

I didn't find Elizabeth. She'd long since moved from the address on that driver's license, and I couldn't even confirm if she'd gone to any US official to report what had been done to her. That slim bit of beneficence was denied me too.

But the serendipitous turn was this: Claire lived at that address then; that was our first meeting. A couple years later I moved to Morningside Heights, and we bumped into each other again. "You look lost, Tom," she said, grinning. And I was grateful, as I would continue to be, for her direction.

"No, Verdecito," the Priest went on. "When you get down to it, this is really the only part you'd do over, isn't it?"

The aria had started over at some point, as if the station played nothing else, and was now rounding off again: *Ah, bravo Figaro! Bravo, bravissimo!*

"A deal with the devil, you think Felipe made for you? No. All deals in this world are still with God. That is what I believe."

"You haven't learned much here, have you?"

"Oh no, Verde, I've learned too much, actually, far too much. I used to believe truth was a benediction, a shining light. But it is blinding. The same way it was for Paul on the road to Damascus—terrible, powerful. As a Jew, you may not know that story. But the lesson is it is a curse as well as a blessing."

"And you still believe you're blessed?"

He indulged a small smile. "I admit I have been made to doubt on occasion. To lose myself entirely, forget what is right and what is not and what side of the divide I am on. Good or evil, even life or death. But there is no faith without doubt, Verde. I tell myself, at the worst moments here, when I would pluck my very eyes out to remove the truth from them, that my faith is being tested. And it is strong."

Just as the music swam back in, the Priest gave the knob of the radio a joltingly fast turn, and it spun off with a staticky beep.

"So now it is my test," I said.

"Yes. In essence. As I understand it, though, it is not your faith that is going to be tested, but your love. Isn't that right, Verde? Isn't this all about love for you?"

He started circling back around the room, continuing clockwise as if he needed to complete a full circuit. I watched him across the wire mesh table without speaking.

On reaching the doorway, he paused. "I do not hate you, Verde, for what it's worth. Oh, I've had moments to be sure—cursed your treachery, your sneaky Jewish nature. No doubt it would give you some satisfaction if I did. But the truth is, none of this has ever been about hatred for me. Always, it has been about justice. And whatever your opinion, I believe you escaped it in '76."

"So do I," I told him honestly.

"Well, then," the Priest said, "don't this time."

He left. And when I followed him out some minutes later, I found myself in Automotores' gloomy hallway again. I went out to the balcony and looked down Venancio Flores at the vacant train tracks, the noiseless school, the shops and kiosks, grated until dawn. Would it be as slow in coming this time as it had been in reality, I wondered, before returning inside, and concluded: Probably longer. Very probably, this night would never end.

NINETEEN

Rubio and I waited a whole hour in the kitchen, our dreary silence broken only when he suddenly got the milk out of the fridge and poured himself a cup. Aníbal arrived in a mood—stomping into his office, hair sleep-mussed and sweaty. He called Rubio in first and closed the door, and I kept waiting, slouched in my chair with my hands spread on the table, attention drifting from the dripping faucet to the grossly stocked pantry—those boxes of cereal and pasta I'd bought, the bags of Wonder Bread and mealy, rotting fruit.

I felt drained—of energy, thoughts, even any sense of danger. Whatever might happen in that office seemed tame compared to the interrogation tactics employed elsewhere at Automotores, and I felt strangely uninterested in whatever might happen to me afterward.

Rubio came out after some twenty minutes, and I went in. Aníbal seemed more relaxed—feet up, shoes off, the moldy odor of his socks infiltrating my nostrils. "Just go over it from the start," he said, and I told the story in rote fashion, answering his questions more mechanically than I'd intended. Only when it came to my apologies could I summon anything like an actor's ability: I offered them frequently, profusely, and genuinely.

"You seem scared," he said at last.

"Of course I'm scared," I told him, and he laughed.

"You fuck that American girl, Verde?" he asked me, still grinning.

I deliberated a moment about what to say. But by then it felt like too much time had passed, and I shook my head. "I wanted her to like me," I said.

Aníbal observed me a minute—sympathetically, I believed, as if he understood such a plight. "I think she'll like you better now," he said, sighing. "You're tired, Verde. I can see that. It's Saturday—you were supposed to come back tonight, weren't you? Well, take the weekend off. Monday too, why not? Come back Tuesday. We'll know what's what then. Go on," he insisted when I continued sitting there dumbly. "It's almost morning. Get some sleep."

I stood uncertainly and staggered out of the office. Rubio had already gone, and others were there to take over our shift. Goat and Nose and two men I didn't recognize—agents from SIDE, I supposed, or more of Aníbal's own creatures, who could keep the incident quiet if he needed. They watched me as I went down the stairs.

There was no train at this hour, and instead of getting a cab I decided to walk. To my foggy mind, it made sense: exhausted though I was, I might not be able to sleep and, besides, I had to figure out what, if anything, I'd do next. The idea of real action still seemed remote, as if it had all been used up already. A *que será será* kind of mentality. Let come what may.

———

FAIT ACCOMPLI. A better term for my attitude during the hours I spent zigzagging northeast between Avenidas Rivadavia and Independencia. Another, from my high school Latin: *Alea iacta est*—the die is cast. *Finita la commedia*—the famous last line of some Italian opera or other. Every phrase that occurred to me seemed to come from a language other than my own. The one that resonated most strongly was the simplest: *Too late.* To me, leaving Automotores for perhaps the last time, it all already seemed too late.

Wide, endless streets devoid of pedestrians, drivers honking as I crossed against a light, blisters blossoming on my heels, kids exiting boliches and staring at me like I was about to keel over drunk or sick or was from another planet altogether. My brain formed impressions more than plans, and what plans it formed were small, a peculiar mix of the practical, the sentimental, and the irrational. Around five in the morning, I made my way to the Colonel's café, Parada Norte. I told myself it was largely coincidence—the closeness to my pensión, its twenty-four-hour air—but no doubt part of me hoped he'd be there with his ham-and-cheese tostados, encouraging pleas for help and confessions.

No one was there, though, except the waiter. "Tomás, no?" he asked at my arrival, and for a second I thought it was the universe mystically reaching out to me, about to say, *It's time.* Then he offered his hand and reminded me the Colonel had introduced us. "Cafecito?" he asked. "Glass of wine?" And I was so demented and out of sorts that I ordered both.

Afterward, I went to Puerto Madero, as close to the water as I could get, hoping to catch a glimpse of the sunrise. But the sky was filmy and gray, the view half obstructed by fencing. I watched the grimy water roll languidly over the garbage in the shallows, caressing the broken pipes and bottles and bathing them all indiscriminately.

I don't know if it was the soothing effect of the water or the suicide's tendency to wrap up affairs, to say good-bye, but from there I went to the train station in Constitución. I glanced momentarily at faraway locations on the departure board—Neuquén, Catamarca, Iguazú, all of which had border crossings with Chile or Brazil—and then got a ticket to La Plata. My mother deserved that much at least, I thought incompletely.

I TOLD HER WHEN I ARRIVED that I'd meant it to be a surprise. My voice was deadpan and unenthusiastic, but she played along, hugging me tightly in the foyer and thanking me for the kindness.

She looked unchanged, which was to say haggard and thin, saggy as an unused rubber band. She asked if I was hungry, and though I said I wasn't, she started to warm up some pascualina, which she remembered as one of my favorite dishes. It was eleven in the morning but it felt like midnight, and I asked for some wine.

"Are you drinking too much, Tomás?"

"You're kidding."

I began to regret coming. I couldn't discuss the fledgling thought I'd had of leaving Argentina—she wouldn't support it, and she wouldn't be of much help even if she did, never having left the country since she immigrated. I didn't know how I'd explain it either: "Sorry, Mami, I fucked up and the milicos may be in touch about it soon"? They wouldn't be, not with her. If they came for me or didn't, either way she'd never hear a word.

Everything I'd learned, from collecting names for Isabel to seeing Pichuca's reaction after Nerea went missing, should have taught me many times over how awful a fate that would be. But in my head—overwhelmed, depleted—nothing seemed preferable. Death might have scared me. But disappearance had shed its reality, and I almost thought it a nice, easy way for all this to end.

After lunch, I told my mother I'd take a nap. I wound up sleeping until the next morning. "Finals," I explained when I came downstairs at last, muttering something about my particular difficulty with oral exams. Not even my mother could have believed me.

Another meal. Another stilted one-way conversation. She asked me if I'd be visiting any friends while I was in town, and I told her I would, that

I should have called them already. She left me to do so, and I called the Colonel instead. No one answered. But the phone rang long enough that I could pretend I'd gotten through to someone, and when my mother returned, I told her I'd better get going, dropping names of people I hadn't been in touch with in nearly a year and heading out as if they were expecting me.

My wandering was largely like the night before last. But my mood was different, the occasional reflection I allowed myself. I remembered Sundays, visiting my grandparents or drinking on a crowded, litter-filled university lawn with my ex until after sundown. It'd been so long since I'd had a proper Sunday. I pictured myself as a child, playing in these tranquil, tree-lined streets with kids my age, going with my mother to the zoo or with my father to the observatory to gaze through the telescope at the celestial bodies he loved telling me about. The memories seemed as far away as those stars had, as twinkly and beautiful and beyond reach.

I wound up going all the way out to the Republic of Children and, in a fit of whimsy or nostalgia, getting a ticket to the theme park. Joining the families roaming the fake, miniature city, with its pink and aqua-blue façades and imitations of Moscow towers, I remembered when my parents had taken me here as a six-year-old. Begrudgingly they'd told me the place was Perón's doing, providing what might have been my first association with his name. My father said the park was just like the man, "all show and no point," and my mother nodded and added that Perón offered asylum to the Nazis—"populist just like them," she said, accurately encapsulating the endless ethical morass that was Argentine politics. The decision not to tell her about my involvement with the Montoneros seemed better then, like I was sparing her. Like it'd be a gift to leave her with the belief that I was just a selfish, ungrateful kid like any other, and none of this was her fault.

Soon the gaudy, splashy colors, the spires rising vertiginously toward cottony clouds, the spectacular fakeness got to be too much. Without finishing the circuit, I went out through the entrance and took the bus back to my childhood home.

I asked myself what I was doing. Reprimanded myself for wasting precious time. But time just didn't feel that precious to me anymore.

———

LUNCH. It was like breakfast except that I didn't lie when my mother asked me if I'd had a good time with Pablito and the others. "I didn't end up seeing them," I told her, to a concerned frown. "I just walked around. Revisited places from when I was a kid."

"You miss it?" she said a bit hopefully, and when I shrugged in reply, "No one likes getting older." She laughed, but with a teary sniffle. "I can't stand it for you. All this—it's no way to grow up."

"Don't worry, Mami," I assured her. "I'll be fine." She nodded and blew her nose. Then she cleared our plates and washed them, and I told her I ought to be heading off soon. "Finals," I said again, despite myself.

"Do you want to take the car? I'm not using it. You should take it. Take it," she insisted, and knowing she'd keep pleading until I relented, I agreed. She went to get the keys from the entry table and I followed her, leaving her little choice but to walk me out.

"I love you," I said, in the half-muttered way I always said it on the phone. "Take care of yourself, Mami. Talk soon."

"Thanks for coming," she said from the doorway, her voice shy, afraid to show too much affection. "You didn't last time."

"What?"

"Last time," she repeated. "You didn't come see me. At the end."

It was like a switch that had toggled on, or one of those flashes in a dream when you realize you're in one before the awareness sputters out completely. In '76, I recalled, I'd stared at the departures board at

Constitución—Neuquén, Catamarca, Iguazú—and decided that my name would probably be flagged at the borders. Then I'd considered La Plata. But I was afraid I'd cause my mother more worry than relief if I came, and I ultimately resolved to go back to the pensión and sleep, think it all through with a fresh mind in the morning. On waking, other concerns took over—should I return to Automotores? call the Colonel? seek out Isabel?—and I didn't consider going back to La Plata again.

I didn't call her from Rome at first either. I was too ashamed, and by the time I got through two weeks later, after a series of unavailable long-distance lines and busy signals, a neighbor answered. She'd volunteered to help clear out the house after my mother overdosed on sleeping pills. An accident, she said, but I doubted it, and those doubts contributed to my almost having a similar "accident" of my own with the Colonel's revolver.

I looked at my mother on the threshold of our narrow little house now and saw her changed: the skeletal features, the stooped back, the general shrunkenness. The bags under her eyes, so dark they looked like bruises, black sockets in a wizened skull.

"It's so good to see you," she said. "But you better go. Otherwise I may not want you to." She closed the door, and I heard the light click of the lock shutting her inside.

Immersed again in the calm, homey quiet of the neighborhood and the bright, clean summer air, I went to the curb and got into my mother's car. It was just a silver Peugeot sedan, nothing special. But at the moment my gratitude was so great that I had to clear my watering eyes before I could start the engine for the trip back to Buenos Aires.

TWENTY

There was something about driving, the clichéd sense of freedom I attached to it growing up, perhaps, that made me feel calmer, more in control. The traffic was light and flowing at first, and I felt, if not quite like I could go anywhere, that at least there were paths still open to me, corners to be turned, however few. Even when the road slowed, and congestion and police lights up ahead suggested an ID check, I decelerated with the detached thought that to many, this was probably the dictatorship's biggest fault—shitty commutes. I didn't even feel relieved when I discovered it was just another car wreck.

It wasn't my intention to continue to Villa Ballester. But by the time I crossed Chacabuco Park, it seemed natural to keep going. Pausing only to study my mother's map and refuel when I got lost in Villa Devoto, I went from Avenida San Martín to Avenida General Paz to who knows how many other streets with military namesakes, until I reached Calle 25 de Mayo.

I wasn't sure what I'd do when I saw them. The vague notion of a warning flitted through my mind, telling them they were in danger. Though what they were in danger of—I couldn't go so far as to articulate that. There'd been many times when the goings-on at Automotores felt behind a curtain, but none quite like this. I imagined more interviews with Rubio, with Aníbal, maybe a call to the Colonel to double-check my background. Or maybe they didn't need to go through all that, maybe they already had me pinned, and were simply waiting for me to return to my pensión.

The more difficult warning to articulate, probably: they might be in danger of me.

—

AS I GOT CLOSER, I was struck by the unpleasantness of the neighborhood, how downtrodden it looked in the evening light. Uncollected garbage, mangy mutts and locals peering at my car suspiciously whenever I slowed at an intersection. I'd barely seen any of this the last time I was here, since I'd been staring at my feet as instructed, and the street itself seemed impossible to find. I zigzagged, doubled back, doubled back again. When I pulled up at their corner at last, I remembered with surging anxiety that I wasn't supposed to be there, to know where they lived. The Gringo had told me that Montoneros disappeared their own just as the military did when they learned of traitors, that they even held their own mock trials before executing them.

From the curb, I saw the landlady's dog in her yard. Just a scraggly collie with a chew toy, nothing to be intimidated by. But the prospect of its high-pitched yelp made me hesitate, the tingly certainty that it would receive me like an intruder. When I got out, though, it remained silent, and as I headed down the driveway, it barely raised its head from its slobbery toy.

The sense of trespass lingered, the pure, hazy wrongness. The unmown grass seemed taller and the Fiat rusty, not the smooth, skylike turquoise I remembered. The shutter on the barred window beside the front door was open, which was odder still. And though I formed a loose, clammy fist in my pocket to knock, I found myself leaning over for a look inside instead.

The main room was empty. But I heard their voices drifting out of the bedroom—his husky laugh, her distinct snort—and, without contemplating what I was doing, I squeezed my way around the side of the house. The shutters of the bedroom window hung wide open too.

There was no nightstand, only a shadeless lamp on the floor where one should have been. It was off, and with dusk swiftly descending, I don't know how I made them out. They were lying naked on the mattress, only halfway under the sheets—her breasts and torso, his left arm and leg. Cigarette cartons and gold-encased bullets were strewn about them, as if during the work of packing the latter into the former they'd gotten distracted. Though how they could have been so distracted as to do so naked, with the shutters open—it was either a cosmic jape at my expense or, after Nerea and everything else, they'd thrown caution to the wind with the same abandon I had.

Isabel was cackling, her head on the pillow, while Gustavo hovered over her. "What's so funny, love?" he asked.

"This, no? I have bullets in my hair and I've never been so happy."

I looked away. At the discolored panels over the window, a broad blank stretch of wall where the beige paint had been scratched off. The pipe running up the side of the house and the stuffed gutter overhead, the graying, soupy sky. It was so ugly, all of it. Yet Isabel found happiness in it, beauty. I couldn't remember her ever saying, amid the branches of the Bosques or the sands of Pinamar, that she was happy with me.

"You should hurry up with this whole pregnant thing," Gustavo said.

"*You* should hurry up with this pregnant thing," Isabel answered, and my gaze drifted back right in time to catch her moving Gustavo's hand farther down. He laughed.

"A couple weeks ago you almost leave me, and now you want to have babies?"

"Wasn't it more like a couple months?"

"I don't think that's the point."

"No? What is the point?"

"I just want to make sure you know what you want," Gustavo said.

"Who the fuck knows that?" Isabel replied.

Gustavo lay back on his side of the bed and sighed, and I thought: Oh, to be able to simply sigh at something like that.

"You remember why I almost left you, Gusti?"

"Elba Hilda Gaudio?"

"No."

"Tomás Orilla?"

"No."

"Isabel Aroztegui?"

She laughed. "Yes. Isabel Aroztegui. I worried you wanted some other version of her, a lie."

"Like Tomás, you mean. Any word from him, by the way?"

She shook her head, sending several bullet casings sliding off the pillow. "I should check the messages. I have to touch base with Miguel about the investigation into that priest anyway."

Who was Miguel? Just another Tomás at another detention center? Or maybe, I thought sadly, Tomás was just another Miguel.

"Poor guy," Gustavo said.

"Miguel?"

"No. Not Miguel."

I half expected them to glance out the window and spot me, as if they knew I'd been there the whole time. But they didn't, and it seemed fitting, another sign that I was merely background to them, barely there at all.

"What was it you said, Gusti? He'd take me as I am, never even blink?"

"He'd never open his eyes, I said."

I remembered the night she came to my pensión, her reference to an argument with Gustavo and that same name, Elba Hilda Gaudio. The drunken talk of lies and acceptance and the backdrop of her fear of abandonment, the steadfast childhood comfort I'd always provided. My conversation with her in the back of their Fiat a month later, when she told me to open my eyes.

"*My* eyes, though," Gustavo said, pinching the sheet around her collarbone and pulling it slowly down to her belly button. "You have no idea how open they are."

She started laughing again. "Not the point either, Gusti."

"Since when do you care so much what the point of anything is?" he said, taking in the rest of her body, drinking in the sight as if there were no more relevant point than that. "If we have a boy, should we name him Juan like everyone else?"

"Shit, Gusti. This isn't about Perón for us."

"Fine, what's it about?"

"Something bigger, no? Perón can go to hell. Besides, I think if we have a boy, he should be Guido. That way I can have my Gusti, my Guti, and my Guido. Sounds nice, no?"

"Sounds like a boludez," Gustavo said affectionately. "Sometimes, Isa, I do wonder about all that happiness of yours here. Is it me, the cause, or just the bullets in your hair?"

"What'll make me really happy is when the bullets are in *someone else's* hair," she said, rolling toward him and holding her fist over his lap. It opened, and gold bullet casings dropped onto him like rain.

"I've created a monster," he said.

"No," Isabel said, bending to kiss him. "You've set one free."

I looked away again. Turned entirely, to stare at the fence I was pressed against, the dull metal lattice with twigs and ivy leaves poking through.

At the neighbor's house beyond the bramble, the linden tree that jutted out from the garden. I was thankful not to be able to smell it from here.

Less carefully than I should have, I stepped past the window and curled back around the house. As I made my way down the driveway this time, the landlady's farce of a watchdog did bark—a violent, toothy yap— but I didn't care. I got into the car and, after several minutes with my elbows propped up on the wheel and my head in my wet hands, I put the key in the ignition.

———

THERE WAS HEAVY TRAFFIC on the way back, and since I also had to find parking, it was almost two hours before I made it to my pensión. On entering, I called the man at the locutorio. Told him it was Pingüino and asked if I had any messages.

I did. Señora Amarga had called to say she heard the auto-repair shop was closing and she wondered if there were plans to open another location. Also, there was going to be an asado Tuesday night, and if I needed a ride, she could give me one. Just let her know.

"Well," the locutorio man said in his perfunctory way afterward. "Want me to let her know?" And when I still didn't answer, "Well? Señor Pingüino?"

"No," I said, then corrected myself. "Yes. Tell her I got another car. I don't need a ride."

I could almost hear him shrug as he hung up, leaving the drone of the dial tone in my ear. I went upstairs, indulged in my ritual of obliterating intoxication, and lay on my bed in my clothes until I fell asleep.

TWENTY-ONE

On Monday I woke early. I hadn't pulled down the blinds, and though my window was porthole-sized and faced another building, which shut out most of the sunlight, it was still bright enough to feel sharp and painful against my eyelids.

I sat up. Shifted so my feet were on the floor. Then got to my knees and pulled out my suitcase. I'd started using it to keep my savings—torture was unsurprisingly a cash business—and with the inflation, they took up space. I counted about thirty thousand pesos. A year or two ago, that would have amounted to six thousand dollars, more than enough for an international flight. Now it was worth less than twenty.

I went downstairs. After waiting for the phone to be freed up, I dialed the Colonel.

"Is he there?" I asked, as soon as Mercedes picked up.

"He's at work, Tomás. The man does work, believe it or not. Is something wrong?"

I tried to picture her: that neat bun of silver-streaked hair, her expert application of eyeliner. Nothing ever seemed to be wrong with Mercedes.

"Can you tell him to call me? I'd just—I'd like to see him," I floundered. "I haven't in a while."

"We had you over for dinner just last month."

It felt like ages ago.

I heard something in the background—long and strident, like a baby's cry. "Sorry, Tomás, I have some people over. Having . . . breakfast," she said, in a last-minute way, as if she'd just remembered the name of the meal.

"That's okay. I have to go anyway," I said. "Thanks for giving him the message, Mercedes." I waited a minute after hanging up in case she called back out of concern. But she never did.

———

I RETURNED TO MY ROOM. To my unmade bed. I hadn't put my suitcase away or even closed it—the cash spread along its bottom would have been glaringly visible to anyone coming in—and I kicked it carelessly back into its hiding place.

Aníbal had said not to come to work until Tuesday, but I decided to go in anyway. I figured I'd look more innocent if I showed up to help—in fact, I should have gone in early, or the day before. Besides, I had nowhere else to go and, I reasoned contradictorily, it was probably too late to save myself anyway.

On the train platform, I found myself pacing; it was the first time I'd ever wanted the commute to go faster. But after I got on, I was hit with a variation of the usual terror. The dingy backsides of buildings, the sweep of greenery flying past in that unstoppable way. The prospect of visiting the scene of my crime, so to speak—it felt like diving straight into a monster's hungry mouth.

When we reached the first stop and the train doors sprang open, I told myself to get off. But the pole felt liquid and cool in my hand, weirdly sedating. Like I imagined a syringe full of sodium pentothal would feel.

The doors opened and closed at Flores, and again I just stood there. Only when the train reached Floresta was I able to move. The idea that I was walking into their arms hadn't left me. But I walked the four blocks to Automotores nonetheless.

THERE WAS NO SIGN of anything unusual outside. The guard in the booth—a regular in the rotation, though his wariness was new—accepted my mumbled "sesame" without comment. I took the half-wood, half-marble staircase upstairs, spotting a nick in one of the steps from where Ramírez must have shot and missed.

Halfway up, I started to hear the bustle—crinkling garbage bags, what sounded like a frantically buzzing shredder. It was coming from Aníbal's office, but the door was closed, and I continued into the kitchen. The drawers and cupboards were all thrown open and plundered-looking.

More startling: the cells were unoccupied. Even the common one was vacant, revealing stained, muddy-brown sections of floor. I remembered Isabel's message for me at the locutorio: she had heard the "auto-repair shop" was shutting down.

In the torture room, I found the Gringo, kneeling in the corner with his ass crack showing under his strained Hawaiian button-down. "Mierda, carajo," he was muttering as he struggled with the picana's electrical cord, evidently trying to work it free from the socket. "La puta que lo . . ."

"Carlitos," I called.

He spun around. Grinned his childlike grin and stood. "Verde!" he shouted happily, brushing his knees off. "I'll just leave the thing jammed. Who cares, right? It's not like these things are actual fucking cattle prods anyway, no one would wonder what it's doing in a garage instead of on a farm." He paused and furrowed his bushy eyebrows. "Say, Verde, didn't you have the day off? What are you doing here?"

"What are *you* doing?" I asked him.

"Cleaning up. Aw, what is it, Verde?" he said, as if to a downcast child. "Feeling left out?"

I glanced around the room. The radio remained, along with the picana and the wire mesh table. But the defibrillator and the rest of my supplies were gone.

"The center's closing?" I asked.

"Gang's breaking up too, at least for a bit, till we get settled. Club Atlético for me. Not sure what's happening to you non-army types..." He trailed off awkwardly.

"Is Aníbal here? Rubio?"

The Gringo shook his head. "Just me and the SIDE folks. Don't get the impression they're too thrilled about the situation."

He gestured over my shoulder, and I saw one of them peering from the far end of the hall, his features indistinct despite the light from the terrace. He stared a moment longer, then withdrew.

"Do you need help?" I asked the Gringo.

"No. Thanks, Verde," he said kindly. "We got it. Mostly throwing shit away, not your kind of thing. Doesn't actually get cleaned up, you know?"

I considered the random, missed items I'd seen strewn about the hallway: cigarette butts, towels, pencils, a syringe. No documents or blindfolds or anything else that could directly give away what went on here, and I felt momentarily reassured by the Gringo's explanation. But then I remembered that no one had asked me to help.

"Don't worry," he told me. "I'm sure somebody will be in touch with you soon."

I nodded. I felt sure of that also.

———

IT WAS THE SAME QUESTION WHEN I LEFT: what to do. Same pendulum too, from panic to indifference, desperate certainty to complete bewilderment. Though the arcs were less definite than that, really, more that of a string, or a yellowed, wavering blade of grass.

I took the train to my stop and continued toward the university. It occurred to me I had an organic chemistry class that afternoon. I hadn't attended classes in weeks, but the droning of a lecture appealed to me at that juncture, as did the complicated molecular formulas that used to put me to sleep. On arriving, though, I found the classroom closed—finals, a reality I'd forgotten after lying to my mother. Since there was nothing else for me to do there, I grabbed some empanadas and headed back like a yo-yo to my pensión.

On my way upstairs, I passed Beatriz, who told me, "Someone came by looking for you an hour ago. Rodrigo?"

"Rodrigo?" I repeated. It rang no bells. "Not Felipe? Or Gustavo?"

She shrugged. "Maybe it was Gustavo."

Could Isabel really have been alarmed enough by my message the night before to send Gustavo?

"He just came and left?" I asked.

She shrugged again. "Said he'd be back."

I took my food to my room and ate on the bed with the door closed, remembering meals I'd made at Automotores, almost missing those duties. At least I'd known how I was supposed to fill the time then.

No word from the Colonel. Only, possibly, from Gustavo. I could check at the locutorio to see if Isabel had left another message, but the truth was,

I didn't want to know. I didn't want to talk to Gustavo either. I didn't ask myself why, merely thought again: Let me go.

Throwing away the last of my empanadas, I went back out to take another walk.

—

THE CITY WAS QUIET, almost like a Sunday, with everyone at family dinners or recovering from the weekend. Few people were about, even in the usually busy downtown areas. Buenos Aires never had a real curfew during the dictatorship, but that night it felt like it did.

My mind was quiet too. Empty, but largely impenetrable: neither the pair of nuns in angelic flowing white habits nor the old man chasing the teenager who'd stolen his wallet made much of an impression. I batted away any reflection I didn't wish to have: Why didn't I get back to Isabel? Give them my warning? Was I really safer from kidnapping in the streets than at home? Instead, I wound up in much narrower lanes of rumination: the ballooning exchange rate and its accompanying, tedious calculations; whom I could talk to about going abroad (Beatriz was Colombian, remember?); how I'd deal with my course credits (I'd have to take this year over again, maybe previous ones too, if I went to a country with different medical requirements). The most substantial question I tackled—fleetingly, without answer—was how, even if I could afford a plane ticket, I could possibly afford life wherever it took me.

The wind on wide avenues, the coppery glow of the streetlights—they made me feel small and alone, removed from everything. Like the center of the world was elsewhere. I remembered Isabel, returning to Pinamar after one of her summers in New York, explaining what was so magical about that city: "The feeling that you're right in the middle of everything, Tomás. Things matter there. Whereas Argentina—it really is the third world for everybody else. Some lost corner. No stakes. No one cares what happens here. None of it matters."

If only it didn't, I found myself musing. If only there were no stakes. It would have been better for us all if we hadn't needed there to be.

———

IT GREW LATE. I wasn't wearing a watch, but it must have been past midnight when I returned to my block. A sinewy-looking man was standing outside my pensión, smoking a cigarette. I made little of it at first—between visitors and the residents themselves, there were often people lingering outside. Then the traffic light on the corner switched from red to green, and as the white headlights rushed nearer, I saw the gilded shimmer of his hair.

"Verde," he called.

I was too close to turn back or cross the street—I worried I'd look too guilty if I did—so I simply stopped where I was.

"Rubio?" I said, and only then remembered: "*Your* name's Rodr—"

"And your name is Tomás Orilla, temporary residence the Gran Atlántico pensión, permanent residence 334 Calle 54, La Plata. That's the truth, isn't it?"

He stepped closer, so close I had to rotate out of his way toward the wall. In the light from a window overhead I could see the flush of his fair cheeks and the sweat that, for once, had mussed his gelled hair. Also the handgun in its holster at his waist. At Automotores, he'd had little need to wear it.

"What are you doing here, Rubio?"

"What are you doing, Verde? It's a school night, isn't it? Don't you have classes tomorrow?"

"Finals," I said like an idiot. "Rubio, I—"

"The truth, Verde, that's all I want. How'd he get the gun, for instance? Pereyra, how'd he get the gun?"

"I don't know. The American girl must have—"

"Found the merchandise closet? In her endless bravery thought she could take the time to find an isolation cell and a fucking ERP guerrilla and give him a rifle?"

I told myself not to panic. My own gun was in my belt, under my shirt—I hadn't left the pensión without it since the escape. I'd fired only the one shot, so there must be more bullets in the cylinder. Mustn't there?

"Well?" he said, breathing hard. He gave my shoulder a shove, and I felt my back press against the coarse bricks behind me.

"You're drunk, Rubio."

"I am drunk. Drunk enough to do something stupid." He removed his gun, and whatever courage I required to reach for my own died, frozen in my hand. "Like you did, no?" He aimed the thing haphazardly in my direction, using it to gesticulate. Cars whooshed past without halting, and what few passersby there were averted their eyes like this was just an ugly everyday occurrence. "You said you were so drunk tying up that American girl. Didn't you say that was how it happened, you were so drunk . . . ?"

Don't panic. Look at him: the perspiration, the heavy breathing, the drunkenness and wildness of his motions with that gun. You know what this is—you recognize it, even in Rubio. You feel it every day.

"You're alone," I said.

"You think I need anybody else to make you sing, Verde? You think I need a picana? You'd piss yourself even without it. You're pissing yourself now."

"If you were here to pick me up, you'd have other people with you," I continued, thinking rapidly, trusting my instincts blindly the way I had with Aníbal, and the Colonel before him. "They're looking at you too, aren't they, Rubio?"

He didn't answer at first. Then whatever pleasure he was getting out of this chaotic exercise appeared to dissipate. Something equally recognizable, more rooted in Rubio as I knew him, took its place. He glared at me in anger. Hatred.

"The truth, Verde," he said.

"Of course," I persisted, almost giddy at the budding realization, the glorious-feeling irony. "You were there that night. You caught her in the first place."

"Verde, the fucking truth."

"You were in charge and didn't even go after them when they escaped. Make me sing? Put me on a table, I'll sing for Aníbal loud and cl—"

It was so quick, his gun across my face. It felt like a knife, it had that speed and slicing quality, and a spray of blood landed on the sidewalk as my head whipped to the side. Another blow followed from the other direction, and I followed that too, to the pavement, smacking my chin. When I fell, I saw people down the street: a young couple, uncertain what to do or whether to do anything, and a woman walking her dog, a goofily groomed Maltese, who marched past us as if we didn't exist.

Rubio's boot found my belly. Again. The air went out of me, and the lights of the night as my eyes rolled upward beyond my lids.

"The truth, Verde," Rubio said, in an echoey way that made me feel he'd been saying other things prior and I just happened to regain consciousness for this. "You want to live, do us both a favor. I'd be willing to listen."

Something touched my face. It was soft, softer anyway than the sidewalk and Rubio's gun, and got stuck to the blood gushing from my lip. I raised a hand and peeled off what turned out to be a piece of paper. I opened my eyes and saw a marred but legible phone number.

I sat up and looked around after lying there for I don't know how long. Neither the couple nor the woman with her Maltese was anywhere to be seen, and there was no newly formed crowd of onlookers to come to my aid or see how I was. In Argentina, you didn't get involved. You saw, but you didn't *see*.

———

I STUMBLED BACK INTO THE PENSIÓN to much the same reaction from what few housemates were still awake. Only Beatriz said anything different, as I passed her room on the way to mine, catching the sound of jazz and the soothing smell of pot; I could already imagine how, with the help of my whiskey, it would numb my pain.

"Careful, boludo," she said. "The landlady might think you're trouble now."

The landlady. I actually laughed, completing what must have been a horror movie image—a bloody apparition, cracking up like something undead. What struck me as funny was that her warning was entirely reasonable. In this country, a single, well-placed phone call from a frightened landlady could get you killed as easily as a military torturer with a gun on the street. If it wasn't one thing, I thought later, in what felt like a mad epiphany but was really just the reckoning of a scared, stoned college kid, it was always something else.

TWENTY-TWO

Tuesday. Wasn't something supposed to happen Tuesday night? I couldn't remember. I woke up stuck to the pillowcase the way Rubio's paper had stuck to my face. There was blood on the sheets. Though it had dried and I knew there was no way to get it out, I decided to wash them and do the rest of my laundry. Usually that was taken care of as part of our room and board, but I didn't relish the idea of someone in the landlady's employ catching sight of the bloodstains, and it was as close as I could get to the consolation of cleaning, besides.

Clearly that was the more important factor, since I ended up doing the wash in the bathroom sink. There was no clothesline at the pensión, so afterward I stuffed some of the items back inside the drawers wet and spread others across the floor, the mattress, and my dresser. Clearing space, I looked at Rubio's bloodied paper again. Small and yellow, the ripped-off corner of a notepad. Nothing but a standard Buenos Aires number.

What was he offering? Hard to believe it was a way out. But if he felt frightened enough, endangered enough? He couldn't kill me; he needed me to affirm that I was guilty and he was innocent. And maybe he knew enough about the false confessions you got using torture to need a different kind of confession from me.

No. Of course not, that couldn't be it; I was reaching. The rest of the crew were likely simply taking their time, deciding how to navigate the politics of harboring two possible traitors, including one with ties to Colonel Felipe Gorlero. There was still only one way out Rubio could offer me.

But I folded the stained paper the best I could and put it in my pocket regardless.

———

NOT LONG AFTER, a knock on my door informed me I had a phone call. I had an urge to stay where I was, pretend I was asleep. But I'd unsuccessfully tried the Colonel again earlier, and with my room still a mess I wasn't going to be able to lie on my bed anyway, so I went downstairs and picked up.

It was Pichuca. I hadn't heard from her since we'd gone to Villa Ballester.

"I heard you were invited to an asado tonight," she said, with a hint of rebuke.

"Busy," I told her.

"I thought you didn't need a ride."

"It's all a bullshit code, Pichu, what difference does it make?"

She was quiet. I thought about that make-believe asado. Was that why I woke up thinking something was supposed to happen tonight?

"The code doesn't make any difference," Pichuca said at length. "But going, Tomás—going could make a difference."

It felt like more code she was speaking in, and something seemed off about it, false. Her voice struck a similar note—it sounded raspier and farther away than it should have, as if she were calling me long-distance.

"What are you talking about, Pichu?"

"You know what I'm talking about, Tomás. The Colonel explained it to me."

"The Colonel?"

"While I was sick. At Hospital Alemán."

That switch toggled on. The dreamlike mistiness temporarily cleared. Recollections lurched back to me, as if from across an infinitely wide divide: her shriveled form in the hospital bed, the muted tones of the mourners. Her granddaughter telling me I'd get a do-over.

"The Colonel told you to call me?"

"He told me he could give you a second chance—give us all a second chance. I didn't believe him at first. But he was convincing. You know how he could be convincing."

I felt no need to say I did.

"You're not the only one with regrets," she continued. "You don't know how many regrets I have. If I'd been a better mother, if I'd kept a closer eye, if I'd sent my daughters to live with their father in New York . . . We all made mistakes, Tomás. Why it's come down to yours, I don't know. I don't know why things ever come down to any one person's choices."

Maybe they don't, I considered saying. Maybe it doesn't come down to anything, and we just tell ourselves it does for the pain, so we don't have to feel so small and powerless. It sounded logical, the kind of argument the Colonel might have approved of. But I could also imagine the rejoinder: Maybe we tell ourselves we're small and powerless so we don't have to feel the pain.

"What do you want me to do, Pichu?" I asked.

"You know what I want you to do, Tomás," she said.

We were quiet a minute, and though there was no disconnecting click or dial tone, eventually I realized the line was dead. Someone had been waiting for the phone, and he gave me a critical look as I hung up—slowly, with the quickly fading, soon-vanished thought that once more I'd failed to tell her good-bye.

———

I WENT OUTSIDE. No blood or other mark was discernible on the pavement where Rubio had attacked me, and people walked past as uninterestedly as the night before, without noticing my swollen lip or scraped chin. Typical porteños, with their red wine and meat and hedonism—they were chatty and smiling, enjoying the warm weather, the approaching holiday. You could already feel them counting down to it—the close of the year, the unpleasant but forgettable chapter that was 1976. I felt it too, if in a different, much less apathetic way: the nearly closed circle, the looming, abstract sense of the end.

I reached into my pocket, pulled out Rubio's paper. Looked at the number again and then uncurled my fingers. Let the breeze pick it up from my palm and take it scurrying and jumping into the air and far down the street.

I didn't expressly know what I meant to do when I went to the car. But I laid out my mother's map of Buenos Aires on the passenger seat as if I did, as if nothing in the world could be clearer than my destination.

———

WHEN I RETURNED TO VILLA BALLESTER late that afternoon, the neighbor's dog was missing, but the Fiat was in the driveway. The sight of it made me angry. All those overnights I'd spent in the torture room at Automotores, and they spent their days fucking with the shutters open.

I approached the door. Knocked quietly, and then more loudly when no one answered. Still nothing, and I had an urge to retreat a second time. What was I going to do, after all? Barge in and say, "You need to flee before they make me sing"? Isabel would probably just hand me a gun and tell me to make sure I didn't sing that way.

I heard a murmur of movement from the window off the living room and knocked again.

No, Isabel wouldn't be so cruel or simplistic. It was something else I feared, the admission I'd be making telling them this, the acknowledgment of what I could be capable of. The truth, in other words. Little was scarier than that.

Still no response. I tried the knob. Inexplicably, it turned. I pushed the door open slowly, and it creaked.

Gustavo was at the stove frying milanesas, Isabel reading a magazine at the table. Neither of them turned in my direction.

"Gustavo?" I called, uncomprehending. "Isabel?"

They continued going about their business while the cutlets sizzled in the pan.

Then the shudder of realization: the hand to my cheek, the recollection of what had actually happened on my sole return visit that week in '76. It was on the Tuesday, and I didn't even set foot on the driveway but darted off at the collie's accusatory siren, as if the dog was a wily servant of fate.

What was it the Priest had said? Things would be messier this time around, more customized for my edification? Perhaps the two of them weren't oblivious; perhaps I was. Standing like Tantalus in a pool whose waters retreated when I tried to touch them, able to use the glassy surface of their lives only as a mirror or not at all.

Gustavo had been putting out items for what must have been a late lunch—bottle of wine, jar of mayonnaise, freshly sliced lemon—when suddenly he stopped.

"Isa," he said.

"Mm-hmm?" She flipped the page—a *Rico Tipo*, the humor magazine that had gone out of circulation some years earlier.

"ERP is done. Montoneros—even you have to admit we're not far behind. Nerea's been gone a month, we haven't heard back from Tomás. I think it's time we talk about leaving."

"Leaving?" Isabel repeated, as if the word were puzzling to her.

"We could go to Cuba. I still have friends there."

"Cuba? Why would we go to Cuba?"

"Why? What do you mean, why? To live there, Isa."

She rested her magazine on the table. "Like you said, Nerea's been gone a month. Clearly she's not giving us up."

"That's not the point, Isa."

"And Tomás is stronger than you think. He's probably just upset with me."

"Not the point."

"You're scared," she said.

"Of course I'm scared," Gustavo said.

"I'm not. Not of death. You're not supposed to be either."

"If the milicos come banging on our door, I won't be. I'd give you that grenade and let you take us all to hell."

They both laughed. Gamely Isabel said, "You won't need to give it to me, Gusti. I'll have it ready."

And then, out of some attuned intimacy or a shift of the atmosphere in the narrow space between them, they both stopped smiling.

"I'm serious, Isa," Gustavo said.

"So am I," she said.

"We could have a good life."

"Do you know how many people in this country have probably told themselves that to avoid fighting?"

"To avoid dying," Gustavo said.

"You can go, Gusti. I won't stop you."

"But you won't join me either?"

"Not in Cuba," she said.

They were silent another minute. There was an explosive pop of grease on the stove, and for some reason that was enough: the tenderness returned, the smiles. All that emotion I was stuck on the other side of.

"How about the bedroom then?" Gustavo said.

Isabel nodded. "Sounds like heaven to me."

She took his hand and led him in without closing the door.

The breaded chicken continued crackling, throwing off bursts of fat. I went over to the stove and turned it off.

From there I had a clear view of the bedroom. But where I expected to see their writhing, ravenous bodies, I saw nothing. Only the shadeless lamp on the floor, the mattress next to it with the sheets tossed messily aside. No bullet casings or other signs they'd been there recently.

"I don't know if it's a happy memory or sad," I heard behind me. The voice was dry and croaky, and before I could place it, I turned and saw whose it was. He'd grown a beard, but it was as graying and splotchy as his sickly, pale skin.

"Happy," I told Gustavo's ghost.

His hips were misaligned, as if he'd continued limping through the underworld. I recalled the Colonel saying that people died as differently as they lived, and wondered if the line between heaven and hell was as thin as that—if everyone came to this place in the end, and everyone simply had different stays.

"I'm not sure," Gustavo said.

"Is Isa here somewhere?" I asked.

"Depends what you mean by 'here.' If you mean in this house, in this room, no. We're never in the same rooms anymore."

"Why not? Falling-out?" I jabbed.

"This place doesn't let us," Gustavo said. "Sometimes I think we could be centimeters apart, even literally on top of each other, and it would still find a way to keep us separate. Invisible to each other. When it comes to love, only the living seem to be within each other's reach. What we get are lies."

"At least you have these memories," I said.

"Memories are dead things," Gustavo said. "You see that here. Maybe that's all you see."

What I'd just seen was vibrantly, terribly alive. Yet here I was unable to do anything grander than turn off a stove. A static feeling had crept into the room, a musty, mothball-like quality, as if the windows hadn't been opened for years. The milanesas didn't give off any scent, and neither did anything else.

"What happened to the linden tree your house had?"

"This isn't our house," Gustavo said. "I told you what this is."

I didn't know if he meant a dead thing or a lie. Maybe they were the same to him.

"So there's nothing to be done then?"

"Done?" he repeated, in the same perplexed way Isabel had said, "Leaving?"

"I thought I could save you," I said. "Tell you to get out—"

"Didn't you hear our conversation? For Isa, there was no getting out."

It should have been obvious. Perhaps on some level it always was. Isabel would never have fled Argentina; there was no saving her that way. There was only one way I could have saved her, only one choice I could have made differently. And that, I realized quietly, with no flash or bang of epiphany, was what my so-called do-over would be limited to: the one proverbial coin I'd ever truly wished I could toss back into the air.

"It didn't have to end that way," I told Gustavo.

"Maybe not that way," Gustavo admitted. "But it would have ended."

I considered telling him I was sorry. I don't know why I didn't; maybe I simply wasn't. Whatever the reason, I didn't say anything when I left, and neither did Gustavo.

———

WHEN I GOT BACK TO MY PENSIÓN, I put the rest of my still-damp clothes away. After I made my bed and everything was as pristine as it was going to be, I went to my dresser. I removed the revolver from my belt and looked at it. So many pointless journeys back and forth—La Plata, Villa Ballester, even my organic chemistry classroom; it was like I wanted to give it a rest, or a proxy for giving myself some. I put it in my underwear drawer and closed it, thinking, I won't need this anymore.

Then I went out for another of my walks.

Rush hour, people going for after-work drinks, students with backpacks headed to libraries or basement hangouts or who knew what other normal things. The air was sweet and golden, rich like honey.

On the tail end of my wandering, I went to nearby Plaza Primero de Mayo, where there was a little pasture used as a dog run. Typically when I visited I stood some meters away and watched as the dogs sniffed one another or ran after tennis balls, their simple happiness a sweet kind of envy for me. This time, though, I went up to the edge of the green and held out my hands, and the kind creatures licked them as if they knew I needed it.

When I returned to my pensión, the green Ford Falcon was waiting for me outside. My palms were moist in my pockets, and I didn't know if it was from sweat or the saliva of the dogs. A man in the passenger seat I didn't recognize—well-groomed goatee, extremely calm, even friendly green eyes—asked me if I was Tomás Orilla. I said I was, and the car's back door opened. I got in voluntarily. A balled-up sock was tossed back, then the blindfold and hood. I put them on myself.

TWENTY-THREE

There were scarcely any sensations to attach to the drive. Dark, imageless, textureless—that may be why memories of it would hide from my nightmares. The men who picked me up were quiet the whole way, keeping the windows closed and the radio off, not speaking even to one another. The machine gun lying across my seatmate's lap and pressed into my side hardly moved, and neither did the hand he'd placed on my head to keep it down. Aside from the itchiness of the hood, the taste of the gag, and the damp, warm smell of my breath on it, I felt almost nothing.

The car slowed to a stop, and I heard the grating of a garage door opening. Breathed the unmistakable odor of motor oil. The hand came off my head and the machine gun prodded me to get out. "Guess you'll be the Garden's last act," one of the men said, before another told him to shut up. Their voices were low and muffled, and I couldn't identify them.

I didn't know if it was the same men or others who led me up the stairs. My assumption was that they'd pass the baton to those who'd want it more—Aníbal, maybe the Gringo, Rubio certainly. Whoever they were, they didn't say a word to me either. Directions were given to me again with the nudge of a gun—up under my arm to tell me to rise, down along my waist to undress, jabbed in the back to march forward. Whenever I didn't understand, a boot or the weapon's butt made the order clear. Their silence felt excessive to me, like a betrayal I didn't deserve. My jailers were presumably people I knew already, so why wouldn't they let me see them? Hear them at least? Why was it so important that I feel alone?

Straight down the hall from the cell where I'd stripped. The gun kept directing me toward the torture room, as if I needed the guidance; I could have made it there like Gordo, by counting my steps.

Someone strapped me onto the table. Removed my gag and threw cold water on me. Some of the wires had coiled and snapped after so much use, and a few stabbed into me—one at the top of my spine, another on the edge of my left butt cheek. The worst reopened a blister on my foot that had just begun to heal.

They didn't turn on the radio. Every expectation I had, every bit of knowledge I'd gained of this process, they upended. Whereas everyone else was made to sing, to say names, my punishment was silence, anonymity. I told myself that maybe they couldn't stand doing it to someone they knew, had trusted. Maybe it was the Gringo hovering there, his conscience quivering like his belly, his shame so great he couldn't say it was him. "Sorry, Verde," I kept waiting for someone to tell me. No one did.

No one applied the picana for a while either, and the delay was strangely terrible. The dread, the endless mental priming, reminding myself over and over again that all I'd have to do was keep quiet. Let them take everything from me but that.

But they never asked me a thing. And as the minutes dragged on, my quiet felt less like a safe haven than like another instrument they'd turned against me. *Verde thinks he knows how to endure this,* I imagined them telling one another as they planned this; *he thinks he can hang on to something. He'll wish we wanted him to sing.*

The unwrapping of a cord, the methodical adjustment of the rheostat. I could hear each individual click of the knob and did the math: 14,000 volts was what they settled on.

The low, droning thrum of the picana gliding ever nearer.

The experience goes staticky then. Not in terms of sound but . . . everything else. The chaotic, inconsistent bursts of pain; the rough, scratchy swerving in and out of consciousness. The flailing of my limbs, the nerve-deep burning of my skin and my organs, like a wildfire inside me.

And the screams. All my incoherent, unfettered screams.

———

CAPUCHITA. At first it seemed like a relief, to find myself in that fuller, blacker darkness of the isolation cell, under the blindfold and hood. At the end of pain, of terror. I could tell myself it was peaceful, in some pure way. Nothing to be done, nothing to worry about. Just plain nothing.

But then that steady trickle. Like nothingness was a hole through which I seeped. I couldn't tell whether my eyes were open or closed or where my body parts were in relation to one another. My thoughts felt like they were scattering, roaming free of my mind. This isn't the end, they taunted me, like schoolyard bullies. This is the beginning. Soon they'll take you back to the torture room. And soon, maybe not the next session or the one after, but soon, they'll start asking you things. And there are things you know.

I tried not to consider it any more precisely than that, to push away the concept of knowledge altogether. Or maybe capuchita did, throwing open doors in my brain, letting drafts blow through to buffet the rickety foundation at my core.

You thought you knew what this would be like? You never got close to it, not really. Even when you were in the room, working the defibrillator or the straps or whatever else, you were listening to the cries from outside.

And the silence afterward—you've never heard it before now either. You don't yet know how loud it will grow.

———

THE SLOWNESS. The way time spreads out, giving every conclusion space to shift direction or be forgotten, become one more drop in the deepening puddle.

I was sitting in one by then. The stench was putrid, but I got used to it, and other sensations took precedence—the taste of my spittle, the sluggish, clogged rhythm of my breaths. The rustle I made with any movement, however slight—they'd put my clothes back on while I was unconscious—and more distant noises as well: sporadic footsteps in the hall, a fly buzzing somewhere, a leak in a pipe in the wall, trickling with perfect precision. How could everything be so clear, I thought, when simultaneously I couldn't see anything?

I had no handle on time. Night, day, the accumulation of either. It remained slow but unhinged, as if counted by a clock without hands.

Sleeping or waking—that difference was also blurry—I continued to lean against my wall. That was how I'd come to think of it, as mine. Like this nerdy kid we had at Automotores from the Institute of Technology who wouldn't let go of a knocked-out tooth of his until the Gringo pried it from his fingers by stepping on his hand. Spend enough time with nothing, and you take possession of whatever you can.

That technology student with the tooth—he lasted a month before they transferred him. Gordo, nearly half a year. Meanwhile, I felt barely able to endure what had probably been a mere few days. I kept returning to the fact that Automotores was supposed to have been cleaned out, that I shouldn't be there at all.

"You are no one," I'd heard the Priest tell prisoners more than once during a session. "You don't exist anymore." The first few times my torturers took a break while I was on the table, I'd hoped the session was over. I came to know better. But among the many thoughts that kept repeating as time dribbled onward, constantly cycled back to me as if on a recorded loop, were those words of the Priest's. Remembering them, my hopes for the end broadened, became all-encompassing. What a blessing that would be, I thought. To be no one.

———

ANOTHER THOUGHT ON THAT LOOP: Those things I knew. They continued to blend with and take the form of things I didn't know. Hardened faiths frayed, assumptions about myself became anchorless, untethered. Was I a good person? Did I even care about morality? What difference does one person make, their love or their death? None of it matters. None of it is worth holding on to.

Easier to look at it that way, more palatable. Philosophical, abstract doubts rather than particular certainties. Nothing to do with my circumstances or the actions I might take to deal with them.

I never looked at those *things* directly. Never mentally pronounced the street or the number or went far beyond articulating the names associated with it: Gustavo Morales. Isabel Aroztegui. Like they were merely entries on a list.

And why shouldn't they be, I asked myself. Again: What does love matter? What does death?

———

SCATTERSHOT IMAGES AND MEMORIES. Elizabeth in her isolation cell, maybe this same one, telling me she missed the hole in the corner. Soapsuds pooling on the torture room floor after Rubio knocked the bucket over. My mother's forcing me to clean after my father died, insisting that the skill would come in handy one day. My photo on my Club Atenas ID, the spot of gloss on my youthfully parted hair. Joking with Isabel about Pichuca's chicken-and-onion soup and its lack of chicken. Isabel's soft knock on the door a couple summers later and her demands that I hold her closer when I was already holding her as close as I could. My tiny twin bed, and her hushed whisper: *You're dreaming, Tomás. Keep dreaming.*

—

FOR THE FIRST TIME since I was in detention: the radio. A soccer game—River against Boca. Whoever was on guard probably couldn't resist.

The game must have been close, dramatic. There was such energy among the broadcasters, in the roaring of the crowd. It all sounded so important—so much more important than this.

Then, a goal. It went off like a series of explosions.

GOAL! GOAL! GOOOOOOOOAL!

Like a trumpet, a herald.

GOOOOOOOOOOOOOOOOOOOOOOAL!

A declaration of the end.

GOOOOOOOOOOOOOOOOOOOOOAL! GOOOOOO—

The radio snapped off.

Footsteps thudded outside.

Everything—my questions and back-and-forths, my unraveled threads of reason—it all vanished. Nothing was left but the fear, the animal drive for survival.

Please, I tried to call, but was stifled by the gag. *Please just ask me . . .*

The click of the lock. The heavy swing of the door.

Ask me something! Please! Ask me anything!

Hands. On my head, my hood. They tugged.

Please! Please just let me go . . .

The hood came off. Light threaded through, faint and diaphanous, tinting the blackness charcoal. Next, those strong, sure hands pulled my blindfold down, so it sat like a neck scarf on my collarbone. Pulled the spit-soaked sock from my cottony mouth.

The figure—he was nothing more to me yet—leaned back. Squatted, it looked like, then changed position to kneel. He waited. Silently, I don't know how long, until I'd stopped crying.

———

AS MY VISION ADJUSTED, I began to piece together his outline: lean, line-like arms, eyes that seemed weirdly round and huge until I realized they must be glasses.

"Can you see me?" he asked. Feebly, I shook my head. "What about my voice? Do you know it? Someone told me once it sounded sad, but I think that was because of my name."

My mind acclimated as well. To the setting, the circumstances, the slow, staccato rhythm of his words, the flatness of one in particular.

"Triste?"

"You had a sad voice yourself, Verde," he said. "In hindsight, I wonder if the only reason people didn't pick up on what you were was because you had me as a foil."

The cell felt stagnant despite his presence, almost airless.

"Who was it who told you that about your voice?" I asked.

"The Colonel," Triste said. "Told me my face was too—a sad, moral face. Straight, stiff features. I told him it was just a face."

"Were you close to the Colonel?"

"You know I wasn't close with anyone, Verde."

"You used to talk to the prisoners," I reminded him.

"True," Triste acknowledged. "That much hasn't changed, I guess."

A pause. The darkness continued gaining texture, as if the amber light from the crack under the door were crawling upward, searching out shapes to curl around. A hinge, a corner. The hood still hanging from Triste's hand like a shadow.

"Is that what this is? A visit like your old ones to Gordo?"

"Most of us, we just find ourselves places," Triste said. "Same as life. At a certain point, you know your orders without getting them."

"And what happened to your life?"

"Drunk-driving accident in '81."

"I don't remember you being much of a drinker."

"Yes, well. Wasn't much of an accident either. Rarely is for our type, isn't it?"

I still couldn't make out his face, only the black circles of his glasses. Yet I felt certain he could see me clearly.

"You regret it?" I asked.

"I regret other things more. Not that I ever felt I had much choice about any of it. I don't think any of us do much."

"We're all just victims of circumstance in your view, aren't we?" I said, remembering my own conversation with Gordo in his cell.

"Maybe not all of us," Triste said. "I don't know, Verde. Everybody's always telling everybody else it's up to them. It's not, though, not the way they mean it. Take your own case. You probably think they got you because of that escape, right? No. It was this pregnant girl they had at Coordinación, something Aroztegui. Held on for a few weeks, then she had her baby. She wanted to get it back, so she gave your name. She didn't get the baby back."

I thought of the goofy star-crossed hopes I'd had around Nerea as a twelve-year-old, before I met Isabel. That our fates were entwined like this instead, that I might have had so little to do with my own—it seemed so unjust. Yes, I was used to feeling like a bystander to my own life—that was part of what had driven me to Isabel, the sense that life was elsewhere, somewhere she could take me. But I'd always believed that I came to this particular fork on my own.

"Who got the baby?" I asked.

"Depended on the center. Knowing Coordinación, probably a dumpster."

I thought of the girl at Hospital Alemán, her dark hair and big brown eyes nothing like Isabel's or Nerea's. "The grandmother didn't get her?"

"Pichuca Aroztegui? I gave her another one—why I remember the name," Triste explained. "There were plenty of babies to go around back then. Not at Automotores, nobody lasted long enough there. But at the ESMA, Campo de Mayo? The Colonel had taken this one home a couple weeks before, to save it from the dumpster, or maybe just because he wanted to, I don't know. He didn't look good when he brought her in—sleep-deprived, bad scratch on his face from their cat. Gave the girl to me in this big crib with ribbons on it and told me where to take her. Said it wouldn't make a difference to those desperate enough."

More recollections. The young girl in the beach parking lot with the might-have-been Colonel, the end of his marriage and his answer to my question about miscarriage—*I'm more inclined to say I did*—the many dead ends in the maze of possibility. My failed attempts to reach him in the days before I was taken, and that cry, like a baby's, the one time Mercedes had picked up.

They didn't own a cat, and I knew without thinking that Mercedes's fingernails were always long and manicured.

"Why'd he give her up?"

"I don't think he wanted to. But we got the call about you, Verde. Aníbal saying they'd picked you up, laying out terms for the Colonel to save you. He probably felt scared, or maybe guilty, I don't know. Aníbal had him by the balls then, me too. His phrase obviously: 'I got you by the fucking balls, Tristecito. I'll have you back in my employment soon enough.' You see what I mean, Verde? You get pinned by some girl in Coordinación, the

Colonel's life and mine turn to shit, and this baby winds up with a random new family. None of that was up to us, not the way we thought. Maybe we get choices, but what good are they when they're like that?"

There were so many ways I could have answered. That it wasn't anybody's fault, or that it was everybody's equally, or that we should have known long ago that choices weren't any good. But it seemed those were lessons you never learned, and all I could say was, "I wish I knew how much was up to us."

"Yes, well," Triste said, "I guess you'll find out soon enough, won't you?"

He rose. Stooped closer, with the hood in his hand. I recalled his telling me he wasn't here to visit, that he knew his orders. Triste had been one of the guards in charge of moving transfers at Automotores. Pedros, they'd been called, after Saint Peter; they held the keys to heaven, was the saying.

"It's almost over now," he assured me. "You don't need to be afraid."

Triste placed the dark cloth back over my head. Lifted me by the armpits and led me from the cell. Directed me carefully, gently even, down the creaky wooden stairs and into the garage.

There another set of arms took over. Shoved me into the car. The men remained taciturn, businesslike, as they pressed my head down in the backseat and rested the muzzle of the machine gun against my ear.

As the engine started, I heard the clang of a cell door shutting, as if Triste had locked himself inside one, and I thought of the words he'd left me with. Repeated them to myself like a mantra, a prayer: *It's almost over now. You don't need to be afraid . . .*

TWENTY-FOUR

I didn't weep in the car. Just sat, my head bouncing periodically off my seatmate's knee. Even when a dim light crept through the hood's fabric, it didn't move me. Didn't soothe or bathe my eyes or give me one last, glowing taste of life. It's only light, I thought dully. There's nothing special about it.

We parked. The guard removed my hood. Nodded his shadowy chin toward the window, while the driver got out to open my door. "There's no point trying to run," he said needlessly.

More light. It was so strong I couldn't look into it, and instead I stared at my filthy sneakers until I could make out their different parts—the tongue and laces, the orange, clay-heavy dirt on the toe from the path I was standing on. That bit felt instinctively wrong to me, misplaced. And when I looked back up, and bright, clean grass and passersby and benches started to take shape, I realized the wall of the cemetery was missing. There were trees where it should have been, and under their swaying green leaves was a woman I'd have known anywhere.

Isabel. Waiting in a park for me, as she'd done so many times before.

She didn't turn as I approached, or when I went to her side. All her attention was fixed on a solitary old woman pushing a walker, moving with the sluggish steadiness of someone who made herself take this stroll every day. Her knuckles were knobby and round as her cheeks, and one arthritic finger had swollen over a wedding band that gleamed in the sun. Her hair was white, and there was a scar on her neck that could have been from anything—a stumble, a surgery, any of the hazards that decades of life eventually throw at you. A silver necklace swayed below it, with the mysterious letter *J* dangling at its end, and though her eyes were clouded with cataracts and time, underneath I could still make out the blue.

"She looks at peace, doesn't she?" Isabel said. Her own appearance was as it had been outside Hospital Alemán: thin, dried-out hair and, under the baggy flower-patterned top, a body that matched.

"She does, Isa," I said.

"There are a thousand other sights like this here, showing lives I could have had: journalist like Nerea, politician, regular old engineer. Married mother of two, sometimes three. Sometimes in Argentina, sometimes in Cuba or Mexico, sometimes not even with Gustavo but with a man I never met, whom I never will meet. None of those sights do as much for me as this one, though. She just looks so full, so full of the whole thing."

"She's beautiful," I said.

Isabel laughed. "That might be a stretch."

"It's not. I'd have still been in love with you at that age."

"Tomás . . ."

"Why don't you ever believe me, Isa?"

"It's a fantasy. It's like me with that old woman. I pine because I'll never have to . . . never have to feel the pain of her joints or the fatigue, or watch loved ones die year after year for no reason but time."

"Time's a better reason to die than yours was," I said.

Isabel shook her head. "I don't think so, really."

She took in the figure for another instant, then started off without warning, leaving me to chase after her as always.

"You must have thought so once if you escaped this place," I said.

"It's true, I've wondered," she admitted, and it seemed she was doing so then as she cast her eyes from the ground to the tops of the trees, the shadows of the leaves playing across her face. "This place makes you. If I didn't fight, if I'd survived one of the centers, lived long enough to become that old woman—yes, I've wondered. It's why I returned when my mother was dying, sought you out. I was wondering again."

The aura of peacefulness that persisted through the park seemed out of tune with her sentiment. The gentleness, the breeze and quiet—there seemed to be no room for contingency here, for such doubts. We started up a hill, and as we approached its top, a familiar sight came unhurriedly, torturously into view: the gate of the Recoleta Cemetery.

"I'm sorry, Isa," I told her.

"I am too. But sadly it's not so simple as that for us, is it? I told you that a long time ago, Tomás. Don't you remember?"

I did. Our last conversation while she was alive. *It's a little too simple a concept maybe, being sorry.*

But the memories swirled again, the Colonel's words mixed in like a cocktail or potion, something blended to just the right proportions to— what? Cast a spell on me? Free me from one? *Much too simple a notion, your regret. Do something, don't do something—as if actions could be reduced to such measly forks in the road.*

"I should have listened," I said.

"You did," Isabel answered.

Another swirl, another ingredient. Darkness but for the glow of a small, cheap hotel lamp, trembling hands, one going to the other to keep it steady, sweat on my temple. The muzzle of the Colonel's revolver slipping off it, and words colliding, arguing in different voices, saying: *Being sorry doesn't fix it. Punishing yourself doesn't fix it. You're taking the easy way out.*

"You mean Rome," I said, hoping she would say, *Yes, this whole time it turns out I saved your life.* Or: *Yes, didn't you know I forgave you?* Or: *Yes. I'm the one who's sorry, Tomás. I should never have done that to you. I should never have made you live with this burden.*

She said nothing.

"And now that you've gone back, you're done wondering?" I asked.

"You're never done wondering. Already I'm back to mourning things I never wanted, dreams I never had. It's so hard to remember who you are. Takes so much will."

"You never had a problem with will," I said.

"No," she admitted. "I had enough to get me back to life, even. But that's a case in point: Once I got life back, what could I do with it? What did I ever do with it? It was never enough to me, you remember. Like I used to tell Gusti, when he asked me why I fought in the first place, what made it feel meaningful. It was the bullets in my hair."

She said it with such fondness. The phrase still broke her heart, I could tell.

"You really don't want another chance?" I asked.

Her eyes circled the trees again, the prettily glinting leaves and the sunny sky checkered by branches, lingered uncharacteristically on each one like every infinitesimal bit of the sight was splendid, worthy of its own farewell.

Was that what she was doing, I wondered as her gaze slowly floated back down to meet mine—saying good-bye?

"Like I said, sadly it's just not that simple. You're never done wondering here." She indicated the entryway to the cemetery with her hand, rolling it out like a hostess at a restaurant or hotel. "We all want another chance in the end. Don't you?"

I looked at the cemetery gate. Underneath it, smiling, was the Colonel, as he was that day in December 1976, when the car drove me here and the hood came off.

Now, like then, I went toward him.

———

HE LED THE WAY INSIDE without speaking. Birds were chirping on the mausoleum ledges and palms were swaying over the walls, the sun giving them an unearthly glow. Everything in view maintained that radiance. People passed by the crypts, pointing, murmuring reverently about the beauty of this one or that, the splendor of the city of the dead. Statues of angels and Madonnas gazed down at them austerely. Gargoyles as well. There were more of them among the spires than I'd ever noticed before.

My smell was terrible, but I no longer noticed that either. And if the Colonel did, he gave no indication.

"May I give you some advice, Tomás?" he began. "May I?"

He was silent after the question, as if he really wouldn't continue without my assent. I could hear the soft blows of a hammer somewhere, likely maintenance on one of the tombs.

I nodded.

"The people you are helping—no matter what you do, they will die. This is not a war their side can win. You, on the other hand—you can live. And you can spare the people you are helping from a fate you know well. The moral balance, here, is on the side of giving me an address. Not a name—we have more of those than we know what to do with, unfortunately. Only an address will suffice here."

I had only the one address at my disposal. It rebounded in my head ceaselessly: *Río Negro 2166. Río Negro 2166.* I saw it on the plaques of the crypts and the signs for the cemetery streets. *Río Negro 2166. Río Negro 2166.* If sometimes phrases lost meaning with repetition, this one seemed to gain it, grow bloated with it. Of course it would be named Black River. Of course it would be easy to remember.

"I don't say it lightly or deceptively," the Colonel continued. "I am a cynic, as you know. But the upside is that I have no real stake in this fight. The war against subversion, the battle for a Christian, Western state in Argentina, not even the remote goal of genuine simple stability here summons my allegiance. What is Argentina, after all? It's not special. Not even this moment is special. There have been coups in Latin America going back as far as the nineteenth century—a Tennessean named William Walker got himself named head of state in Nicaragua in 1856, joder! No, Argentina, this moment—it is all just one more drop in the pond of world history.

"What this is about to me is *people*, Tomasito. Precious, simple little people. *You* came to *me* asking to work at the ESMA, remember? Do you think I didn't have some inkling why? I didn't know how bad it would be there, but even so. Better to have you under my eye, I thought, than under someone else's who wouldn't be protecting you. And I *was* protecting you, Tomás. I have always been protecting you. Even now, right now, at this very instant: you know what they will do with you. But if you give me an address, I can save you."

He was my *angel*, a part of me recalled. The breakdown was complete, the dividing line between past and present collapsed like a bridge, leaving nothing but water, the indistinguishability of waves.

"I know these rebels are not so dangerous, really. But I know they put you in danger with that request. I do not take that lightly either."

I didn't take that lightly either, a different part of me thought. One tethered to that moment, to my anger in it, my tremendous sorrow.

I didn't want to be there, that part of me continued. *I should never have been in that fight.*

It's not my fault.

Please! Please just let me go . . .

"You wouldn't have them detained?"

"It will be quick, Tomás," the Colonel said. "I promise it will be quick."

He didn't lie, another, farther-off part of me recalled. *He was my angel.*

"And me?"

"Freedom. Of a kind, anyway. You would have to leave Argentina, of course, but wouldn't you want to after all this? Go to some other country, start another life? Cut ties, clean slate. You could meet a woman, a safe, stable one. Have children, a family?"

Poots and chortles, shoulders toweled off after a shower. I was doing my best, yet another part of me insisted. I really was.

"Live, Tomás," the Colonel continued. "My point is that. What will it matter what you do? You will live."

I don't know how much time passed, how many circles we walked around the crypts in silence as I wrestled with it, my neck alternately hot in the sun and cool in the breeze, the chatter of the tourists in my ears. I'm not positive what I was wrestling with exactly either: My pain, my sense of betrayal? My fear of going back in the hood? Dying? Was I even really wrestling at all?

I don't know. I only know that soon enough I stopped. I told the Colonel Villa Ballester. Gave him the address.

It was such a beautiful day.

Afterward he handed me a bulky manila folder and a fake U.S. passport, which had a plane ticket tucked into its pages. The Colonel explained that immigration to Italy was easier than to Spanish-speaking countries right now, since they were eyeing those like hawks and he couldn't arrange travel to America on such short notice. Besides, Rome harbored other former revolutionary types, and if I wanted to get in touch, he'd given me a number, along with a bit of cash. The exchange rate with the lira was decent, he added, in what felt like a brutal irrelevance.

"Listen, Tomás," he said then. "I know this will seem like the breakdown of everything. I know that. First time I had someone killed, I remember it was the same—it was like I had broken too, shattered. But time, Tomás—you remember what I told you about time? There's no proof of it without these things falling apart. Which is to say there's no life either. You see that, don't you? Dying is just a cost of living."

"You get comfort from this shit?" I asked. Again I couldn't make out if it was the past or the present, or which version of the Colonel laughed and slapped me on the back.

"Ja, no, perhaps not. But I try to comfort myself with it all the same. Thought it might help you."

"Help me," I repeated.

"Tomás, Tomás. You think it's just bullshit, don't you, just a lot of speeches, don't you? All I'm saying is this is the way it goes. That's all I'm saying. You're neither the first person nor the last to do something like this. It may not get better with time. But it should get clearer."

"I'll look forward to that," I said, but asked myself: *Had* it gotten clearer?

"Go home, have some whiskey, put on some music. Trust me. Before you know it, you won't hear yourself anymore. So tell me," he continued, when I said nothing. "What will you listen to when you go home, Tomás?"

"I don't know. The Beatles? What does it matter?"

"The Beatles!" he cried, in sincere dismay. "No, please. Let me give you some advice: Listen to Gardel. He's the musician of memory. And you will be remembering this far longer than you wish." He patted me on the back again. "The Beatles! Ja!"

He went ahead. Left me in front of an uncared-for crypt with no detectable family markings and one of its inner shelves halfway caved in. I stared into it a long while before starting my departure as well.

—

I FOUND THE COLONEL at my side again. It was the ghost version of him, but he looked worse, hollowed, like in our exchange he had lost something too.

"I thought you said actions couldn't be reduced to such measly forks in the road."

"Well," he said. "They couldn't, could they? In the end?"

We walked slowly, the way I had alone. I gave the tourists a wide berth, as if afraid they'd catch my stink or something worse—whatever look you must have after you've done something like this. Despite the space I put between us, their leisurely, indifferent babbling still rang inside me, along with the click of the Colonel's shoes.

"You didn't walk me out that day," I recalled.

"I'm not going to today either," he answered. "Not really."

A profound loneliness came over me, not unlike what I'd felt when I left in '76. It was as if I'd already been aware of all the years I'd be alone with this, how isolated I'd feel, snapped off like a twig from a tree.

"Was it all a game?" I asked. "Something to teach me a lesson?"

"Maybe it was something to teach me a lesson. Maybe there are no lessons. I don't know, Tomás, not even we do, really. Haven't we all tried to tell you that?"

A group of cats was following us. Among them, that Siamese with crossed blue eyes that looked benevolently, almost wisely befuddled, as if there were much grander questions at stake than ours.

"I still don't know what I got out of this," I said.

He shrugged his shrug. "Time. If nothing else, you got more of that. There's shockingly little, remember. Goes by like that—poof. A puff of air."

We passed the mausoleum of Arturo E. Gómez and Family and turned onto the lane leading to the southern gate. The same Virgin Mary watched from atop the Dasso crypt, and in the same decrepit condition. Did time ever really pass at all?

"I guess we'll meet back here soon enough then," I said.

"I'm afraid not, Tomasito," the Colonel said. "Once you're here, once you're here in truth—there are no more meetings, really. Just long farewells."

We were back at the gate. The Colonel halted, and the cats did too.

"Well, Señor Shore," he said, "you should have everything you need."

"I don't need this," I said, indicating the fake passport. The top of the plane ticket remained sticking out of its pages as it had a decade before.

The Colonel gave another shake of his head. "Rather a stupid kind of intelligent, Tomás," he said, and closed the gate behind me.

TWENTY-FIVE

Hardly anything seemed different outside. The day was hot and lustrous, and people continued buzzing around me as if I were invisible. The only immediately discernible changes from when I'd left the cemetery in 1976 were the destination and date on the ticket the Colonel had given me: New York and December 5, 1986, respectively. The name, however, was the same: Thomas Shore.

The transition was as seamless and anticlimactic as that. When I glanced back through the bars of the gate, the Colonel was gone. And when I went to a kiosk off the plaza to check a newspaper, I saw that the date was the same as on my ticket. Existence didn't offer any more proof than that to welcome me back.

I walked from Recoleta to my hotel in Palermo. I needed to clean up and pack, to get a move on generally. Death might wait on me a little longer. But life wouldn't.

—

WITH THE EXCEPTIONS OF MY LETTING the front desk know I'd need a cab in a few hours and there being no gun in my underwear drawer, my return to the hotel was reminiscent of my return to the pensión that day in 1976. The length of the shower and the sensation of melting under the water, the lazy scrubbing despite how dirty I was. The ridiculous lines I rehearsed in my head in case the landlady inquired where I was going with my huge suitcase or the hotel clerk asked why I was checking out early. The difficulty I had actually packing, stuffing everything inside, and the wish, in one case, that my mother was there to help me and, in the other, that Claire was.

There were the disjointed sounds outside my room as well: In the hotel, it was the ring of the elevators and guests in the hall, the knocks on doors before housecleaning entered. In my pensión, it had been music. I didn't put on either the Beatles or Gardel as the Colonel had recommended— though I did have a joint and several whiskeys—but through the walls I heard Beatriz's record player. "The Girl from Ipanema." So light and pleasant, romantic vacation music if ever there was any. And when the woman's voice came in, singing, *Tall and tan and young and lovely,* I finally cried. Isabel wasn't any of those things, I thought, trying to console myself and stop my tears, before I remembered: She was certainly young. And lovely too, in her way.

And when she passes, I smile, but she
Doesn't see. She just doesn't see.

I was drinking out of a styrofoam cup. Which led me to another thought, namely: Isabel was right. I should have been drinking out of glass, something I could break.

———

NOT LONG BEFORE IT WAS TIME to head to the airport, the phone in my hotel room rang. It sounded obnoxious, like an alarm, but maybe that was because it had no place in my memories of '76. That day, I made the calls. They weren't to my mother or to Pichuca or to anyone from the university.

Instead, both were to our messenger at the locutorio. Two brief, garbled pleas—I was unambiguously drunk and high by then, otherwise I would have known the effort was futile—to call the Profe and Señora Amarga and tell them Pingüino said to get out of their house as soon as possible, to go anywhere else, it didn't matter where, that I was getting out too and I—

He didn't have their number, the man reminded me. They just called him for their messages.

I hung up. Then I thought better of it and went through the same thing again. This time, practically weeping himself, the man at the locutorio told me he didn't want to be involved. "Please," he said, his usually automated-sounding voice breaking into human tones. "Please, just let me go." And ultimately I did.

The phone in my hotel room continued ringing. Finally I answered. It was the front desk, informing me that my cab was downstairs.

———

I WASN'T NERVOUS about what the immigration officers would say regarding my fake passport this time. In '76, it had been my last moment of terror, watching the eyes roll up and back down, listening to every crinkle of a page, wondering if it was sturdy enough. Now, though, I felt like nothing could stop me, like I knew how the story would end. Or, more accurately, how it would continue: another airport in which I'd be anonymous, with no one to pick me up. I hadn't told Claire I'd decided to come back, and who even knew if she'd let me. Though I vaguely pondered telling her about the whole experience, considered writing it out in English for her and framing it as a kind of love letter, a testament to some tenuously re-newed faith in life, the truth was, this might be yet another way things turned out to be too late.

The officer studied my passport, then stamped it. Handing it back to me, he warned me it was about to expire; I'd better renew it soon, before it was too late.

—

WHILE WAITING IN THE BOARDING AREA IN '76, I'd tried to convince myself that the locutorio man had succeeded in reaching Isabel and Gustavo. That at the very least, the phone had screamed as the milicos got there, so they knew I'd tried to warn them. I also pictured grander elements to the scenario: the exchange of glances as they saw the Ford Falcons pull up and decided what to do, grabbed their guns and readied themselves, or took a grenade out to the garden, to set the shed and the rest of their dreams ablaze.

But those two puny words still found their way to me, as they did now and throughout the years between: *too late.* The phone almost certainly hadn't rung, and even if it had, it likely would have been to an empty room or over their corpses.

Only after time had passed did I begin to reckon with that aspect: the way their bodies were disposed of. It was hard to believe that whoever killed them would go through the trouble of dropping them at sea if they were already dead and starting to decompose. Chances are it was simpler—quick, like the Colonel said. Driven down some back road in Villa Ballester or nearby San Martín and tossed into a common grave. Chances are, in fact, that they're still there, buried lazily beside their peers.

—

WAITING FOR TAKEOFF, I tried to shift my thinking, force my perspective to face forward, so to speak. The future was still out there, presumably, behind the setting sun and the pillowy darkness enveloping the sky, and I gazed out the window as if trying to find its outline among the blurring silhouettes.

I couldn't, of course. I couldn't even locate my reflection. A decade before, I'd stared at the murky, gaunt face in the glass like it wasn't mine anymore. Maybe that's good, I'd mused then; maybe I'll become someone else. Escape not only the country and the past but my whole being. Three months later, as I headed to New York, the notion had given me some false reassurance, a mistaken sense of casting off chains. It had seemed liberating, even, to arrive in America amid all its myths of new beginnings, able to claim that Tomás Orilla had disappeared.

I told myself this time would be different. That I'd return undisguised, with acceptance if nothing else, a sort of robust clarity. But with the horizon quickly dissipating in the deepening twilight, there was so little I could glimpse through my window. And whether for that reason or because something distracted me—people jamming their bags in the overhead compartments or the flight attendants checking the aisles—my attention returned to the inside of the plane. The recycled air, the lack of room for my legs. The stillness, more than anything. I didn't hear the other passengers or see anything when I fruitlessly closed my eyes to sleep. Even with the roar of the engine and the wheels starting to turn underneath us, I still didn't feel like we were moving.

ACKNOWLEDGMENTS

This book was inspired by my half sister, Isabel Loedel Maiztegui, a Montonera who was disappeared on January 17, 1978, at the age of twenty-two. The novel could not have been written without her sacrifice.

Many other family members and friends contributed to this project with their stories and support. My profound gratitude to my father, Eduardo Loedel, and my siblings, Enrique and Bonnie Loedel; to my mother, Susan Lucks; to Juan Carlos, Isidro, and Mercedes Maiztegui; to Nelly Lopez, Daniel Di Giacinti, Gustavo Villar, Virginia Urquizu, Maite Heras, and Paula Luttringer.

Extensive research went into this book, and certain sources were invaluable, especially *A Lexicon of Terror* by Marguerite Feitlowitz, *Prisoner Without a Name, Cell Without a Number* by Jacobo Timerman, and of course the *Nunca Más* report from CONADEP. I am also very grateful to all the people working at the memorial site for Automotores Orletti, who gave me such extraordinary access and insight.

My vast thanks to my agent, Marya Spence, whose guidance and enduring belief will always awe me, and to Clare Mao, Zoë Nelson, and everyone else at Janklow & Nesbit. To my brilliant, wonderful editor, Becky Saletan, and the rest of the magnificent team at Riverhead, especially Jynne Dilling Martin, Geoff Kloske, Kate Stark, Catalina Trigo, Helen Yentus, Lauren Peters-Collaer, and Anna Jardine, and to the copy editor, David Koral.

Many thanks to my early readers: Kate Barry, Emily Barasch, Kelly Farber, Daniel Magariel, Stefan Merrill Block, Mark Russell, Daniel Sterba, and most of all, for her incomparable patience, help, and wisdom, Julia Lee McGill. Thank you.

Finally, for supporting this book's journey through publication in every other way, my deepest thanks to Emma Ramadan.